"'Stonewall' is pitch-perfect."
—Thomas Lawrence Long, PhD, editor,
Harrington Gay Men's Literary Quarterly,
University of Connecticut

As Stonewall turns fifty and Jack Fritscher turns eighty, I have with a curator's sense of finality collected in this "Stonewall 50" edition the original nine keepsake stories with the original introductions by Richard Labonté and the late Mark Thompson from the fortieth-anniversary edition. I have added a new version of "The Story Knife" along with a new tenth story, "Three Bears in a Tub," finishing the anthology with a new essay, "Lost Photographs, Found Genders," telling the backstory of how the author's one-act play, "Coming Attractions" came to be produced in 1976.

Mark Hemry
Editor

Also by Jack Fritscher

Novels

Some Dance to Remember
The Geography of Women
What They Did to the Kid
Leather Blues

Short-Fiction

Rainbow County
Corporal in Charge
Stand by Your Man
Titanic

Non-Fiction

Gay San Francisco: Eyewitness Drummer
Gay Pioneers
Mapplethorpe: Assault with a Deadly Camera
Popular Witchcraft
Love and Death in Tennesssee Williams
When Malory Met Arthur: Camelot
Television Today

www.JackFritscher.com

STONEWALL
Stories of Gay Liberation

Jack Fritscher

**Introductions by
Mark Thompson
Richard Labonté
Mark Hemry**

50th Anniversary Collection

Palm Drive Publishing

Cover drawing by A. Jay ©1969 and 2008 Estate of Allen J. Shapiro, administered by Dick Kriegmont, used with permission
Cover design by and ©2019 Mark Hemry
"Inheriting Our Stonewall Legacy" ©2008 Mark Thompson
"Tribal Words, Our Queer World" ©2008 Richard Labonté
"Suddenly That Summer" ©2019 Mark Hemry

The "Stonewall" story was first published in *Harrington Gay Men's Literary Quarterly*, Vol. 8 #1, 2006. "Chasing Danny Boy" was first published in *Chasing Danny Boy: Powerful Stories of Celtic Eros*, 1999.
Published by Palm Drive Publishing, San Francisco CA
Email: publisher@PalmDrivePublishing.com

Library of Congress Control Number: 2019940145
Fritscher, Jack 1939-
   Stonewall: Stories of Gay Liberation / Jack Fritscher
   p. cm.
   ISBN 978-1-890834-21-0 [print]
   ISBN 978-1-890834-22-7 [eBook]
   1. Stonewall—Fiction. 2. San Francisco—Fiction. 3. Short-Stories—Fiction. 4. Gay men—Fiction. 5. Gay & Lesbian Studies. 6. United States—Fiction 7. United States—Social life and customs—20th century—Fiction. 8. Gay marriage. 9. Mapplethorpe, Robert, 1946-1989. 10. Woolf, Virginia, 1882-1941—Influence fiction. 11. Joyce, James, 1882-1941—Influence fiction. 12. Williams, Tennessee, 1911-1983—Influence fiction. I. Title.

Printed in the United States of America
First Printing June 2019

www.PalmDrivePublishing.com

For author history and literary research
www.JackFritscher.com

For my Mrs. Dalloway,
Virginia Day Fritscher,
my mother, the Irish storyteller
1919-2004

Stonewall
June 28, 1969

"Bliss was it in that dawn to be alive,
but to be young was very heaven!"
—William Wordsworth,
"The Prelude"

CONTENTS

Introductions

Stories

"Hilarious, exquisite, empowering stories about how fabulous we are."

Inheriting Our Stonewall Legacy

Mark Thompson
Former Senior Editor of *The Advocate*,
author of *Gay Spirit*

"Forty? Forty?" Volcanically spewing smoke and ash, Bette Davis bitched about her fate in *All About Eve*: "I'm not twenty-ish. I'm not thirty-ish. Three months ago I was forty years old. Forty. Four O." In gay years, "Forty" spans two or three queer generations.

One night I met a jaded man sitting on a barstool. Now, this was no ordinary man. (Think George Saunders in *All About Eve* playing "Addison Dewitt"—but on steroids.) And certainly not a typical place. We were in the basement bar of the San Francisco Opera, sipping flutes of champagne between acts of a dreadfully boring piece by Rossini. At least I remember it as boring, because "Addison" told me so. And that's not all.

"Look, you're a cute young thing, so let me tell you something," he said, slightly slurring his consonants. I could tell this wasn't his first cocktail of the evening. "Don't ever grow old. You hear?" I compliantly nodded, because anyone standing within a ten-foot radius could hear him perfectly well. With another flourish of his glass he continued. "It's hell to be forty and gay. Don't let it happen to you."

The man adjusted his seat and patted down his graying pate. He intoned his narration so like "Addison" doing his arch voice-over in the film that I couldn't help but think of La Davis as "Margo

Channing" stuck in the snow bemoaning her fate at "the big 4-0." Like her, this man was blasting smoke too. At a little more than half that age, I couldn't imagine how I was going to stop getting there. Still, I listened.

"Age does have its privileges though," he admitted, suddenly shifting tone. "I was at Stonewall, you know. One of the lucky ones. Ever hear of it?"

I replied that, yes, of course, I had heard of the famous riot — the gay riot that supposedly set us all free. I'd met so many people who said they were "there" it would take Shea Stadium to hold them all. And yet, with the benefit of the doubt, I politely deferred. Leaning forward to ask him more about those famous June nights, we were both saved by the bell for the final curtain.

Ah, Stonewall at "Forty." 4-0. Stonewall. That magical, mystical place which resides somewhere between Broadway's *Camelot* and *Brigadoon* in our queer consciousness. So near, yet so far ago. What do any of us really know about it?

With verve, a steady hand, and admirable audacity, Jack Fritscher tells us everything we ought to know about those tempestuous times in June 1969. The little girl who sang "Over the Rainbow" had so suddenly just died. Only as quickly to be replaced by a new kind of queen — a queen, as Jack Fritscher writes, with "a bitch slap heard around the world."

Stonewall wasn't the first such action, or rather reaction to a police oppression as evil as ever known — just the most famous. It helps when the offices of *The Village Voice* are down the street. That said, why would anyone suddenly care about another gay murder, or suicide, or phony arrest? The river of ruined queer lives was as wide and deep as the Hudson by then. Only this time it made headlines. And just because, Jack Fritscher posits, of one small slap in one big face. That's all it took. But the faces of the haters always look bigger until they get figured down to size. In this case, it took a mighty large queen with nothing to lose to do the calculating.

I'll let author Jack Fritscher fill you in on the details of that particular night. But here's a few other things you might want to know. The New York slap that led to a global civil rights insurgence had been practiced elsewhere a few times before. In May 1959, in a shabby Los Angeles coffee shop, queens in Capri pants let the

LAPD goons have it for perhaps the first time. Officers from the city's notoriously homophobic police department were harassing the denizens of Cooper's Doughnuts yet once again when tensions snapped.

At first it was the doughnuts that came flying through the air towards the cops. Then paper cups and coffee stirrers and just about everything else that wasn't fastened down by a hair clip. More squad cars were called. Sirens wailed and streets blocked off. A lot of queer folk were arrested and jailed during what was probably the first gay riot in recorded history.

A few years later, in August 1966, it happened again in San Francisco. A bunch of cross-dressed hustlers in Compton's Cafeteria decided that they'd had enough of shakedowns too. Someone threw a cup of coffee in a policeman's face. Yet another slap that resulted in broken windows and a fire. The sissies in the Tenderloin were tired of being picked on and they weren't going to take it anymore.

It was time for a revolution, a riot or two. Perhaps in Barcelona they hurled empanadas, in San Paulo each other, in Tokyo maybe just plain old shame. But wherever they were, and whatever they had, the queens flung it hard and fast.

In Greenwich Village, angry protestors marched down the street singing "We are the Stonewall girls. We wear our hair in curls. We wear our dungarees above our nellie knees!" And that was just during the first round of that historic three-night rebellion. Singing defiantly. Right after they had finished ripping the parking meters out of the sidewalk in front of the rattrap bar forever to be celebrated as the motherlode of a movement.

Comically stirring, Jack Fritscher's pivotal tale of the start of the Stonewall Riot is first of the many worth reading in this Stonewall anniversary collection. His ten tales are about gay liberation before and after the June 1969 rebellion. He writes about time and place, and finding one's grace in them. The author is a man of many voices, each exquisitely calibrated to the subject. His "Mrs. Dalloway" may go "that-a-way" picking her flowers at a certain point of time, just as Stonewall had to happen in 1969. But Jack Fritscher gets us in every season: we queer men who are under, at, or above that all-defining marker known as "Forty."

I'll take our gay tribe at any age—as sometimes frightful but always fabulous we are. And so does Jack Fritscher, who revels in writing the unvarnished truth. Not only are his stories frequently hilarious, his angle is empowering to know.

This very political year of 2009, driven by the battle for "gay marriage," is no time to shy away from the forty-year-old fight for gay liberation. Life at 4-0 has just begun.

Bette Davis' "Margo Channing" may not have understood the positive side of "Forty." "Addison DeWitt" may not have grown into accepting "Forty." But Jack Fritscher's "Mrs. Dalloway" knows a thing or two about gay survival. As does that other unforgettable doyen of modern letters, "Molly Bloom," whom the author references via James Joyce in "Chasing Danny Boy" in this collection—as well as in his character "Solly Blue" in his memoir-novel *Some Dance to Remember*.

Forty years on, we inheritors of the Stonewall legacy, understand why the nearly-forty "Molly Bloom" has the wisdom to declare that all is good by saying, "And yes I said yes I will say yes."

Mark Thompson
Los Angeles

**There is more diversity
in this sterling collection of short stories
by one author than there is in some anthologies
with a dozen authors."**

Tribal Words, Our Queer World

Richard Labonté
A Different Light Bookstores,
www.BooksToWatchOutFor.com

We have always had our words.

In the centuries before print, "men met men" and "women met women" through glance and touch and whispered words that led us to each other.

Then words were written — within our lifetimes, enough words that entire gay bookstores can be stocked with them.

In Greenwich Village in 1967, first came the "Oscar Wilde" bookstore with shelves of "words" by literary titans such as James Baldwin and Truman Capote, Tennessee Williams and Jean Genet, Christopher Isherwood and Gore Vidal, John Rechy and Paul Bowles.

Emboldened by the Stonewall Rebellion of 1969, more bookstores followed: "Glad Day," Toronto, 1970; "Giovanni's Room," Philadelphia, 1973; "Lambda Rising," Washington, D.C., 1974; and "A Different Light" in the Silver Lake neighborhood of Los Angeles, a store long gone — but celebrated in memory for itself and for its offspring — for a time in New York, and still in business in West Hollywood and San Francisco. The "Outwrite" bookstore founded in Atlanta, 1993, continues the tradition of selling queer words in queer books by queer authors to a diversity of readers.

These post-Stonewall bookstores, and the words stocked on their shelves, have been a catalyst for a Gay Liberation Movement that was inspired by the drag queens, the gay boys and girls, and the leathermen—by the queers—who took to the streets outside the Stonewall Inn to protest the "words" used against us. "No more."

Forty years ago, there was no Internet. Gay bookstores were the chat rooms of our queer nation. The books on the shelves, the magazines providing news, the encouraging staff behind the counter—that was how our words were passed on, from one person to the next, from one generation to the next. The revolution started in the streets, but it spread through typewriters and printing presses. It seems quaint, in this era of instant online access and books-on-demand and one-click shopping through the sterile interface of a desktop computer—but, in their day and even today, bookstores and the words they contained brought gay men and gay woman together, served as social centers, and as information resources.

We can celebrate the Internet: young queers come out sooner, meet each other more easily, plug in to knowledge bases in the privacy of the bedrooms, read copious book reviews if they choose, learn that they are not alone. Using the Internet, elder queers keep in the swim of words and books.

That said, bookstores still matter, as repositories of literary history, as places where books can be handled, browsed, discussed. Breathed in, even—that's *really* quaint. Books like this one, which does what queer words do best: bring our past to life, put a fictional twist on queer fact, entertain us intellectually, emotionally, vicariously, viscerally, sexually. Imaginatively.

Jack Fritscher has been doing that work with words for five decades, though dozens of books and hundreds of short stories and thousands and thousands of words, chronicling successive gay eras with a wordsmith's sure touch.

As I have written about one of his other solo anthologies, I can repeat: "There is more diversity in this collection of short stories by one author than there is in some anthologies with a dozen authors."

"Stonewall: June 27, 1969, 11 PM," the centerpiece story of this sterling collection, perfectly captures the bitchy bravura of that moment in time, of that particular night, of the defiant queens and queers who fought back: it's fiction that encapsulates fact, and expands it, and explains it.

The crowd being herded out the front door (torn from its hinges), turns, curious, muted, shocked, at the precise instant Sylvia hits the cop, again, with an open-handed bitch-slap heard round the world.

Indeed. Through the wonder of words, we are there, we who weren't there, we who were not even born then, we who — books live on — have not yet come out.
We will always have our words.

Richard Labonté
Bowen Island, Canada

HEADLINE NEWS:
Stonewall Riot Ends Prehistoric Gay Period,
Begins LGBT Civil Rights Movement...

Suddenly That Summer
1969

What It Was Like to Be Gay and Alive
That May and June

Mark Hemry, Editor

"At Stonewall, gay character changed."
— Jack Fritscher, *Gay San Francisco*

Do you remember where you were during Stonewall? Are you younger than Stonewall? Half a century ago, Stonewall grew out of our larger American struggle for civil rights in the 1960s during the sexual revolution sweeping the world. "Stonewall" was happening everywhere before the June 1969 riot broke out at 63 Christopher Street. On April 23, 1961, a crowd of gay men's voices was recorded for the first time cheering uncloseted on the live-concert album of *Judy at Carnegie Hall.* On the West Coast, queens stood up against the cops in Los Angeles at Cooper's Doughnuts (1959), and in San Francisco at the Why Not? bar (1960) and Compton's Cafeteria (1966).

Almost five years to the day before Stonewall, the June 26, 1964 issue of *Life* magazine documented San Francisco's gay bar, the Tool Box. Jack Fritscher wrote in *Drummer* magazine, "That *Life* article was like an engraved invitation to queers everywhere to come out of the closet and immigrate to major cities where there was strength in numbers." *Life* threw down a gauntlet: "A secret world grows open and bolder. Society is forced to look at it—and try to understand it."

Against the odds of straight history, the Stonewall Rebellion of June 28, 1969, became the epicenter of a Queer Culture Quake that ended our "Last Prehistoric Gay Period." At Stonewall, we showed our true rainbow colors. After a week of riots the media could no longer ignore, the *New York Daily News* headlined on July 6, 1969: "Homo Nest Raided, Queen Bees Are Stinging Mad." Ouch!

Jack Fritscher was not in Sheridan Square at the Stonewall rebellion, but he was professionally prepared to be an eyewitness to the media coinage and coverage of the events. At eighty, he is the San Francisco writer, storyteller, and historian whose sixty-year career predates Stonewall itself. Published as a teenager in national magazines in 1957, he wrote the first doctoral dissertation on Tennessee Williams in 1966, and as a university professor began writing gay fiction and reviews about gay popular culture in 1967.

In his essay "Homomasculinity: Framing the Key Words of Gay Popular Culture," he wrote: "Reporting the Stonewall uprising six hours after the first stone was cast, a reticent *New York Times* in ten short-shrift paragraphs used the words *homosexual* once and *young men* twice. The *New York Post* in five paragraphs used *homosexual* only once but actually dared quote the framing chant of *gay power*. In its Independence Day issue (July 3, 1969), the *Village Voice* nailed the gay gravitas with the headline feature 'Gay Power Comes to Sheridan Square.' On November 5, activists successfully picketed the *Los Angeles Times* for refusing to print the word *homosexual* in advertisements. By June 1970, thousands of gay militants—veterans of the civil rights, women's lib, and peace movements—marched past news cameras with signs reading 'Gay Pride' and 'Gay Power' at the first Christopher Street Liberation Day in Central Park."

"So how," he asked, "did a routine NYPD raid on a Mafia-owned gay bar in Greenwich Village morph from a bar fight into a symbol for the gay civil rights movement in much the same way that the march across the Edmund Pettus Bridge in Selma, Alabama, on March 7, 1965, became an impelling roots moment for the black civil rights movement?"

"Even though Stonewall wasn't the first rebel act in the gay war of independence," he wrote, "it scored the best news coverage to date. In the twenty-four months after the Stonewall riot, it was activist journalists thinking and writing about the shifting paradigm in gay social justice who did the pre-historical math, created the origin myth, and framed the importance of its commemoration in order to organize the screams, bottles, and bricks into the rally cry of resistance and enlightenment inherent in the *Realpolitik* of the Stonewall rebellion."

Assessing writers working inside gay culture before, during, and after the happening of Stonewall, Willie Walker, founder of the GLBT Historical Society of San Francisco said, "Jack Fritscher, a prolific writer who since the late 1960s has helped document the gay world and the changes it has undergone." Before Stonewall, Fritscher had written a dozen published short stories and his first novels *What They Did to the Kid: Confessions of an Altar Boy* (1965) and *Leather Blues* (1969), as well as his dissertation *Love and Death in Tennessee Williams*, and his 1969 review of *The Boys in the Band* for the *Journal of Popular Culture* (January 1970). And he was already journalizing the text that became his novel *Some Dance to Remember: A Memoir-Novel of San Francisco 1970-1982*. In February 1969 he had begun researching his nonfiction book *Popular Witchcraft* (1972). In a signature eyewitness way, Fritscher's fiction and nonfiction connect Stonewall and Castro Street.

In *Gay San Francisco*, he recorded his participation in civil rights with Saul Alinsky in 1962 on the South Side of Chicago, and at the August 1968 Democratic Convention in Chicago when hippies and yippies and gays, including Allen Ginsberg and Jean Genet, fought in the streets against the Chicago cops clubbing the surging convention crowds who chanted in self-defense to the live TV cameras, "The whole world is watching." He wrote, "You don't have to be Rosa Parks to figure that the people's resistance against the cops at the Democratic Convention in Chicago 1968 was a precise model and encouragement ten months later for the queens' rebellion against the cops at the Stonewall Inn. Without Chicago, Stonewall may not have happened."

The spring of 1969 was a wild time in the Swinging Sixties. On June 9, 1969, eighteen days before Stonewall, gays thoughout the world hosted parties celebrating 6/9/69. On June 20, 1969, seven days before Stonewall, Fritscher, an openly gay professor teaching at university since 1964, turned thirty. He was a constant observer in his journals of the gay push forward in the revolutionary 1960s. Four weeks before his birthday, he had returned from Europe where "in Holland a wild sexy Dutch boy" had recruited him "into a student takeover of the University of Amsterdam." The excitement of that rebel melee swept him further to La Rive Gauche in gay Paree. He wrote: "Paris still vibed 'red' with a peoples' revolutionary brilliance that May 1969 after the riotous Prague Spring of 1968 when student strikes had shut down old-style Paris and post-war Europe. The most popular music worldwide on jukeboxes in gay bars was the explicit pair of whispered duets by Serge Gainsbourg and his pop goddess Jane Birkin anointing 1969 sexually in their shocking '69 Annee Erotique' and 'Je t'aime, moi non plus.' Oh, mon amour!"

About Paris in 1969 in the 5th arrondissement, Fritscher wrote about the "gay wave" sweeping western culture: "the bedroom windows reached from floor to ceiling," and he "...fell in, and out, of springtime love, and the Dutch lad shapeshifted one night at Le Keller's bar near the Bastille into a young Brit whose leather-biker good looks swept us both across the Channel to London which was suddenly that summer way more queer than the straight scene of the Beatles and Carnaby Street because of the decriminalization of homosexuality in 1967. Our gay London was the leathery Coleherne pub in Earls Court, the cruisy movie theaters in Piccadilly, the squaddies of Studio Royale, the nighttime sex in the wild woods on Hampstead Heath, and the steaming pleasures of the ancient Turkish baths tucked under York Hall on Old Ford Road. Those Victorian working-man's tubs, next door to the Museum of Childhood, were perfectly situated for a little extra cottage sex in the busy, dank public toilet outside the Bethnal Green tube station. And from London, the amazing gay wave rolled on to New York and the Rambles in Central Park, the Off-Broadway *Boys in the Band*, the Everard Baths, the afterglow of the 1966 Mattachine Sip-In at Julius' swellegant bar, dirty 42nd Street bookstores, Fire Island, Bernadette Peters in *Dames at Sea*, Warhol at the 55th Street Cinema, leather bars, the Ninth Circle, and the counter-culture of the Village. During that erotic spring just before that dramatic summer's Stonewall and Woodstock and Moon Landing and Manson murders, gay novelist James Leo Herlihy and gay director John Schlesinger turned *Midnight Cowboy* from a conventional buddy movie into a complex male love story that won the Oscar for best picture. And lots of us gay men shouted 'Bugatti!' as we fell in love with the divine Vanessa Redgrave dancing as the divine Isadora Duncan in Cinemascope, naked and wrapped in the star-and-sickle of the red Soviet flag, fucking handsome young Russian Communist poets and revolutionaries. The underground gay world of the Swinging Sixties was an on-going worldwide orgy long before Stonewall turned sex political."

Two days after his thirtieth birthday, and five days before Stonewall, he felt "the sorrow most gay men suffered when Judy Garland accidentally overdosed, age 47, in her home in London on June 22, 1969." He wrote, "As thousands of grieving gay men queued up in Manhattan to stream past her laid out like a queen in an open coffin during her all-night wake at Campbell's Funeral Home on Madison Avenue, June 26 turned into June 27. The mixed emotions and motivations hit a gay nerve and then exploded four miles south at the Stonewall Inn as June 27 became June 28. If Judy Garland, the ventriloquist of gay code, had not died," he added, double-billing her with the Democratic Convention, "Stonewall may not have happened. Nowadays it's a gay joke that if the mob of people who claim to be veterans of the Stonewall riot are not lying, the crowd would have been greater than the 400,000 who showed up six weeks later at Woodstock."

*****

As Stonewall turns fifty and Fritscher turns eighty, I have with a curator's sense of finality collected the original nine keepsake stories with the original introductions by Richard Labonté and the late Mark Thompson from the fortieth-anniversary edition. I have added a new version of "The Story Knife" along with a new tenth story, "Three Bears in a Tub," finishing the anthology with a new essay, "Lost Photographs, Found Genders," telling the backstory of how the one-act play, "Coming Attractions" came to be produced in 1976.

What might the LGBT world feel as Stonewall reaches middle age? Or old age? "Stonewall 50" deserves a huge celebration, and may perhaps, especially in our age of political resistance, initiate a true renaissance of LGBT culture that, even after Stonewall, has suffered so many years of oppression at the hands of fundamentalists. "Even as we gays disappear," Fritscher wrote, "we reappear. Twenty-five years ago marking 'Stonewall 25,' hundreds of thousands of us appeared on June 26, 1994, marching in worldwide Pride parades to reappear as millions for 'Stonewall 50.'"

"If in 2019," Fritscher said, "one in ten people is gay on our globe, with a population of nearly seven billion, well, that's inching close to one billion gay folk who are more linked, and therefore more powerful and able to create change, than the small crowd at Stonewall who succeeded beyond their wildest dreams when there was no Internet, no texting, no instant messaging, no viral call to action, no Facebook, and no video footage of the riots on Youtube. That small band of twentieth-century folks with analog voices, all of them, whoever they were, working with what they had, gave us at Stonewall a teaching moment about the on-going revolutionary responsibility we twenty-first-century folks with digital devices have to amplify and complete our liberation in our time of rising fascism if there is to be a 'Stonewall 75' in 2044 and 'Stonewall 100' in 2069."

For myself as editor striving to present information accurately, I must, in transparency as a longtime media producer, say that I have known Jack Fritscher intimately since the 1970s as his lover and as his domestic partner and as his spouse of forty years. As a reader, I'm also a fan which is why I think of this anthology of gay entertainment as a worthy project capturing the spirit of Stonewall. As actor Ian Richardson repeated so famously in the British series *House of Cards*, may I say, "You may very well think I have access to the author's most intimate thoughts and private papers, but I couldn't possibly comment." As with the Woolfs and Bells in Bloomsbury, who better to be an eyewitness than a spouse sorting out how things went that-a-way behind a writer's study door?

This *Stonewall* anthology surveys a fictive essence of Fritscher's sixty-year career capturing the character, dialogue, nuance, arts, and ideas of the gay culture he loves. Guided by a veteran elder's canonical sense of gaydar, he celebrates gay "drama," diversity, and magical thinking in these ten tales scanning the curvature of the Queer Earth—from the 1906 earthquake in "Meet Me in San

Francisco" through the camp-fest last hour before the NYPD raid in "Stonewall: June 27, 1969, 11 PM" on up to gay marriage in "Mrs. Dalloway Went That-A-Way." The settings range from Christopher Street in Greenwich Village to a Midwest movie palace, and from an Alaska cruise ship to a Castro Street teeming with gay refugees from the American culture wars. His characters manage to survive, like Stonewall itself, against all odds.

Elaborating on the changes caused by Stonewall, and writing stories told with a humanist's feel for the way we are, Fritscher uses an omniscient narrator's voice to inflect his stories with humor, irony, and drama. He is a prose stylist who can turn a phrase with a flip that surprises and delights. His dialogue seems as lively on the page as it is in the plays and screenplays he has authored. The following thumbnails may reveal how some of his stories worked for me personally over the years, and professionally during the time my task was to select the stories for this "Stonewall 50" anthology.

The title tale "Stonewall: June 27, 1969, 11 PM" is a drag comedy with *All About Eve* dialogue that *Will and Grace* never dared try. True to Aristotle's classic unities of time, place, and action, "Stonewall" unfolds in the precise "Last Prehistoric Gay Period," the final sixty minutes leading up to the NYPD raid on the Stonewall Inn. It was encouraging to me that the first publisher of "Stonewall," Thomas Long, editor of *Harrington Gay Men's Literary Quarterly*, wrote: "Fritscher's 'Stonewall' is pitch-perfect." Flying the rainbow flag, these literary short stories bring Fritscher's stylistic mix of humanism and eros to the gay literary canon. Two of the stories, "Stonewall: June 27, 1969, 11 PM" and "Chasing Danny Boy," give me special delight in sharing. As entertainment, these stories reflect our evolving gay hearts and minds and illustrate Fritscher's Woolfian observation: "At Stonewall, gay character changed."

- "Stonewall: June 27, 1969, 11 PM" with its comic "sixty-minute countdown," camp-fest characters, "snap" dialogue, and homosurrealistic style, might very well be, as *Advocate* editor Mark Thompson said, "a nominee as one of the twentieth century's best gay short stories."

- "Chasing Danny Boy" gayifies the Celtic mythology of the

author's own Irish roots, camping for *craic* on the *Complete Irish Mythology* of Lady Gregory with streaming bits of James Joyce. His four young millennial punks explore their polysexuality with sex, drugs, and rock in the underground world of Dublin during the last summer of the twentieth century. "Chasing Danny Boy" was first published as the title story in *Chasing Danny Boy: Powerful Tales of Celtic Eros* featuring "Last Rites" by Neil Jordan, director of *The Crying Game*.

- "Meet Me in San Francisco" is a romantic Valentine of teen boys in love, separated in the deadly San Francisco earthquake and fire of 1906 when 3,000 people died and eighty percent of the city was destroyed.

- "The Unseen Hand in the Lavender Light" is an existential profile of a movie-mad young gay boy abandoned during World War II by his waitress-mother at the Bee Hive café. Disoriented and confused, he comes out in a dark movie theater where, lit only by the light of the projector, he survives as an usher, and tries to make something of himself as the conformist 1950s of corporate Hollywood movies evolve into the swinging 1960s of personal underground cinema.

- "The Barber of 18th and Castro" features two characters locked in one's struggle to come out. This black comedy about sex worship dramatizes how gay pop-culture photography in "physique" magazines drives the coming-out process. Think Alfred Hitchcock directing a psychological thriller about existential fear and erotic fantasy on Castro Street in 1973, four years after Stonewall.

- "The Story Knife," noted historically by *Men on Men* editor George Stambolian, is the shipboard rom-com of a redheaded Irish-Catholic priest who as an ordinary guy struggling in an age of AIDS discovers that temptation has turned him into a sex-tourist beguiled by a cabin boy from Genoa; so what does he do with his new video camera? The new *pentimento* version in this edition has been re-imagined cinematically by the author from the 2009 edition.

- "Mrs. Dalloway Went That-A-Way" is a touching vernacular story of gay marriage, eldercare, rising matriarchy, and failing patriarchy in the last summer of the millennium. The narrative helix, delicately wrapped around a gay man's mother, Princess Diana, and the film version of Virginia Woolf's *Mrs. Dalloway*, teases out a tender gay love story as appropriate as Michael Cunningham's Woolf homage, *The Hours*.

- "Three Bears in a Tub" is a breathless one-sentence comedy of a summer evening on a lake in the Ozarks when three good ol' boys in a rowboat mix and match under the full moon and find family in each other.

- "Sweet Embraceable You" is a comedy about two couples—two women and two men—in the first days of gay gentrification on Castro Street surrounded by people self-fashioning new gay identities in the wonderful 1970s window between penicillin and plague.

- "Coming Attractions: Kweenasheba," the stage adaptation of "Sweet Embraceable You," is the author's 1976 one-act play produced by the Society for Individual Rights (SIR) for San Francisco's Yonkers Production Company

- "Lost Photographs, Found Genders" is the author's history of the social changes around the San Francisco production of his play, "Coming Attractions."

Mark Hemry
San Francisco 2019

Stonewall
June 27, 1969, 11 PM

JudyJudyJudy. All over the television, *JudyJudy,* all over the radio, *Judy,* all over the headlines, *Judy Garland Dead,* and all over the juke box — against which leans Aretha Iago.

"She's the flaming, burnt Toast of Chicago, darling. Very South Side."

"On loan to Manhattan, Greenwich Village, the Continental Baths, and the Stonewall Inn."

"No deposit. No return."

"I never repeat gossip. So listen carefully. You know what I'm saying?"

"I can dig it."

"Groovy."

M. Iago is singing along (at 43 rpms) to (the 45 rpm) "The Man That Got Away" catching some sniffy notice from the early birds doing laps through the Stonewall's two rooms. Growing up staring into her mother's three-way mirrors, magnified twelve times, M. Iago faces reality. Inside every drag queen is a man that got away. M. Iago, stoned at the Stonewall, believing Judy/being Judy/belting Judy, is gay happy-sad.

Early on a Friday night, the joint is jumping like a high-school hop. It's that hour of the optimist in any gay bar, only eleven o'clock, sixty minutes before the wee bitching hour when everybody who is anybody changes into somebody else to make their entrances.

M. Iago is exhausted after two hot June nights standing in line, crying and pushing and shoving (groping), craning her neck among the throng of men dragged up in boots and heels on the sidewalk outside Campbell's Funeral Chapel at Madison Avenue and 81st waiting like a — what? — huge conga line snaking (one, two, three, kick) in to view the famous corpse smothered in yellow flowers, and hoping to catch a glimpse of Judy's poor babies, Lorna and Joey and Liza, the Red Menace.

The first night—or was it last night?—lost in the army of thousands of waiting men, Iago latches onto the flurry of Candy Darling's pink-chiffon entourage, featuring Holly Woodlawn and that Jackie Curtis, all of them daring to drag illegal drag (*tah-dah!*) into the public street, and is positively swirled up inside the muffled interior, into the *ruzzabuzz* of voices passing the casket of Frances Gumm who three days dead looks better than, well, to be kind, ten percent of her mourners. What *ruzz* was she doing in London, *abuzz* loaded in that hotel bathroom, with that last husband—her groom of ninety days!—who could be *ruzz* forgiven for being clueless but not forgiven *abuzz* for not being glamorous. He should be slapped. All her husbands should be slapped. Louis B. Mayer should be slapped. The Wizard behind the curtain should be slapped. Somebody should be slapped.

If Miss Garland hadn't been with what's his name, if she had been with us, she'd be alive tonight—although Iago insists that at a snotty soiree in an Upper East Side apartment in May, six weeks ago, Judy had been a tiny tipsy when the hosts persuaded her *JudyJudyJudy* to lean into the curve of the piano and croon a little tune of Dixie, but what was worse Iago says is that the living legend smelled, uhh, dead, but that's just Iago's high ego bragging that she that night stood as close as she could get to Judy Garland whose vodka glass fell accidentally into Iago's purse, and is now a collectible (if not a holy relic) worth, with its red lipstick smear, at least twenty-five bucks or half a lid of killer grass.

"Midsummer magic," Iago says. "The moon is full, and I'm not even high."

The crowd swims towards booths and tables through the humid Inn. A school of tropical fish darts left. Another school drags right around three young leathermen, each standing alone on the dance floor (squared off with puke-yellow tiles), as if no one else exists, sweating in their leather shirts and jeans. Two are a pair detached out of *Easy Rider.* The other is a stunning Kenneth Anger blond. Hippie ringlets fall from his leather cap to the broad shoulders of his *A Star Is Born* T-shirt; he rubs his packed black lederhosen to show off his hairy blond legs well turned in his sharp (red) stiletto heels. Skirting him, couples with eye-make-up dance shaking their hip-huggers to "Hot Fun in the Summertime."

At the coat check, a man batting Bette Davis lashes says, "Hey, look. Somebody threw away a perfectly good slave boy."

"But I feel high," Iago sniffs at clouds of cologne mixed with poppers. "Everyone is so emotional. What will we do now? We've always had Judy to get us through." She wipes a defiant Garland gesture through the bright psychedelia of black lights, day-glo posters, beer signs, and a mirrored ball flashing like one of Judy's sequin concert jackets. "When she sings 'Over the Rainbow,' I always stand, like, the gay national anthem." Of which Iago sings a snatch. "What a dump," her hands sweep the Inn. "Who said that?"

"We say that. We all repeat shit like that. We all say the same shit over and over and over. Like *Boys in the Band*. Like it's, like, always fresh."

"Shut up, Brain."

"My name's Brian."

"Fuck you and the evil twin you rode in on."

"Judy had a long life. She was forty-seven."

"A limited engagement!" Iago grimaces like the mask of tragedy. She had studied acting one semester in high school when Mister Janeway, the drama teacher, cast her (him, Tyrone Washington) opposite Othello and Desdemona, because "a black Iago tips the play." To say nothing of a queer one. Which Mister Janeway could never say. "This dump was a dump when the guidos opened the door two years ago. If one of these flaming creatures catches fire, head for the front. Always shout *theater* in a crowded fire. Who said that? The rear exit is welded shut, but, darlings, mine ain't." Iago bumps and grinds. "My guido told me."

"Your Mister Man must lu-u-u-v you," Brian says.

"Love me? Love? Me? The Afrikkin' Kveen? No, doll. I was pushing on the door, which was formerly famously open to the alley. I was in a tiny panic to go out back to score some Quaaludes, and my guido holds up a baggie and says, 'Stop pushing, doll. No exit. I'm holding Vitamin Q.' My guido's connected."

Iago brags she's a born depressive who lifts her mood with higher stakes, wilder sex, outrageous make-up, dangerous boyfriends. Just like Judy. "She's the queen of masochism. That's why we all love her.

You don't have to be into whips and chains to understand Punch and Judy. She's got shoulders padded to carry our dreams, our anxieties, our sins." Iago's radar, constantly scanning the door, catches a pouf of (hit it!) limelight. "Enter," Iago announces, purposely punning her nemesis, "Norma Desmond, pursued by a boa."

Stout and stately, Norma Dessun, opera queen, enters through the Stonewall crowd that parts to let her parts go by, Iago thinks, like a (marcelled de-camped) nude descending the stairs.

"Get a load of Funny Bun tonight."

"She forgot her broom and monkeys."

Norma's face is stretched by her all-conquering past with no future even at 11:02 by the clock. In gay years, she is in middle-age, pursuing what once had come quickly to the fourth runner-up in some drag bar in San Francisco. "Hello, infidels and daffodils!" She exists with no visible means of support. Two seasons ago, briefly, she was a comb-out *arteeste* for the wigs in *Cabaret*. Norma, true queen, presenting plucked face to a follow-spot she is certain exists, holds court *en route*. "Judy is exactly that song about Elsie in Chelsea, the happiest corpse I've ever seen." Norma, fresh off the funeral line, had been at the same Upper East Side drag party with Iago. "Judy was happy to let go. I know for a fact the names…," Norma floats like the Pope above the crowd, "…of more than one sleazy hotel in Hollywood, where she used to take her rough-trade tricks. And I don't mean Chateau Marmont."

"Norma's had her cake," Iago says, "twenty-eight cakes, pushing twenty-nine."

"Miss Dessun is dragging thirty-six," Sylvia Rivera says passing by with two soft drinks. "After I fucked her, I looked in her wallet. She's twice my age."

"Liar."

"That flower child is what's left of the last of the hippies."

"We're all the last of the hippies. Norma just seems old. She can't get over never going on as understudy for *The Madness of Lady Bright*."

"Type casting, *puta*." Sylvia walks away impersonating "The Girl from Ipanema."

"Norma," Iago yells, "you tacky mannequin! Weren't you Goebbels' mistress?"

Norma Dessun has the vapors. "Darlings, I cruised six of the cutest cops drinking coffee out in Sheridan Square. If the Sixth Precinct had a ball…"

"Those aren't cops," Iago says. "They're Hitler Youth. Leather queens. Hanging out to go down to Keller's. Did I tell you I lost my thing for cops last summer…"

"*Oy!* Here comes her litany of Jack and Bobby and Martin Luther King."

"…during the Democratic Convention in Chicago."

"Darling, you're a rebel without a dress." Norma oozes cuckoo bravado. She fabulously dispenses free beauty tips. "LSD is the fountain of youth. It stops mental aging. Take acid when you're nineteen," she tells her tricks, "and stay nineteen forever." Norma accidentally came out into stunt-double drag in Mexico, on the beach at Mismaloya, standing in for some of the biddies on the set of *Night of the Iguana*. Between takes on the bus driven by Richard Burton, Norma, who was still Norman Dempsey, hears Tennessee Williams comment to Liz Taylor, "Why is every stuntman two hundred pounds of meat in a blond wig?" Then Tenn says to Norma/n, "Have you met my friend, Victor? That's short for victim." And Norma/n says to Tennessee, "I'm Norman. That's short for enormous." Tenn takes one long smirking drag on his cigaret holder, and exhales his message like skywriting, "Norman is short for Norma."

Fingernails, red with polish, delicately drop a dime into the spinning psychedelia of the Wurlitzer juke box, and push the buttons for C-9, Mickey and Sylvia dueling out "Love Is Strange."

"This dump really is a dump," Iago says. "Amazing how you can take black paint and a red light bulb and call it a gay bar."

"This dump," Brian says, "is a high-school sorority. Legal booze would keep out all this drag chicken. I dig the Hayloft on 42nd Street. Gay sex and beer. Now that's a private club."

"This dump," Iago says, "is not private enough—if the doorman let you in."

Frankie the Goon: "Members only. Sign your name. Five bucks. Get a ticket for one drink." Frankie squints. "I don't want no trouble. Show me your draft card."

The guidos pay off the cops who they try to screen out at the door, because the undercover pigs are, like, moody about private clubs serving unlicensed liquor, and unpredictable about enforcing the law that every bar in New York City keeps a proper ratio of men and women.

"Sooner or later everybody comes to Rick's." Iago speaks in quotes from movies. She sizes up her chances with the crowd, big for this early on a Friday night. "Fuck 42nd Street. Location is everything. This is the spot. 53 Christopher. You take Christopher Street, you take West 4th, or Seventh Ave, or even cruise down Waverly Place, and you always end up here, dear, where we're queer, dear, at this dump, where all yellow-brick roads lead to Rome — dig the guidos or not."

Norma Dessun heads back to the toilet. "I'm visiting the black hole of Calcutta."

"You are the black hole of Calcutta."

"Is there nothing you queens will not mock?"

Marcia Garcia intones the 1930s ditty, "We are the Roxy girls."

"Each and every one a virgin."

"We wear our hair in curls." Marcia Garcia and three queens (including Bessie Mae Mucho) dissolve in laughter singing. "We roll our dungarees way up above our knees."

At the sink behind the bar, one of the managers, one of the better looking of the junior guidos whose job is watering drinks, picks up four Coke glasses with each big hairy hand and dips the eight glasses (1-2-3 fast dips) into gray sudsy water, and then again (3-2-1) into a murky rinse. "My God," Norma says, "that water's the color of jaundice." She calls back over her shoulder, "Sylvia, darling! Another glass of Coke?"

"Envy me." Sylvia Rivera swims away trailing a pool of color through the dim light. "Hibiscus is in town for Judy's funeral. I may become an honorary Cockette." Sylvia the street hustler is in mix-n-match drag because the law, enforced by Frankie's fast eye (yeah, you) and faster hands, requires anyone with a dick to wear at least three articles of men's clothing or risk being arrested for impersonating a woman. "Hibiscus says San Francisco is still all hippie flowers in your hair. So fuck you, my darlings."

"Sylvia, you are the world's only reusable *pinata*."

"Outside that chapel," Iago says, "there were so many friends of Dorothy they looked like an army of ballerinas. I shouted out, 'Boys! Boys! Your dance class leaves at dawn!'"

"You could have laid them end to end."

"Butt—of course! I had every tenth one. I confirmed Kinsey's count. Every tenth one was queer. And so was every ninth, every eighth..."

"Stop bragging. The radio said twenty-two thousand..."

"I haven't had them all, doll. Yet."

"...said twenty-two thousand single men—they called us single men—were there."

"What would you suggest they call us? Bachelors?"

"Considering..., I'd say we're lucky."

"I was there," Brian says. "I cruised by earlier tonight."

"Something was in the air."

"Yeah, babe, cheap cologne."

"Everybody was there."

"And those who weren't will swear they were. Every queen that ever was claims she saw Judy at Carnegie Hall."

"Tonight was historical."

"You mean hysterical."

"Queens thrive on hysteria. Judy was hysteria on a stick. We're all Blanche on a hot tin street car."

"I'm Judy, suddenly, this summer." Brian makes Fosse jazz hands around his face.

"You are such a phoney. That first artificial heart last month? Who knew you got the transplant."

"I'm so Tin Man."

In the toilet, Norma Dessun surprises two recent graduates of one of the finer Ivy League schools taking seesaw turns blowing each other. Gay sex is one way to keep out of the draft for Vietnam, but they look swish enough for immediate deferment. Both wear powder-blue Orlon sweaters across their shoulders with the arms tied loosely across their chests. They jump as Norma enters. One pats his styled hair. The other wipes his lips with the back of his hand.

"Perhaps I can be of service," Norma says. "I'll watch you while I guard the door against that big bad manager."

Norma, ever queen of the universe, lights a joint, huffs a hit, and offers the two sweater-queens a toke which they take and re-breathe into each other's mouths. Their dicks bobble between them. Locking lips, tangling tongues, the two jerk each other off in a sensuous preppie palming that raises the heat in the humid toilet. One of them has doused his balls with a choke-hold of Jovan musk oil. The tiny window is boarded up the way the front window of the bar is boarded up to hide from the street the kinds of shit that scares the horses.

"I feel faint," Norma says. She pops the glass of her yellow-mesh amyl capsule, and falls to her knees securing her heels tight against the door. She pushes her face between what she fantasizes (more popper) are two young college athletes who take the opportunity offered by the opportunist and double-fuck her face cuming together in…

"…My hungry hole," Norma says returning victorious from the toilet, lipstick fresh. "Film at eleven. Oh my. It's a little after eleven…which I'm always after."

The guido manager shakes a familiar finger at the impossible Norma. "*Gavone!*"

"Uh-oh," Iago says, "Maria's not an asset to the abbey."

"At least, she's not dragging toilet paper stuck to her shoe like Jackie O."

"This place only looks like a gay bar. It's really an eye-talian bar."

Norma Dessun has a secret taste for linguisa which she indulges starting late one night—early last spring—when the lone guido closing the bar, like, leans back against the cash register and unzips his black gabardine slacks which causes Norma's knees to grow so weak she takes the uncut invitation deep down her throat and hums thirty bars of "Come Back to Sorrento."

The guido's shirt hangs open by three buttons. Around his neck, a gold chain rests in the tangle of thick black hair on his pumped chest. Hot enough himself he's made hotter by the thought of the powerful anonymous interests he works for.

It isn't so much that the guido lies and tells Norma he'll tap her head before he cums (in her mouth) that disturbs Norma.

It's more the gun that Norma's fingers feel strapped to the husky guido's right calf that cautions her to barely mention what was for some weeks an unspoken date that always ended ("Mambo Siciliano") with the guido getting off squeezing Norma's cheeks to make sure she swallows his eye-talian ice.

"That's his trip," Norma says. "I tell him, I don't know who you work for, but I know *you.*"

"Oh, listen," Iago says to Norma, "they're playing your song: 'Kind of a Drag.'"

A boy duded up (young, dumb, and full o' cum) like Joe Buck in *Midnight Cowboy* lights a cigarette, exhaling with exasperation, "My john said he'd be here at eleven. It's fuckin' ten after." His shirt hangs open. He has a bluebird tattooed on each pec above each nipple. "Fags are always waiting for something. So why am I waiting? Do I look like a fag?" He flashes the panther tattoo on his forearm. "That's the difference between me and you brownie queens. I don't wait."

"Smell him," says one of a matched pair of androgynous Pratt brats out slumming for the night, sucking energy like the lost love-children of Jim Morrison and Mick Jagger. They have art-school vibes silk-screened all over them. One seems like a girl passing as a boy. The one that seems like a boy carries a concealed camera — the one thing most taboo in a gay bar — because the Polaroid is his most valuable possession and he fears leaving it in their crash-pad at the Chelsea Hotel.

"Do something," his twin says. "You're so boring."

"I'm not boring."

"I don't see anyone standing around wondering what you'll do next."

"Babble on, bitch," says the number one Pratt brat. He turns to the cowboy. "You ever gone to Max's Kansas City?"

"What?"

"You ever have to go, like, every night, to Max's Kansas City?"

"Fuck, man, yeah. I been to Kansas City."

"What's your sign?"

"I'm a dollar sign on the cusp of ten bucks."

"Are you ready for your close-up?"

"You got ten bucks?"

The brat ignores the remark. He prefers pictures to sex. He says,

"Slow night. Full moon. You wanna make a happening, something, anything, like, creative, happen?"

On the dance floor, the uncoupled crowd jerks akimbo to Creedence Clearwater pounding out "Proud Mary."

"This place ain't happening," the cowboy says. "This dump is fucked."

"So this *is* a dump." Iago is rowing herself around the floor in her invisible gondola. "But I pretend this is so much grander than doing sailors in the toilets at the Port Authority Bus Terminal."

"What you lookin' at," the cowboy says.

"I'm admiring the view."

"I ain't your view."

"You would be if you straddled my chest." Iago touches imaginary pearls.

"Fuck off. I ain't into you." The cowboy nods to the brats. "I'm gonna cruise down to the trucks. Where the action is. You wanna come?"

"Come? Cum?" Iago is jealous, and, turned on (turned down) by another man that got away, paddles up river. "This dump isn't hell." She looks at the clock that seems stuck at 11:20. "It's Limbo."

The cowboy tells the brats, "I got a party in my pants."

"I got a couple hits of acid in mine."

The brats and the cowboy merge into a tight threesome who shuffle their way making puppy licks over to the dark cubby hole behind the bright cigarette machine. They bump past a bleached blond beehive inserting forty cents for a pack of Virginia Slims.

"Vagina Slims," the cowboy is a snide asshole, "You've come a long way, baby! And it ain't far enough."

"Darling," the beehive snaps, "you obviously grew up in something aluminum and tow-able."

Through their clothing the three-way makes furtive gropes at breaking laws against loitering for sodomy and deviant sex. The cowboy's dick burrows up a 3-D outline of the Texas Panhandle inside his jeans. A wet circle of pre-cum darkens his denim where Amarillo would be. Since the nude scene in *Hair*, or is it because of the Summer of Love, nobody wears underwear anymore.

Inside the whirling Wurlitzer juke box, the needle scratches into "Town without Pity." Norma is cadging drinks. "For ten dollars, I'll count down the Gay Hit Parade. 'Secret Love,' 'Secretly,' 'Strangers in the Night,' anything from Cole Porter, everything from Noel Coward—all capped by the be-wigged, be-jeweled, be-gowned Diana Ross bullying the be-dragged Supremes into 'I'm Gonna Make You Love Me.' She can't threaten me that way. But you can."

"Two weeks ago, at a 6/9/69 party," Iago says, "that fagalicious day and date celebrated everywhere in the gay world, I blew that cowboy. What a love-in. Now he pretends he doesn't remember me."

"6/9/69 I filled up my dance card and my diary. It was a night to remember." Glorious Wantsome, who thinks Warhol's *Chelsea Girls* is *Our Town*, is the make-up girl for one of the actors who knows Gerard Malanga who knows Paul Morrissey who works with Mario Amaya who was shot when Valerie shot Andy last June. Glorious Wantsome was standing on the other side of Andy, and wants her fifteen minutes, and she has been speeding exactly one year and twenty-four days since two bullets went *pop-pop* like a cartoon into Andy's spleen. She's speed-queen friends with Bridget Polk, and she traded (for a load of meth) her Warhol drawing of Judy's red slipper filled with flowers. "I'm an outdoorsy Pisces out of place in Manhattan. Andy refused to cast me. He said I'd leave a stain on the screen." She wears a gingham pinafore shirt knotted above her bare midriff and speed-talks. "The trucks are a man's world. Just like Keller's."

"What's your point," Iago asks Glorious, and then squeals out to a passing face, "Sabrena! You gash! So groovy! You blow my mind!"

"Help me," Glorious says. "I've been up all night."

"It's only eleven-twenty-two."

"Up. Up. Up. Ever since Judy died. Last night. Again. Every night. Fuck her self-pity. Fuck her *oi vey* songs. Fuck the man that got away. I could ream someone a new asshole."

"And ruin your pinafore?"

"I'm so insomniac. I have jet lag. Without traveling."

"Flight 69 now departing for *The Valley of the Dolls*."

"Who do I have to fuck around here to buy some Quaaludes? All anyone has is speed."

"Your mood ring is gonna explode."

"Out of my fucking way."

"Down boy."

"Don't you *boy* this girl. No to all that." She steams off to a rear corner in the bar, stewing in the shadows, near three guidos standing in the alcove at the back end of the bar—all talking at once with their hands. She drops her purse that spills open with a two-ton arsenal of bobby pins, compacts, curlers, and metal lipstick tubes.

"Thank God," Iago says, "I'm not a drag queen. I only look like a drag queen. I'm really a manazon. In fact, I saw several manazons among the friends of Dorothy in Judy's funeral army. And why not? Judy was a manazon."

"What's eating Glorious?" Norma Dessun asks. "She hasn't been the same since that anti-war be-in last March at Grand Central Station. The one the cops busted because of the pot. She claims two cops dragged her by her wig into a paddy wagon."

"Darling, I know that scene!" Iago says. "I was arrested for lewd acts in that raid on the Continental Baths last February."

"Fags are like blacks. Always arrested."

"This frikkin' African ain't whistlin' 'Dixie.'"

"Sooner or later. *Oy* and *vey*. Rounded up."

"The cop identified my towel."

"The Continental towels are all the same."

"*Mais oui, cherie.* But I was lewd, am lewd, will always be lewd." Iago lights a cigarette. "I been arrested nine times. Peace marches. The Ramble in the park. An erotic subway ride. I don't care what people think about me."

"My God, it's hot out tonight. With the humidity, it must be a hundred."

"Half of Fire Island came back to the city to see Judy." (Iago knows Judy's death is all about Iago, because *IagoIagoIago* is always the bride at every wedding and the corpse at every funeral.) "Christopher Street is shoulder pad to shoulder pad. Julie Julius' was jammed this afternoon."

"You trespassed into that bar and mortuary? That's where Judy should have been laid out. Even you are too young for that Wrinkle Room." At Julius' Bar around the corner, the clientele, dragging forty and pushing sixty, is *too, too much* in a decade trusting no one over thirty. "What was Julie's having? A sip-in? A die-in?"

Young guido and mick cops get off strutting into Julius' to hassle the old queens they arrest for soliciting if the old dears so much as stand at the bar facing out rather than leaning in.

"What was I doing?" Iago pauses (poses). "I was ticked off. My brother's wife said I could come over as long as I didn't say anything gay, and I said I'd come over if she didn't say anything straight, which snapped her bra. The Swinging Sixties have not liberated my sister-in-law. I should have gone over anyway and kicked down their door. (You can stop arresting me, officer — I've cum!) I don't care if I get arrested as many times as Mae West. Umph." Iago, who swears Mae West is a man, does West's vamp. "Why doncha come up and see me sometime?" In her wallet, Iago carries an Illinois driver's license (expired), a draft card (with a high number), and a medal (miraculous) of the Virgin of Guadalupe tucked in with membership cards to the Hayloft, Mattachine, and NAACP. "I give massage now," Iago says.

"You sell handbags in Filene's basement," Norma says.

"I also do massage. I make hotel calls. Closet calls."

"You're hustling."

"But Judy has me thinking about singing in nightclubs."

"Your name in lights over the Plywood Room."

"I'll change my name to Jetta Kay, tickling my twin keyboards in the lounge of the TWA Terminal at JFK. 'Fly Me to the Moon.'"

"Darling, you have no talent. You sing into your hairbrush."

"Fuck you, Mary. I can sing."

"Lip-synching isn't singing."

"When I lip-synch, I sing along. In living color. When I was six years old, I wowed the Christmas pageant at Saint Jude's. I lip-synched Judy at Saint Judy's." Iago sings, "'Have Yourself a Merry Little Christmas.'"

"What the hell is that racket?"

In a blowup, two of the guidos hassle a patron, a short skinny sixteen-year-old she-he wearing a Che Guevara T-shirt. They strong-arm the poor baby out the front door. "Beat it, Munchkin."

She shouts back, "The Dwarf is not saying goodbye."

"Poor Dwarf. How did these guidos take over our world?"

"Gay bars can't exist, sweet-cheeks, without the guidos paying protection to the fuzz."

"Fuck it," Iago sighs, "There exists a future time when we will already be dead."

"Spare me."

Iago sings the blues. "Judy has me crying in my beer. That quivering tremulo in her voice. We're all just Judy waiting for some man to come through that front door, or kick us out the door. Where's the sassy black queen with the huge Afro who's supposed to hold all this together?"

"That would be you."

"Me? Am I still black? Am I? Black? Still? Once I was colored, but I grew up Negro."

"I feel one of your arias coming on."

"Judy had soul. Belting out 'Swanee' and 'Mammy' and 'Rock-a-bye Your Baby.'"

"And 'Battle Hymn of the Republic' on her TV show when JFK died."

"All those white spirituals that sound black."

"She also swam a lap or two around the island of Lesbos. What kind of woman sings 'For Me and My Gal'?"

"Lesbos isn't an island. It's a cunt-inent." Iago vamp-sings Kander and Ebb. "The cunt-inent of Lesbos is so wide, mein Herr." She hates herself, her constant lip, her trivial quotes, her repeating everything a thousand times. "Well, shut my mouth!" Self-loathing (spreading through Iago's body) ignites masochistic desire. "Depression is my only hardon. Can I go down to Keller's to meet a leatherman? Can I go to Sanctuary and dance? Can I go up to the West Side Y to charity-fuck old farts in the steam room? Can I borrow five bucks to do the Everard Baths? Will white boys ever top me—and my ten inches of depression?"

The Stonewall has no past and no present. Gay hot spots hang in a constant future of hope and despair. The clock is always ticking toward closing time.

"What makes this night like no other?" Iago cannot stop her manic-depressive swing. "One thing," Iago says, "Judy's dead." She sings another snatch, "The hopes and fears of all the years are met in thee tonight." She turns, "Why don't I put a dildo in my mouth and pull the trigger."

"Iago, darling, as a B-movie, you're an A-Plus. For a revolutionary, you don't quite grasp the power of queers. It's like Black Power, only different. Smoke a doobie. Get a grip. Be cool."

The Wurlitzer needle drops on Betty Everett slapping out "You're No Good, You're No Good, Baby, You're No Good."

Brian pulls Iago. "Come dance with me."

Norma evaporates.

"I need rough sex," Iago says, "like Judy needed rough sex."

"You're safe here in our little daisy-chain universe…where I slept with, mmm, him who blew her who fucked, uh, him who slept with you who never slept with me."

"Thank you, Barbarella."

"I'm much more Bette Davis or Joan Crawford."

"Don't play drag poker with me," Iago says. "I'll see your Bette Davis and I'll raise you two Diana Rosses."

"You can't beat a full house: two Streisands and three Mae Wests."

"Read 'em and weep." Sylvia Rivera crashes up, cruising through, always on the game. "Four of a kind. I got four Garlands."

"Let's go up," Iago says, "to that porno theater on 42nd…."

"The Cameo?"

"…and blow some seafood. The Fleet's in."

"The *Times* says sailors are deserting in droves since the Tet Offensive."

"The *Times* fails to report they're hiding in back rows at the Victory."

"I loved ushering at the Victory."

"Not the Cameo, doll, and not the Victory."

"Those balconies, those toilets are so *mondo*!"

"It's called the Masque. Between 9th and 10th. Where they stop the fuck flicks at midnight, and Lady Ludlam performs *Turds in Hell*. Live on stage! And *Whores of Babylon*."

"I auditioned for both."

"You're ridiculous enough." Sylvia Rivera is pissed. She is eighteen, living in a squat, raging when she's not ragging, and bitching about being shoved around by johns after they cum. "Do you believe these musclebound guidos giving Dwarf the gate?" The four-foot she-he often hustles protected by Sylvia whose stock in trade is her motto: What's hotter to a john than discovering a transvestite's penis? "My God, girl," Sylvia takes a long and not unsatisfying look at Miss Aretha Iago, the crusty Toast, "you look like shit. You need a drink. Sashay your bones to my table. Sylvia will magically turn your Coke into a rum and Coca-Cola. Fuck the guidos. And fuck me. We all need a cock…(rim shot)…tail."

Norma Dessun, reigning at Sylvia's table, is interrupted saying, "Judy fought with everybody: MGM, managers, directors, husbands, hotels. She didn't take shit from anybody." She assesses Iago. "*Garcon*, two more chairs!"

"*Garcon* screamed the gargoyle." Iago parries.

Norma thrusts. "My limit is three drinks a day. It's past midnight. Bring my next three."

Sylvia pulls a flask from her Capri slacks, puts a Coke glass between her knees, and pours in a double shot. "That will be one dollar," she tells Iago. "A girl's got to live."

Dwarf scoots into the table. "Frankie the fuck can't keep me out."

"Toto returns. Hello, Meeskeit."

"I says to him," Dwarf says, "'You Don't Own Me.'"

"Thank you, Lesley Gore."

"Attention Kmart shoppers! Fresh meat." Norma Dessun says. Her three crepe necks periscope up. "Get a load of him. Hot new talent entering the front door. Now that's a Mister Man."

"In this dump," Iago sips her drink, "nothing beats a new face."

"You could use a new face."

"I don't like his face," Sylvia says. "He don't look like a paying customer."

"He's a tourist out for a spin from his closet."

"Ask him to dance. Straight guys don't dance. Here's a dime for the juke box. Play E-16."

"What's that?"

"Hello, I Love You (Won't You Tell Me Your Name?)"

"Judy," Iago announces, "was a manazon."

"Who isn't?"

"Don't look now." Iago holds her rouge compact close to her

eye (up periscope) and aims the mirror over her shoulder. "Another tourist."

"Check out the number in the booth by the door. He's been ogling us since a quarter to twelve."

"So ogle back. He's hot."

"Forget E-16," Iago says. His blood pressure ramps up. "Go play A-12. 'Susie Q.'"

"'Susie Q'?"

"Susie Queer. Susie Queen. Susie Quaalude."

"Why?"

When things go wrong, everything changes quickly.

"Because that tourist is the cop who busted me at the Continental Baths…"

"Not this tired bullshit." Sylvia has the instincts of a kid born hustling Times Square. She came out working when she was eleven — under a table at Horn and Hardart's.

"…and I'm gonna ask him to dance. If he dances, cool…."

"My nipples are getting hard." Sylvia slides down into the booth pushing her flask under the cushion.

"We pay the guidos plenty," Norma Dessun says, "to protect our little sanctuary."

"Payoffs ain't what they used to be."

"Who needs an ambush?"

A palpitation ripples from Iago through the *JudyandMickey* musical comedy of the Stonewall. Faces look up from tables. Heads turn on the dance floor. As if it trembled. A red rush of instinct causes some of the seated to stand, some of the dancers to stop. Like a crowd in a theater at the first faint smell of smoke. The noise drops ever so, under its own roar of the crowd. Something ancient rises. Primal fear at a noise outside a cave. The snap of a twig. Those seated lean into one another. Those standing move one step closer. Alert. For a moment everything is pantomime. Everyone continues gesturing, talking, laughing, dancing, smoking, drinking because this surge of panic is coded in the bones and blood, and often is little more than a contagious rush that comes to nothing, and to notice it, acknowledging its hour-by-minute-by-second presence would seem, so, well, darling, paranoid. Drugs do that, and queens are ever so hysterical. Just like Judy.

Under the suddenly dazzling mirrored ball, even though everyone looks the same and acts the same, the gay guido notices the mood change from major to minor. He leans hard against the locked back door, as the front door explodes inwards with six big-deal plain-clothes cops led by a cop in uniform. "Aw, fuck," the guido says.

"Omigod!" Norma Dessun is unnerved. "This is a very bad scene. I'm ankling this joint."

Iago's cop-tourist yanks the plug on the juke box.

Silence.

Some screams, grumbling, hissing.

The uniform shouts, "This is an illegal membership club with no liquor license."

Low booing.

"Hey! It's the Keystone Cops."

Catcalls.

"Pigs!"

"Don't get your panties in an uproar."

"Woop woop."

"Okay, ladies, line up. Let's clear this fucking dump."

"My opinion poll is complete." Iago stands up.

"Give me that dime," Sylvia says to Dwarf. Sylvia threads her way through the crowd. She pushes opposite to the flow of panicky queens funneling toward the front door where a cop says, "One at a time. One at a time."

"Hey, Officer Krupke!"

"Three pieces of picture ID, you fucking degenerates. Get 'em out."

"Nobody has three photo IDs."

"You're certainly a prick."

"You think so?" the cop says. "You ever had a football shoved up your ass?"

"Didn't I blow you at the 6/9/69 party?"

The cop dodges a lipstick thrown hard at his shoulder. "Motherfucker!" He grabs hold of Norma's arm.

"Please, officer, sir, officer," Norma whispers. "Can I be the man that got away?"

Iago watches three or four huge sections of Norma Dessun cave in, very *nude falling down the stairs.* "The fatter you get," Iago snaps, "the more submissive you become."

Glorious Wantsome reapplies her makeup. "I'm ready for my close-up. I want all my minutes of fame, plus yours, his, and hers. I do not intend to blend in with the locals." She throws a shower of hairpins that hit the plain-clothes cops like shrapnel.

They cuff Glorious (bruise her wrist, break her watch) and push her (resisting arrest) to the front door where shouting can be heard out on Christopher Street.

"I adore bullies."

"Officer! Officer! There must be some mistake. We are the Roxie girls."

"Hey! Arrest me. I don't want to go to Vietnam."

"This is the bad and the beautiful."

"Get rid of your drugs."

Uppers, downers, joints, pills, coke (folded in origami papers), poppers, baggies, tabs of acid hit the floor.

"You fuckin' freaks," a plain-clothes dick says, "Don't you look at me like that. You look at me like that, I'm gonna kill you, and tell God you died."

"I been hearing all that jazz since grade school, but not with such bad breath."

Sylvia makes it to the Wurlitzer and pulls the console out from the wall.

Dwarf crawls behind the jukebox, sticks the plug into the socket, finds a quarter on the filthy tile floor, quickly peeps for more spare change, finds a hit of acid, and swallows it.

Sylvia pushes A-12.

Dwarf twists the volume control on the back of the Wurlitzer and turns it full tilt boogie.

The jukebox lights up bright, whirring alive with a whine, raises its metal arm to grab A-12, plops the 45 rpm down on the turntable, and drops its needle right on the revolving lip of "Susie Q" that blasts like a shockwave into the crowd.

"Kill that fucking jukebox!" A detective tries to shout above the din; he pats his gun.

Cops shove jittery, rattled, petrified patrons toward the double door that's breaking open.

Bright lights (red, white, and blue) from squad cars (black and white) sweep in from Christopher Street (hot and humid), sweep in past Frankie (pissed off), sweep in past the coat check (fat chance), sweep in splashing the walls, splashing the faces (red, white, and blue).

"Susie Q!"

Iago (flashing back on the Democratic Convention) chants "The whole world is watching," and hustles up a scrum, "C'mon, girls," who lock arms around the Wurlitzer. Iago tosses Sylvia a red-silk purse full of dimes that Sylvia feeds into the jukebox, punching, A-12, A-12, A-12, over and over. Iago yells at the blond leather hippie in the (red) stiletto heels, "I like the way you walk. I like the way you talk."

The crowd around Iago shouts back, "Susie Q!"

"What a blast!" There's two great things: to fuck and fight. "Susie Q! Susie Q! Susie Q!"

The uniformed cop charges the jukebox kick-line like a football fullback, knocking down four chorines and the leather hippie, and grabbing Sylvia's wrist, squeezing the dimes out of her hand. "You fucking cunt," he says. "You," he yells at Dwarf, "unplug that thing."

Dwarf flips him the finger.

"You! Tiny Tim! You're under arrest. And you, you fucking deviate," he turns to Sylvia whose wrist he is trying to hurt, "you're under arrest."

Two plain-clothes cops swat their way to the jukebox and kick it into silence.

Sylvia, tempestuous even on a slow night, does not like the cop twisting her arm, forcing her down to her knees, like one john too many. "I spit on you," Sylvia says.

The cop straddles Sylvia and tries to cuff her.

Sylvia conjures every frame of every fabulous Maria Felix film she's ever seen. She twists between the cop's shoes on the dirty floor. She knows this movie. She's got one take and she screams. "Don't make the mistake you can treat me like a woman. Under this drag, *puto*, fucker, there's a man who's a woman, and she ain't your bitch."

"Pull this cunt out of here."

Iago steps between Sylvia and the plain-clothes cops. "Black Power turns pink!"

"Try me, you knuckle-draggin' fuckin' monkey fruitcake."

The Pratt brat, very *La Dolce*, very *Vita*, aims his paparazzi Polaroid at Sylvia knocked down on her knees. His flash explodes a tabloid-expose rectangle—very *mondo*, very New York *Daily News*—around the tiny little drag queen, nylons torn, lipstick smeared, splayed splat on the yellow-tile floor with the gum and cigarette butts. Very *JudyJudyJudy*.

A cop grabs the camera and smashes it on the hard edge of the bar.

The twin Pratt brats grab a zygote-hold of each other.

"You wicked old witch!" Iago screams at the cop. "You fuck!"

Sylvia, seeing blue dots from the flash, twists on her knees, wipes her hand across her mouth, and works her way to her feet.

In slow-motion, she rises up out of *papi*'s lap, up out of the movies, up out of ten cents a dance, up out of the streets, up out of centuries, up out of nothing to lose.

In slow-motion, she rises up the knees of the cop, rises up his blue-serge thighs, rises up past the gun slung low on his hip, up past the leather belt and buckle at his belly, and up past the badge on his chest.

In slow-motion, she punches him in the face.

Everything speeds up.

The crowd at the juke box cheers.

The cop is stunned.

The sequins on the mirrored ball shoot psychedelic light shards (red, white, and blue) that explode overhead like (frag-grenade) fireworks on the Fourth of July.

The room falls deadly silent.

Sovereignty teeters.

A pin drops.

The crowd being herded out the front door (torn from its hinges), turns, curious, muted, shocked, at the precise instant Sylvia hits the cop, again, with an open-handed bitch-slap heard round the world.

Glossary for *Chasing Danny Boy*

Place: Ireland, Dublin, City Centre, Temple Bar
Time: January-June 20, 1999
Characters: Dermid
Oscar O'Sheen
The Brothers O'Morna:
    Goll O'Morna, Conan O'Morna
The Yanks from Chicago:
    Wethers, Frankie X, Knuckles, Patch
The He-She Banshee
Gran (Grania)
Brigid, Dermid's sister
The Conjure Bride

23 June 1993: Irish Government legalized homosexuality and the age of consent doing away with the laws that sent Oscar Wilde to prison.

Wilde One's Pub: Oscar Wilde meets Marlon Brando; Irish dramatist Wilde (1854-1900) jailed for homosexuality; wrote *The Importance of Being Earnest* and *The Picture of Dorian Gray*.

Banshee: the screaming banshee, often androgynous, signals imminent death

Cuchulainn: Ireland's most famous mythic warrior, formerly known as Setanta, swelled up to huge proportions in battle, and was killed by the wicked Queen Maeve's sorcerors. His statue stands in Dublin's General Post Office on O'Connell Street commemorating the Irish martyrs of the Easter Rising against the British occupation in 1916.

Dermid and Grania: the Romeo and Juliet of Celtic mythology

Dolphin's Barn Junction: a neighborhood in Dublin

DART: Dublin Area Rapid Transit system of light-rail trains and subways

Eamonn Owens: redheaded young Irish movie actor—with the map of Ireland on his face—in films, *The Butcher Boy* and *The General*

Great Famine: the potato famine of 1845-1848 killed more than a million Irish and forced another three million to emigrate, mostly to the U.S., thus making emigration into a feature of Irish culture. Presently, 3 million Irish live in Ireland itself; 7 million Irish nationals live temporarily elsewhere, extending Irish culture and genes throughout the world.

Glossary continued

Firbolgs: an ancient tribe in Ireland
Gardai: police
Aer Lingus: an international Irish airline
Lir, the Children of Lir: Lir's four children were turned into swans by their
    wicked stepmother's spell which also gave them the extravagant gift of song.
    (Lir is pronounced "Lear")
Mickey: like "Mick," an American derogatory term for an Irish person
Otherworld: the night world of myth and legend where heroes, enchanters, trick-
    sters, and fairies live
Paddy Goes to Holyhead: a satirically named rock band
eejit: idiot
Tuatha de Danaan: originally the people of the gods of Dana, the tribe who
    arrived in ancient Ireland on the feast of Beltane, May Day, landing at Con-
    nacht, displacing forever the earlier tribe, the Firbolgs
shebang: party, the whole thing, a celebration

Sources: "Chasing Danny Boy" is based around the Irish mythological tales
    "How Diarmuid Got His Love Spot" in *Oisin's Children*, "The Fight with
    the Firbolgs" in *The Coming of the Tuatha de Danaan*, "The Landing" in
    The Coming of the Gael, and "The Flight from Teamhair" in *Dermuid and
    Grania* collected by Lady Gregory in *Gods and Fighting Men*, London: John
    Murray Publishers, 1904

Chasing Danny Boy

Love hides where? The question dogged Dermid on the hunt. His gang of lads, slumming through Dublin, looked for love hiding inside the pubs, revealing in doorways, cruising through the pathways of St. Stephen's Green. Across the clipped lawns and cobbled quads of Trinity College. On Bachelors Walk beside the black water of the Liffey flowing under O'Connell Street Bridge. Night times, pissing in a construction dumpster on the corner of Dame Lane where one door led up to a Turkish sauna and another door, guarded by beefy hooligans, opened into the crowd of lads at the Wilde One's Pub.

Chasing scores down in Dolphin's Barn Junction, the south inner city, where a crowd beat some AIDS junkie to death. Right in the street. Fifteen rib-kicking anti-drug vigilantes cheered on by a scrum of women and children. Steel-toed boots striking sparks on the cobbles. Junkie blood on the steel shutters. In the Barn, anyone who risked the vigilantes and dared the dark streets turfed out by the dealers could score grass, acid, ecstasy.

Dermid and his boyo's were full of themselves with the success of their hunt. They had outsmarted the dealers and outstepped the vigilantes. Inside the Wilde One's, the queer pub air hung thick in a silken blue cloud of smoke that shimmered with the thump of the disco beat from the dance club upstairs.

"Was that love?" Dermid, at twenty, was a pub-wonder at discussing a premise in detail, standing with a pint among his friends. A pearl of foam hung on his short-clipped dark red goatee. Not a single freckle marred his perfect white face or cheeks ruddy as rowanberries.

"Was what love?" Oscar O'Sheen asked. He was happy with their raid into Dolphin's Barn, hunting and scoring sixteen hits of acid he could sell for double to the kids in from Galway for Saturday night outside, two blocks away, on the trendy streets of Temple Bar.

"Was it love when that old AIDS junkie threw his skinny fucking body across his twenty-three-year-old partner to protect him from the steel-toed shoes."

"Get over yourself," Oscar said. "Maybe it was love of family, yeah, driving the men to kick the shit out of two dope-dealing heroin addicts ruining the neighborhood." Oscar was a joker always playing tricks and acting out: *Move the fuck out of the Barn!*" Oscar, who was very tall, drove his hands down in the way he learned from hip-hop American rap artists on Sky TV.

Dermid laughed and his blue eyes laughed. He liked the hunt, the drink, the talk, the fact of the lads all together.

"In those flats in Dolphin's Barn," Conan O'Morna, who was twenty-two and the darkest of the lot, said, "the addicts are dealers and the dealers are users and it's fucking clear what they love."

"But the junkie," Dermid said, "when he was dying bleeding on the cobbles said, 'Keep away from me: I have AIDS.' Was that not a kind of love of your neighbor even when he's killing you."

"Ain't you just a fucking Jesuit," Goll O'Morna said. "A truer Irish statement of suffering was never made."

At twenty-four, Goll, the older blond brother of the dark Conan, was touted a dare-devil for all his adventures, and the three others had looked to him since they had been boys walking through the wet woods down in the Wicklow mountains, hunting wild rabbits and quail with snares, playing guns on and off the old Military Road that wound like a scar through the mountains to the south of Dublin, long before they had practiced smoking cigarettes and shaved their heads down to a rasp and played at being post-U2 Iggy Pop rockstars calling their air group, Tuatha de Danaan.

Long before Goll had been sent off for six months to the Priory, which was what Conan and Goll's Da politely called the prison, where Goll had turned fifteen and learned much more about men's bodies than ever he learned about not stealing tourists' cameras down at the Irish Sea side in Bray where their fathers worked.

They had discovered their bodies together tutored by Goll. Curious. Sizing up. Joking. *You're fucking gorgeous.* Measuring up. Competing. Hardening up. Shooting first. Cuming last. White flesh slip-slapping. The serious dare to put that in your hand *your mouth* your ass longest deepest hardest biggest. What they had done in quartet, in trio, in duo, and back to quartet, circling, jerking, arguing, wrestling, which dick *which face* which hole, sucking with quick sucks each other's nipples, pumping shooting, pals lads rebels rockers mates friends for fucking ever.

The Tuatha.

One for all and all for one staring at the piece of paper Goll pulled from his pocket with the address of a man in Dublin who was a friend of a convict mate in the Priory who wrote down the name and told Goll that fags were a soft touch a lad could use if the lad weren't a fag himself.

A punch in the face could prove the Tuatha rebels weren't fags.

Together, stripped naked, they took grooming turns shaving each other's heads, standing barefoot in the pile of Dermid's red hair, sculpting black sideburns on Conan, and goatees on Oscar and Dermid, and on Goll a chinstrap blond beard.

Conan took a needle from his Ma's sewing kit and pierced their ears for gold rings Goll had filched. The three of them had held Dermid down to the floor and pierced his right nipple with a gold ring and he called them cunts and they rose up wrestling and laughing, hard and sexy and surprised, turned on in the mirror at the sudden changed image of themselves. The small bedroom exploded in a flash of revelation.

They were boys no more. Their manly heroism was in their pride and joy in each other. They were bigger than their little seaside town. Neither the amusement arcades and the fish-and-chip shops, nor even the casual summer trade of Brits lazing along the strand willing to pay for quick sex, could keep the lads long in Bray which was a red dot on the DART rail network that couldn't roll fast enough on up the commuter tracks into Dublin.

"Don't look now." Oscar punched Conan on the shoulder.

Conan in turn punched Dermid. "Your search for true love, Dermid, is over."

Goll stubbed out his cigarette, exhaling hard, snorting a laugh. "There's a Whore at the Door."

The blue air in the Wilde One's split apart opening a path down the bar through the crowd of regulars from the door to Dermid's feet.

"It's the He-She Banshee," Conan said. "coming to take you

away. *Goo-goo goo joob.*" It was the man to whose Temple Bar address Goll had taken them six months before.

Dermid winced.

The He-She Banshee was an irony of nature: one of Ireland's high-hearted queens and the most handsome man in the underworld of Dublin, dragged up in a smart black suit of impeccable taste, with skin so fair that no light but night or fog had ever touched his face. He was a sort of gangster, not of the usual politics, but of porno, with ties some said to Amsterdam.

He was the owner behind the manager of one of the sex shops upstairs over a vacant lot on King Street offering Czech videos, and American gay magazines wrapped tight in plastic, and Taiwan toys inflatable and insertable. The shop existed beneath the radar of the Dublin Gardai, which gave Dermid and his friends the deluded idea that they too existed like an outlaw band outside the view of the police, free as the Banshee to do what they liked.

"It's a free country."

"Aye, and getting freer."

Even being queer was suddenly legal. Vertigo spun the whole shebang. All of them could feel Ireland, poor little Ireland, no longer an isolated island, shrinking under the Euro and the Internet and the Aer Lingus planes direct from Chicago. The Gardai were busy running bomb-sniffing dogs and drug-sniffing dogs through the strangers and tourists and daytrippers taking the jet-propulsion ferry back and forth from Holyhead in Wales to the Dublin port at Dun Laoghaire where the Banshee was always greeting someone or seeing someone off to the tune of "Paddy Goes to Holyhead."

The Banshee fancied Dermid, but he was forty, an old man, a dirty old man to the lads. Still, as the convict had predicted, he had money and, one by one, Goll and Conan and Oscar had, each more than once, trekked up the stairs to the rehabbed loft the Banshee kept as a pleasure penthouse on Wellington Quay looking back over Temple Bar. His interest in the muscular Goll was intensified by the sizeable Goll's wee stay at the Priory.

His appreciation of the sensuous hue of Conan's bog-dark looks had turned into a jape the lads used to provoke Conan who got his Irish up merely being reminded that the Banshee had told him the story about the Spanish Armada going down off the coast of

Ireland: "From the looks of you, Conan, at least one of the greaser sailors made it ashore to at least one Irish whore's bed."

For the Banshee, as for everyone, Oscar, hip-hop, with pockets full of drugs, was always the life of any party. "A cool life," Oscar said, "is always played cooly before cool spectators."

Truth was, the Banshee after his fashion loved Dermid, but loved the pursuit of Dermid more. He chased the young man but purposely never caught him, as if captured, Dermid might vanish. Always the Banshee stopped the hunt short of erotic seduction. Or something stopped him. Curious. Were forces at work somewhere over, above, around, and through Dermid? Love hides where, indeed? And what hides love?

The Banshee noticed a peculiar thing. Dermid was unaware that he was the most cruised youth in the City of Dublin. Nobody ever won him or could buy him. Dermid's sex was confined within the brotherhood of the Tuatha. Those other three, fucked with drink and sex, were hard cases who had walked Dermid, like their vestal virgin, down to the commuter train tootling out of Bray. Four handsome wild boys from the Wicklow mountains.

The Banshee was an expert listening to pillow talk, hearing Goll's bragging, and Conan's whispering, and Oscar's mooing over all the sex rashomon among the four Tuatha.

He imagined the lads of the Tuatha in the fast-forward, slow-motion, and freeze frame of the porno videos shelved in his shop. *The hot wet mouths of those handsome handsome handsome four swan-like boys lipping down slow then eager on jutting cocks spit wet tongued fucking pink butt yes like dogs taking every shape cum spurting on lips nose eye lashes stripped naked in the shed barn woods no no no yes linen sheets stained with shit dewlaps hot young sweat browning each other those four drip cum into me cum into you fuck into you fuck me oh yes wipe it on me eat it eat it swallow more more fucking yes you and you and you those four ah ah ah.*

The Banshee, flushed with the winter's night, walked through the Wilde One's crowd straight up to Dermid.

Goll stepped in front of the Banshee, and said, "Ain't you just the Lord of the Fags."

"Why hasn't," the Banshee said, "the Gardai arrested you yet!"

"Because I ain't yet fucked you to death," Goll said leaning in and kissing the Banshee's cheek.

"You'll have to wait," the Banshee said. "I can't stay." He turned to Dermid directly. "My, ain't you deadly good tonight."

"You spotty fuck." Goll laughed at the Banshee. He was jealous. He thought maybe Dermid had got a leg up by not fucking the fag.

The Banshee laughed back. "I said I can't stay. My dogs are outside. That great big doorman, with his girlfriend, is holding my hounds, mmm, leashed. I've come down simply to tell you four you must come up to my place tonight. Some Americans are in."

"Yanks?" Dermid said. "Why for fuck's sake, Yanks?"

"Because they're all rich," Conan said. "They smell like dollars."

"Faith and begorrah," the Banshee croaked like a stage Irishman, "they be comin' here to Ireland chasin' Danny Boy." He turned, chin up, for his exit, and threw back. "I have some white powders that will take you to the Otherworld."

"You're a right prick!" Goll was happy.

The Banshee gestured grandly to the pub full of men. "It's paradise this." He waved. "See you at the stroke of midnight. Cheers!" He disappeared out the door in a silken cloud of blue smoke.

"One time," Oscar said, "everyone left Ireland. This time, everyone's coming back."

"Jayzus, Jamie," Goll said putting his finger up his nose. "Yanks." Ireland was full of tourists looking for their roots. "The poor creatures."

Dermid followed the Banshee out the door to pet his dogs. The girl holding the three leashes smiled at him. He pet the dogs who licked his face and he smiled up at her.

"I'm Gran," she said looking freezing shoulders in her little tittie tanktop.

"Aye, you are," Dermid said. He rose up to his full height, and walked back into the pub, leaving her revealing herself in the doorway, vexed.

Oscar looked at Dermid. "Yanks are no problem," Oscar said. He signaled for pints all around. "Are they?"

For a fact, they all agreed, Saint Patrick's Day fucks Yanks up. Especially the queer ones. Those boyo's, coming out of the States, think, *don't yeh know*, wearing green at a parade and drinking piss-pints of Guinness, *puttin' on the Irish*, qualifies them for a duty-free trip to Ireland where life is One Great Big Fucking Saint Paddy's Day.

Drink up, lads.

Their travel agents all so eager to take the VISA and book them round-trip smack into one of those shimmering green fantasy posters of the Emerald Isle that turns out to be a night in Sligo. Ha!

Gimme a cigarette.

And, oh, it pains a man a bit. Them rich Yankee queens pretending they're married, out on their Irish honeymoon, buying Waterford crystal, swinging their cameras, hanging by their heels to kiss the Blarney stone, combing the highways and back-combing the byways, cruising for Eamonn Owens, standing posed like movie stars in Aran sweaters on the edge of windy cliffs, pissing out whiskey *too good for them* into the hedgerows by the roadside, leaning next to their Tour Bus, staring out like a bunch of Ryan's daughters at the westward sea.

Pretending they're standing in their immigrant great-grandfather's shoes, making jokes about always loving potatoes, talkin' imitation Irish, *starvin' far patatas*, taking panoramic snapshots of green fields crisscrossed with them rock fences, *bless us and save us*, that look so romantic to Yanks imagining stone fences built by red-headed men with uncut cocks white as perch.

Finish up, boys.

A fella has to love them, the American cousins, flying back economy class, tourists without irony, looking up long lost relatives who didn't particularly know they were lost, working as they are at computer companies in Cork and belonging to the EU. The Banshee's waiting with some easy marks, so's remember to lay on the brogue and the charm and say "wee" a lot and don't tell them Yanks we never eat corned beef.

"So," very droll, Goll said, "here you are your first trip to Ireland."

One of the four Yanks said, "To Dublin actually."

"Actually," Goll's ear spun the funny-sounding American idiom. "Dublin *ag-shoe-alee*...as opposed to Dublin virtue-ally."

"Dublin. Yeah," Conan said.

"Where the love that dare not speak its name first learned to hiss." Goll licked his finger.

"Boys, boys, boys," the Banshee said. " Let's forego the old Dublin irony for some Irish hospitality."

"Ain't 'hospitality' the new name for a fuck," Oscar said. He inhaled deep and blew a spew of cigarette smoke into the Yanks' faces, musclefucks one of them was, with big biceps and a stalactite crystal hanging very new-age between his bulging pecs. "You took your shirt off, I guess, because…?"

Attitude caused the posh furniture in the penthouse at the top of Wellington Quay to shift. Chic white chairs and plush white sofas and glass-top tables clittered back against the egg-white plaster walls. Red Berber rugs rolled up revealing the waxed pine of rough-hewn floors. Across the high ceiling, 12-volt track lights scooted into position. Candle flames guttered in the rising incense. Outside, below the windows of the penthouse, Dublin lit out in a maze through the ink-black Saturday night where anything was possible.

"Mmmm. Excuse me!" The Banshee moved like a stage director to arrange the eight men standing in the room. "Dermid and Oscar," the Banshee said, "and Conan and Goll, this is Mr. Wethers."

Wethers stepped forward, solid, impressive, thirty, and himself a redhead. He offered his big hand all around. "You fucks and my boys are gonna get along," Wethers said. He pointed and named Knuckles, Frankie X, and Patch who nodded their heads atop their thick necks and said nothing.

"Tough guys, huh?" Conan checked out the tattoo on Frankie X's neck.

"Patch is from the Patch in Chicago," Frankie X said.

"Why's Chicago need a patch?" Oscar cracked.

"Wise guys, huh?" Knuckles said. "Who do you think you are? Sean Penn?"

Wethers laughed and when he laughed, all his boys laughed.

"You wanna know the Patch is the Irish northside," Knuckles said, "and you wanna know why I'm called Knuckles." He locked his thick fingers together and made snapping sounds like little gunshots.

"Brilliant!" the Banshee said. He pointed to a table. "Food. Drink. Et Cetera. Name your poison. Especially on the Et Cetera."

Like a magician, he aimed his black plastic remote at a CD player and music exploded in volume and beat beat beat filling the penthouse with pulse and blood pushing the rhythms of the eight men sitting down *zip* smoking leaning pacing slamming a whiskey *ahhh* walking around one another looking *zip* checking sniffing *oh yeah* touching punching unbutton stroking rubbing the inside leg squeezing *don't go there* groping sizing slow-stripping laugh snort *hey* pose smack smack smack *yeah fuck dude come on*, Wethers grabbing *zip* Dermid's *zip zip* crotch: "*Show me what you got, Danny Boy!*"

"Don't fuckin' call me Danny Boy!"

Fighting words. Dermid's goodlooks flushed blue, warriors from the weir possessed when confronted, *yeh fuckin' shite*, punches tossed and blocked, lust rising, the room spinning round, men half-naked ripped naked, cocks gorging hard and rising, whiskey glasses dropped down on tables, *c'mere you little shit*, smoke inhaled deep, torn off shirts shed, nipples grazing nipples, the fighting stance of love, half nelson full hammerlock, penis poking butt slapping, *momentum, baby*, a harder dance rocking the room, *going farther faster than the fastest horse than the fastest jet than the fastest Internet because sex between men, even if it goes slow itself, goes swifter in the end than the swiftest thing in the world, for men's desire is a natural river that never stops while horses die planes crash satellites fall* and over the tub-thumping music the TV screen of silent Prague pornos shoots *digital bits of analog sex* into a room of grease lube oil spit shine sweat sheen O'Sheen red goatee tongue hunger *fingerknuckles nipple plucking* suck on me you him *fucking cocksucker* friendly thighs suctioning *rush the enemy naked* possessed with warp spasm of Cuchulainn into the *outrageous rage of the river of eros flowing*, the evening rising hard high clear brilliant, *sex sparkling like water gaining speed over rocks.*

"Everybody seems," the Banshee said, "sufficiently stoned." He looked with pleasure at the eight young gentlemen roaming his penthouse, sitting naked on his white furniture, walking naked about his table he had casually catered with plates and knives and paté and white wine and biscotti because he had forgotten bread.

Oscar, thinking of the sixteen hits of acid in his trousers

hanging on a lamp across the room, rejoiced to be a bit wrecked on someone else's stash.

"Drugs is the fucking glorious Otherworld," Conan said.

Dermid, always thinking of the hunt for the clarifying force of love hiding maybe somewhere in the penthouse, looked at the Yanks comparing them to his lads and his life and feeling weird.

Goll, thinking of the Americans, naked, circumcised, taking a break, well fed, huddling together laughing joking, liked their gangster style, four or five years older than him, tattooed, buftie boys, and imagined himself living back in the Patch in Chicago, an emigrant success at last, not like his Da and his grandfather and great-grandfather and all his family before him who'd never been able to get off their doffs and escape the emerald-green backwater of filthy gritty stupid old Ireland, and migrate out where there was money and sex and real luck.

"Danny Boy is a stupid fuck," Goll yelled. "A stupid fuck for staying stuck."

They all laughed at Goll standing naked and hard, throwing little amateur boxer punch-up punches, biff biff biff, in the middle of the room.

Wethers said, "Go fuck yourself, Danny, you stupid mick, cuz nobody else will."

"Fuck up, you," Dermid said. "You fucks only come to fuck us."

"Hey, fuck!" Knuckles said, "do we look British?"

Dermid stood up, blood boiling cock erect, hard, red, veined, big, thick, long, proud, stabbing into the sweaty air. He pointed at his prick, its big head mushrooming out the purple-red cowl of foreskin. "This what you want? This what you're chasing?"

"Fuck no," Wethers said. "Turn around. Show off your fucking cunt butt."

Dermid stuck his snotty fuck virgin butt out pulling his round white cheeks apart to the deep line of red furze growing thick and moist in his crack making kiss kiss kissy smooches. "You can kiss it."

"Pucker up," Patch said.

"Fuck you," Goll said.

"Fuck yourself, mickey," Wethers said. "Once me and my boys

fucked a United States Marine Corporal while I made him sing 'From the Halls of Montezuma to the shores of Tripoli.'"

"Fucking droll," Conan said.

"Like me and my boys are gonna fuck the four of you…"

"I'm wetting myself," Oscar whinnied, "fucking ass-bandits."

"Shut up," Wethers said.

"Yeah." Francis X stood up.

"Yeah." Knuckles stood up.

"Oh, yeah." Patch stood up.

Goll pointed. "Look, ain't they a fucking Hollywood western."

"And the movie ends," Wethers said, "with me and my boys fucking you four river-dancers while you sing 'Danny Boy.'"

"I love musicals," the Banshee said, drooling over the raw male energy in the room.

"I'll make you a bet," Wethers righted the room with good-natured belligerance, "that I can make you want to do it."

"Name your bet," Goll said.

"Never dare a Dublin man," Conan said.

"We ain't Eurotrash," Oscar said.

"Fucking us," Dermid said, "will be stepping up for you, because what you've been doing will make you blind."

He started laughing, and he was figuring fast what to do to rescue the lads and his ass, and his laughing and the whiskey and the grass stepped him out of time, slipping to another time, another Yank, who had come on strong, taking him on a long drive in a rental car out from Dublin City Centre north along the road to Howth at the northeastern end of Dublin Bay.

The ride had been lovely, really. Dermid had never been the few kilometers north, looking out east over the Irish Sea so familiar from down south in Bray, and then back west toward Dublin, but that City view over that posh neighborhood had disappeared, driving back, when the honestly handsome Yank had cut off the road and driven though the dunes along the beach, grinding gears through the sand, his hand on Dermid's knee.

The tall grass spotting the rolling dunes gave way to the miles-long flat sandy shore of Dublin Bay marked off in the distance by the twin stacks of the electricity works guiding in the jet planes to Dublin International. The car sped across the smooth sand, daring the broad lazy inrolling green green green waves of low tide, leaving wet tire marks behind in the white froth.

What was it with these Yanks showing off?

The beach was deserted. The car roared. Then stopped. The Yank, with a rasping black stubble of a three-day beard, came on strong, stronger than in town, with wet tongue kisses, demanding Dermid's ass, and Dermid thought of his mam telling his sister Brigid going on a date to always take bus fare home just in case.

When his sister made it home, she was, she was, she was very, and she said she was going to keep it. One time, that taboo would have been the end of a girl's name and the shame of a family, but in the vertiginous new times, pregnancy was a style and paid for and given little knit booties and pennies enough for a ride in the stroller to MacDonald's.

Only one last taboo remained, and that too was a style, and legal, except when paid for, which is what, in that car on that beach, the Yank with the expensive American teeth had told Dermid he'd do. For fun, Dermid had said *how much*, knowing no matter what bumboy price the Yank put on his hole, he'd refuse, but at least he'd know how much a Yank thought his Danny Boy ass was worth, which, when he heard the price in Irish pounds, was almost mystical news.

That time the wisdom had come to Dermid of how to save his ass. The handsome Yank, grabbing and groping, was all big-dick talking big-dick big talk, because really what the Yank wanted was Dermid fucking him, which Dermid did, in the car, in the sand, on the beach, in the late afternoon, feeling brilliant at turning the tables and driving his dick in and out of the athletic-built Yank in a fierce fuck that brought the Yank to tears, shooting his cum, untouched by hands, crying, putting his hands on Dermid's rosy white cheeks, touching his red red goatee, staring into his blue blue blue eyes, saying the kind of illuminated fuck-poetry men with stars in their own crossed eyes say after sex, "Some men have a look other men recognize, but you are as yet unmarked," and Dermid was told later by the Banshee that the Yank meant that Dermid had not yet ruined his body with the usual poisons of the adult world.

"Fucking you," Wethers stepped into Dermid's face, "may be I'll become a permanent resident up your Irish hole..."

"Ah, the bragging of the wee folk," Dermid said.

"…and make you want it," Wethers said.

"Don't tease tossers," Goll said. He stood shoulder to shoulder with Dermid facing Wethers' three boyo's. "As for this back-up group of wah wah sissies," Goll said. "We're the Tuatha!" He strummed his headbanger air guitar. "Waaaah!"

Dermid looked at Goll. The four Tuatha looked at each other, *fighting lads we are*, then looked at the four Yanks, *fucking Firbolgs*, then looked a warning at the Banshee, the would-be queen of the Tuatha, and ran like berserkers, shouting, across the room, jumping the Yanks, surprising them, and a terrible row shook the penthouse, arms and legs tangling, yelling, *wankers*, chest to chest, heads butting, cocks and tongues and bollix swinging, *we are the champions*, the hounds of the Banshee yapping barking, flailing fists gut punches pec slaps *you want a piece of me* music thumping Depeche Mode *wrestle this* thighs spread feet dug in sharp jabs soft palms strong fingers interlocked *get down* veins startling on forearms *on your* cockheads unsheathing excitement *knees* body slam onto couch shoulders into pillows, tongue-puking Yank deodorant, leg lock fierce breathing tight choke hold *choke on this* porno video bits jerking sweat rising smoke from ashtrays candles incense ram it *Dermid!* battling across the floor up against the wall *ouch goddamit* pressure of flesh drive of thigh sweat in the small of backs dust spiraling up in the fuming cones of track light *watch your fucking teeth* rising in pairs then threes *Goll Goll!* falling back in pairs physical primal animal *jay jay jaysis* teeth bared cocks rampant, Wethers rising, huge engorged blue veins *fuck* jab 'em thrust *boys* cries ravaging triumphant fluid *what forces work* spear impale, steam billows from the bodies clouds the smokey room, onscreen actors in the Prague video freeze in violet haze of digital bits, the dogs howl, muggy penthouse windows inside sweat with juice, outside a mist drifts lifts rifts through the high orange light glowing cumulus over Temple Bar and a dark fog rolls up from the cold black waters of the Liffey carried in by the ancient tide from the Irish Sea on the cum cum cum cries of night birds.

Three weeks later, Dermid wondered how his butt that night had become part of the Irish tourist industry.

Wethers himself had popped his cherry.

Coming out of the Infirmary, Dermid gave thumbs up to Oscar sitting with Goll and Conan on the long wooden bench. "The nursie says I'm okay." They all laughed nervously. "Ain't we just the mystic knights of the Fianna defending Ireland from foreign troops." The English doctor, who had drawn their blood and swabbed each of them front and back, had told them they showed no signs of any social disease.

Yet.

Conan said Frankie X had whipped out a condom before he fucked him. Oscar claimed Patch shot dryfucking his thighs, and Goll admitted to no more than Knuckles had fucked his face. Then Oscar remembered that Patch had cum twice, *mmm*, once inside his butt. Dermid noticed how Goll denied that Knuckles had screwed Goll as well.

"It was all so fucking furious." Dermid studied Goll's expression.

"We was all so fucking stoned," Goll said.

"The doctor wants to check our blood in three months." Conan said.

"Fucking AIDS," Oscar said.

"Fucking suspense."

"Fucking Yanks."

"Fucking us."

"Fuck."

At a curry cafe where they were not known, Dermid said, "Wethers and his boys put us well underfoot." He looked at the plates of sizzling tandoori. "I'll be changing my tune."

"What are you on about," Oscar said. "You turning down a life in Vaseline Alley?"

Goll sat a bit moony. He was remembering Knuckles who had whispered sweet nothings to him. What good did it do him to be sitting in Dublin with these gits when he could be working back in Chicago with "Wethers Bros. Bricks, Paving & Landscape."

He had drawn his brother, Conan, in on the intention, as much as the thought, that they two should be off to the States. Some fancy it was, but whether the Wethers or not, Goll was figuring his good old Dublin days were about over. He and Conan could lay bricks. In his pocket, he had two green card immigrant work applications, and Knuckle's Chicago phone number on a slip of paper.

Who was chasing who?

Goll looked at the other three lads. They looked at each other. What feeling was shame—suddenly at a soul-piercing glance—turned to a loud exploding laugh of relief.

"Waaaah! It was a fucking teen sex comedy," Goll said, "… starring us!

"Fuck us!" Oscar said.

"Fuck the Banshee!" Conan said.

"Indeed, fuck us," Dermid said. He raised his glass. "Fuck the Banshee! Fuck the Yanks! The doctor said we flirted with death."

"Jay Jaysis, Dermid," Goll said already imagining himself leaving Ireland behind. "Lighten up, dude."

Six months later, in summer, Dermid's shaved head was grown out to a lustrous red. He felt like a new man. He rubbed his long fingers over his moustache and goatee. He faced himself naked in the full-length mirror at the Sauna on Dame Lane. What a fire trap. His body was tall and lean-muscled. His skin clear and unmarked. Eyes bright. He was happy the doctor told him his blood was clean. He looked at his cock hanging soft and thick and long between his thighs. He flexed the muscle between his bollix and his asshole to make his cock bounce. He looked only at himself, neither to the left or the right, ignoring the eyes watching him from the lockers and the showers.

Life in Dublin had speeded up too fast for him.

He could not go back down to Bray and live like Bridget with her kid in their parents' house. He had found a room without a bath close to Dolphin's Barn where he lived alone. He toweled his shoulders and back. He had slowed his life down to a discipline.

Men could live without a bath or a kitchen.

He was tuning into the inner language of men.

Moving quiet around Dublin, ignoring what temptations he noticed, becoming a solid man, he said, working as a waiter among the starving young artists at the Idée Fixe Café, the good old *IF*, on Fowne's Street off Temple Bar.

"You've become a fucking monk," Oscar said. He was working for the Banshee. He had money. It was Oscar who brought the Tuatha de Danaan together one last time. He paid for the taxi to drive Goll and Conan out the M1 road to Dublin Airport.

Conan was worried about leaving the country, scared about climbing on the Aer Lingus jet, wetting his pants afraid about landing in Chicago and getting fucked all over again.

Goll was exuberant justifying himself. "Seven million Irish can't be wrong living outside of Ireland!"

"Meaning what about the three million of us living here," Dermid said. "Do you think this is the land time forgot?"

"Love hides where?" Goll imitated Dermid. "Love hides where?" He shoved his hand along the taxi seat under Dermid's buttocks and laughed.

"You're a right prick," Dermid said.

"But together we're deadly grand," Goll said.

The Tuatha de Danaan laughed. All together. One last time.

In the taxi heading back through the warm June night to Dublin City Centre, Dermid wondered what it was that drove so many Irish out of Ireland. Himself, he was staying put. He looked at Oscar. Also staying put, he figured.

Oscar was a good friend. His sister Brigid had taken a fancy to him despite his hip hop phase. And a convenient thing it was, them both being from Bray, knowing each other since kids, and Brigid's boy looking so much like Oscar, it was a wonder to think about.

Brigid herself was a dirty old mouth, invited by Oscar, coming to that curry house for the Tuatha farewell supper, saying goodbye to Goll and Conan, laughing and wishing them well, and saying mystically later at the pub, well into her second pint, "The secret Irish purpose is spreading Irish blood all around the world." And what barbed thing had she meant, saying, "Wasting Irish blood," looking hard at him, "is a crime against the Irish nature."

"If being Irish is all a person is," Dermid had answered.

With Goll and Conan O'Morna headed out over the North Atlantic toward America, Oscar in the taxi let Dermid climb out at Temple Bar.

It was half-ten and the crowds of kids, five years younger than Dermid, sat smoking and running and jumping on the steps of the plaza. Tourists from Galway and the States were strolling out of the small experimental theaters around Andrews Lane and heading to the expensive pasta restaurants like Paolo's where he'd like to work.

Dermid wandered on down the cobbled street of the pedestrian mall. Ninety minutes to midnight and the last light of the high summer twilight had finally darkened the lower sky.

Off Eustace Street, on the five-story outside wall of the Irish Film Centre, Dermid watched the rippling canvas screen wave under the huge Technicolor motion picture image of Liza Minnelli and Joel Grey dancing and singing loud over the crowd seated below in the courtyard enjoying the movie and the warm summer night. Middle-aged American queens were standing in the back rows singing along to *Cabaret* like it was fucking karaoke.

Maybe he should have gone back with Oscar to Bray. Maybe he should have flown off with Goll and Conan to America.

Down the street he walked through the crowds milling outside the music pubs from one spill of music to another. What a scene. One last tour of the street was all he promised himself, and maybe a midnight pint over at the Wilde One's, when his ears pricked up, and his eyes lifted up, and he saw eight young girls singing on the corner, "We're Goin' to the Chapel and We're Gonna Get Married."

Something drew him to them. Their voices. Their innocence. Their fun.

Seven of them stood around a dark-haired girl whose head was swathed white in yards of net bridal veil. She was beautiful. The light of her beauty was shining on the walls of the small shop front as if her glow was the light of a candle.

Dermid watched several tourists watching her. Something was going on. People were putting money in the bridal box at her feet. He was curious. He walked up to the girls who were calling out "Sir, sir, madam, madam" to the tourists who walked by staring captivated, but a bit timid at stopping, figuring the girls might play them like street mimes somehow for public fools. Dermid walked straight up toward them.

"Sir, sir," the girls called to him. Their pretty hands played through the white white white bridal veil floating around the dark-haired girl.

He smiled at them.

"Come here. Come here."

Dermid ventured up.

"Sir," the girls said, voices laughing talking saying singing sighing everything all together. "Sir. Please. Buy a piece of her wedding veil. She needs the money to buy herself a wedding dress."

Two Irish women standing by, four white plastic bags of groceries hanging straight-arm down from their four dumpling hands, said, "Ha Ha Ha."

"Ain't youse just the performance!" Dermid had seen everything at the *IF* Café.

The dark-haired bride with dark eyes smiled directly at Dermid.

"Brilliant." He grinned.

One of the girls held a scissors. "I'll cut you a piece. Yes? It will bring you luck on your path."

"With the looks on him," the two women standing by cackled, "he don't need luck."

"Aye, OK," Dermid said. He reached into his pocket for coins and looked at the dark-haired girl and pulled out a pound note. "This is rich."

The two women standing by said, "All these eejit girls want is seed and cash."

The girl with the scissors cut a three-inch piece of veil into a patch.

"Come here," the dark-haired bride said to Dermid, "and I will put a love-spot on you…"

"Are you a witch now?" He laughed and played along and went over to her.

"…that no one will ever see without giving you love."

She put her hand on his forehead, and she touched the piece of net veil there, and minutes later on his way home, in the high June midnight, walking the long walk toward Dolphin's Barn past the Wilde One's, Dermid, already forgetting the incident, feeling cocky in his pants, strolled past the beefy hooligans guarding the pub door where, lighting a cigarette, the girl Grania in the little tittie tanktop stood, calling to his back as he rambled by, "Where you been hiding, lover?"

Meet Me in San Francisco

San Francisco, April 25, 1906

Dear Benny,

It's yer old (ha ha) pal Jimmy writin you from General Delivery in Frisco. Where you might of heard back in St Louie we had a little earthquake on my birthday Wednesday last. What a way to turn 19 (ha ha). No birthday cake for me like the one we had two years ago when we had that special birthday party at the St Louie World's Fair before I lit out for Frisco on the train. I ain't forgot what we did. Sorry I ain't writ you much but I bin thinkin about you, &, pal o mine, I wish you were here, but I'm glad yer not. What I seen in the last week could break a man's heart. This whole city it ain't gone, but sorely wounded. Ma Sloat's boardin house where I live is all gone down South of the Slot an so is all the buildins South of the Slot. It's all us workin men down here an pore families because nice San Franciscans never cross South of the Slot in Market Street. Remember I toll you last letter that the cable car slot ran down the center of Market Street from the Ferry Buildin west toward Twin Peaks like a line between us an the rich folk we work for. It were terrible after the shakin woke us all up yellin in our longjohns runnin out into the streets at 5:12 in the AM. The Chronicle paper says 60,000 us souls live down South of the Slot, & we was all runnin for it, tryin to get away from the fire that started in a Chinee laundry near Ma Sloat's at Third & Brannan. It just spread & spread through all the broken wood & gas mains shootin flames into the air. I don't want to make you sick, dear Benny, but there was lots of men, some of um I knew, trapped in the wreckage & beggin at first to pull um out till they was beggin anybody to shoot um, & they was shot, because they was about to be burned to death. It was a vision of hell. Nothin none of us could do to keep somethin like 3000 souls alive in our disaster. Somethin like 500 looters was shot on site includin 2 fellas I knew who was just tryin to get their pants out of the wreckage. Gun fire & flames & smoke & explosions. I left Ma Sloat's with nothin. I don't know where I'm gonna live, despite rumors of Tetrazzini singing at Lotta Crabtree's fountain for us survivors at Geary & Market, as I am now campin next to a tent in Golden Gate Park which you may recall I once told you you'd like since I could see us walkin there, hand in hand through Paradise. So I was wondrin if you wanted to come out here to the ruins (ha ha, but I mean it) because you said you were needin work & there's lots of it. Just so's you know—I been takin my once-a-week salt-water at the Sutro Bath that's as fine as any building at the St Louie Fair. Maybe we could work for room & board for Ma Sloat. She says she's rebuildin over on Folsom Street upstairs over where her brother Hallam has a piece of property for a new saloon because he believes in the future of Frisco even South of the Slot. She says he believes in the future of thirst, & he be namin the little street next his after their father the older Hallam. If you have work there in St Louie then maybe you could send your old secret chum a couple bucks to help out, but, dear Benny, if I have to start over, & I do have prospects, I'd a damn sight rather start over with you by my side here in Frisco cause you never know what's gonna happen next, but this survivor can tell it's gonna happen here, & it would be good for us because our kind has to know how to take care of ourselves if you get what I mean. I can't meet you in St. Louie, Louie, but I can meet you at the Golden Gate. & you might want to see Tetrazzini as much as me (ha ha). Down on Folsom Street I found some French postcards like you never seen. I love this place, but not as much as you know who. Put that in your pipe, dear Benny, & smoke it. Two bucks would be fine. Your face an other assorted parts would be better cause I'd like to show you my South of the Slot.

Your devoted pal,
Jimmy

The Unseen Hand
in the Lavender Light

REEL ONE
His life was a silent movie

His mind craved flickers the way his mouth watered over salt-grit popcorn. In the early nineteen-forties, while the World War raged from Europe to the Pacific, the doll-faced waitress who was his mother snapped her gum in downtown Peoria's famous Bee Hive Cafe while she fielded her counter tips into an issue-by-issue collection of *Photoplay* magazine which he read between the daily double features.

Each afternoon she paid his nine-cent admission to the Apollo Theater. Each dinner time, after the matinee double bill, he left the balcony to eat supper on the last counter stool at the Bee Hive, and thought it not at all odd that his mother's regulars called her "Countess Betty" because she never waited tables, always working the faster turnover of the counter.

She flirted with the men from the County Court House across Main Street, and the factory workers from Caterpillar. She turned nickel tips into quarters. The War Department had retooled Caterpillar Tractor Company into a defense plant. Peoria, in the middle of nowhere, became strategic. Landing Ship Tank Boats, built up the Illinois River, cruised downstream past Peoria, with soldiers waving, sometimes coming ashore, headed for the war. The nightly blackouts and air-raid drills made everyone feel important. The Caterpillar men, exempt from the draft, built Army trucks and heavy equipment. He liked them—more than he could say—calling his mother "Betty Grable." She was their very own Countess of the Counter Stools.

She was the star of the Bee Hive Cafe. No one even knew her real name was Helen which was the only name she let him call her, and only in private in their rented room in the Flatiron Kickapoo Hotel above the Pour House Tavern where, tired from gabbing all day long under a war poster warning "Loose Lips Sink Ships," she wanted no talking at all, taking off her shoes and her makeup, and watching out the window the soldiers and sailors leaning in the lamplight and whistling at the girls going in and out of the Pour House.

His mother, a take-charge arranger nobody dared cross, saw to his free meals the way she arranged his evening admission to the Apollo with the manager, a young man come downstate from Chicago to learn the ropes of the movie-theater business. His weak eyesight kept him from the draft and kept the movies on screen out of focus. One way or another, his mother was sure, even with a "Four-Eyes" 4-F man, a living was to be had in the movies, if not on the screen, then behind it.

Beggars, she shouted over her busy shoulder to her customers, and she meant herself, can't be choosers. Some people, he had heard her say to new waitresses, are born to be actors and some are just plain born to be the audience.

She never spoke directly to him.

Anything she had to say to him he overheard her telling someone else.

He got the point. He looked like his father.

She knew their place in life, his and hers, and she vaguely shamed him, too old for baby-sitters and too young for the draft, fending for him until he could fend for himself. He knew she wanted to divorce his father who was somewhere off in the war, but she was too patriotic to write him a "Dear John." So she acted, vague, like she was no longer married, and ambiguous, like her husband was dead, which was a convenience of war and the real hope behind her pretty doll's face.

No matter. He got the point his father had probably always missed. His mother, only fifteen years older than him, was a star, but despite her Hollywood longings during the endless war in Europe and the Pacific, none of the slick succession of young managers ever took her away or even convinced the home office in Chicago to install sound in the silent grind-house of the Apollo.

He longed to walk around the corner of Main and Jefferson to the brightly lit jewel of the Rialto Theater where big Hollywood pictures blazed across the silver screen in Technicolor and thundering sound. But his mother could not arrange things at the Rialto.

So he had sat, stuck in the Apollo, staring at the mute screen, out-of-fashion, out-of-sync, under the clack of the silent projectors. Even before he could read the dialog on screen, he had learned, without even trying, to read lips. He found no contradiction that the written dialog often said one thing while the actors said something else. He began pretending he heard words coming from their moving mouths, not knowing his mother was making arrangements and cooing sounds, with whoever was manager that month, behind the tatty screen where pigeons perched on the high dusty beams of the tired old anachronistic Apollo that everyone said was a tax dodge for a Chicago gangster.

Then quite suddenly, because of the war shortages, everyone said, the Apollo went dark. He was the last one left standing in the empty lobby. At the Bee Hive, his mother sighed something almost grateful about the end of that flea pit that should be torn down for scrap, but within a month the Chicago owners had sent in what his mother, leaning close into her mirror to tweeze her arched eyebrows, called, with a sneer, a Rosie-the-Riveter team of women painters and carpenters who remodeled the old girl, because movies, with the war and all, were bigger box office than ever.

Sitting alone in the balcony of the new Apollo the night of its grand reopening, he thought he had died and gone to an Arabian palace in heaven. The handsome new manager, another 4-F flatfooted floogie with a floy-floy, so his mother, always scoring laughs at the Bee Hive, reported, turned on the new projectors, and with the blaring sound track came the 1944 *Pathé News of the World*: a blitzkrieg montage of world leaders, beauty pageants, faceless troops, crazy inventions, atrocities, circus acts, advice on spotting saboteurs and spies, and fashion-ration tips, narrated by a man's enthusiastic voice, showing pretty young women drawing a line with an eyebrow pencil straight up the middle of the back of their long bare legs to create the illusion of a hosiery seam in a world that had run out of nylons.

Everyone was war-crazy.

He was too young to be of any more use than collecting tin cans and lard from patriotic housewives even in the last desperate year of rationed gas and food shortages. He lived out the world-nightmare in the balcony of the Apollo, the hundred lights of its marquee strategically blacked out. He liked the friendly way the newsreel soldiers, who danced wild athletic jitterbug contests, hugged each other. But the violent exploding newsreel battles scared him. The bombed rubble of destroyed cities frightened him. The long lines of refugees in rags, trudging icy roads past burning tanks, shocked him because they looked like him. The tortured children hung up by their thumbs terrified him. The shot, grotesque, frozen dead bodies petrified him. Each week the newsreels grew more bloodcurdling.

The audience around him was weeping.

The Apollo was sobbing.

Women and men.

And him. Alone in his seat. Crying in the balcony.

He felt there was only one finale to these real news movies between the feature movies. In the mad world of war, both sides were going to kill each other until no one was left. He was so scared the exploding World War no one could end was about to spin out of control, about to leap off the screen, leap out of Europe, leap out of the Pacific, that night after night he woke wet with dreams of breathless gagging sickening panic.

The news from the front was so bad, the patrons of the Bee Hive grew strangely quiet.

Behind the counter, even his mother shut up. Then, as if by force of collective will, the terror ended.

Suddenly, in the next wet April spring, the war in Europe was over. Even more suddenly, the following muggy August, the war in the Pacific ended with a surprising blast of radiant energy that made grown-ups cry with gratitude. People, screaming, laughing, joyous, crying, dancing, drinking, celebrating, filled the streets of Peoria, crowded shoulder to shoulder, traffic stopped, tossed toilet paper unrolling like ribbons out of office windows, horns blaring, singing, hugging, kissing, walking across cars stalled in the human surge of happiness into the streets, delirious, unlike anything he had seen, so happy, they were, he was, the fear gone, sitting by himself on top of a car under the marquee of the Apollo Theater whose lights in broad afternoon blazed away in rolling electric waves of American glory and joy and freedom with one word the Apollo manager himself had hung in huge letters: PEACE!

Then one suppertime, later that hot August after VE Day and VJ Day, he sat eating alone at the Bee Hive. It surprised him not at all that the waitress who was his mother just upped and casually vanished.

The last he saw of her she was carting a tray of four lip-sticked soda glasses through the double-doors of the sweltering kitchen.

She disappeared deeper into the cooking steam each time the doors, one fanning in as the other fanned out, clipped each other to shorter and shorter arcs.

Finally, the energy of her push evaporated and the doors seamed to a halt.

It made equal sense later that evening to find a new manager at the Apollo, a stern-faced woman whose steely-clipped hair told him without being asked that she had never heard about arranging his admission. He stood back from her and considered that since he at fifteen knew nothing of life, he must watch the movie-shows to find how people lived. The waitress who was his mother had never talked to him and all that was left of the man she named as his father was an eight-inch red vinyl record with sounds of someone laughing and whistling and trying to sing "Amapola" like he was dying drunk at long distance in a far-off phone booth.

Through the box-office glass he saw the stern-jawed woman point to him under the marquee, as if he were skulking, which he wasn't, not till she pointed at him, and then he could not help starting to skulk he was so embarrassed, because no one had ever pointed at him before, not even his teachers.

No one had ever noticed him.

The woman, who looked like the woman who had been foreman of the Rosie Riveters, said something he could not hear to the ticket girl who squinted her eyes to look at him. She said something back to the woman who pursed her lips, raised her chin, and humphed approval that someone at least knew his face.

He wasn't nobody. He was the audience.

She smiled at him.

Embarrassed, he shoved his hands into his corduroys, but he could not turn his back on the celestial bright of the marquee. He was one of those people who belong inside a movie theater.

In that moment's pause he decided he must arrange things for himself. The woman smiled again and he walked toward her the way a camera approaches a movie actor. The patrons in line, had they watched, could have seen them talking behind the heavy glass doors of the lobby. The woman led him across the new red movie carpet into her office. Thirty minutes later he emerged dazed in black slacks striped down the side with satin. He wore a maroon jacket which was a size too large and he carried a flashlight. The woman touched her hands to her hair, pointed him toward the balcony, and fixed her lipstick. A living, the waitress who was his mother had said, was to be made in the movies.

REEL TWO
Transformations

He was a bumper, a toucher, one of those kids who can't make it through a store without fingering every pencil and pen and magazine within reach. He grew to expect the clerks to follow him. He wanted one of them, particularly the one whose badge read "Mr. Coates," to collar him and take him to the security room of Clark's Department Store, second-best to Block and Kuhl's Department Store. He wanted desperately for Mr. Coates to accuse him of shoplifting. He wanted the police to be called and he wanted to be stripped down to his fifteen-year-oldness and searched and proven innocent. He wanted people to look at him and see he had never taken anything that was not his, or even laid claim to anything that was. But as it was, no one thought he had anything that was stolen, or even somehow remarkably different, and the very distinguished Mr. Coates never said a word. He simply shot his cuffs efficiently down over the black hair on his thick wrists and ignored the boy he knew as the usher from the aisles of the Apollo Theatre.

He spoke to no one except the moviegoers who asked for the time of the next feature or the direction to the loge or the lounge. Every night of his life with the waitress he had spent at the movies, so it had never occurred to him to ask for a night out when the manager herself made the suggestion. He did not argue. He pulled off his maroon jacket and hung his flashlight in the cabinet inside her office door. She smiled at him and handed him two passes.

"Perhaps," she said, "there is a pretty little someone you can take to the show."

He shook his head. She was deliberately confusing him. He knew she was right, suggesting that he ought to do what other people do. He had watched a million movie dates and it ought to have helped him. But somehow he hadn't the click for it.

He was no dummy.

He had ushered the balcony long enough to watch the back rows while on screen two lovers kissed in the evening mist and the world stood still except for trains rushing into tunnels and trees bending in the wind and waves crashing on shore. Enough glow spilled from the triangle of light shooting from the small window of the projection booth down to the screen. He had orders to stop anyone from getting fresh in the balcony, but he could never bring himself to flash his light into the snuggles of couples who learned fast enough that when he was the usher no one would bother them. From his station at the top of the balcony aisle, he watched over the audience and stared down at the screen.

During the rolling credits at the end of each feature, he opened the doors. Slightly disheveled couples pulled themselves together, whisking powder off suit-jacket lapels and patting hair into place. They filed out through a long gauntlet of new couples held back by his red velvet chain. Some customers entered the balcony alone. One, a woman who reminded him of his waitress, regularly tipped him ten cents for showing her to the seat he saved for her each Tuesday for the last double feature.

An evening to himself threw him for a loss.

He lingered longer than usual at the Bee Hive, where the owner, sorry for him that the waitress who was his mother had disappeared into the steam of the kitchen, had allowed him to arrange his own discount meal ticket.

He pinched three paper straws from bottom to top. He alternated the pinches at right angles one above the other. He said she-loves-me and she-loves-me-not and never once wondered who the she was as long as she did more than she didn't. He reached for a fourth straw, but the waitress, who was not at all like his mother, playfully slapped his hand.

"Those cost money," she said. She pulled his empty plate away. Her name was Crystal. "More java?" she asked.

He looked at her and felt the two passes in his pocket. He smiled and she poured the strong boiled coffee up to the green ring around the outside lip of his heavy china cup.

She looked possible.

A wisp of blonde hair escaped from her black snood. Her lips were red as Technicolor. She looked like she could use a movie.

He smiled again.

"Want some pie?" she asked, knowing he missed her teasing double meaning.

He decided to ask her. He could take her past the box office, through the lobby, and up the stairs to the balcony. Unless maybe she wouldn't go to the balcony. Unless, maybe, this first time, they ought to sit in the loge.

"Well, do you, or don't you?" she said. Her hand made a petulant little fist on her aproned hip.

He smiled and held up his passes.

She stepped toward him. "Gee," she said, bussing up his glass of bent straws.

He handed them closer to her.

She was definitely balcony.

"You work there, don'tcha."

He tried staring directly into her eyes, but she looked straight at the passes. Like a hypnotist, he waved them back and forth and closer to her face.

She blinked, took the passes from his hand, and kissed them a light hello as she breezed them into her pocket full of tips. "Thanks," she said. "Here I always thought you were a pretty odd guy, always standing in the back of the balcony, watching everything that goes on up there. Shows how wrong a girl can be."

He felt the blood rush to his face. He wanted to say that was not what he had meant at all. The passes were not her tip. His breath seemed gone and the walls of the Bee Hive seemed to split at the seams and fall back and she kept wiping the counter around his coffee cup as if he were her best customer ever.

"I spent my last dollar on this really cute gold ankle bracelet at the dimestore," she said. "It was a dollar-nineteen, but I split everything with my best girlfriend Angela."

He reached for his coffee to hide his face and make it small behind the cup as he tilted it to his mouth.

"I'll get to wear it tonight since I got these two tickets to the show."

He set his cup down in the saucer and wished for a director who would yell "Cut!"

"Here's a piece of pie," she whispered, sliding a fork into his fingers. "I'll forget it on your check."

He slid backwards off the counter stool.

"You don't want the pie?"

He pulled the correct change from his black usher's slacks and laid it on the counter. He slipped from the Bee Hive into the street.

"Brother, what a jerk!" she said, just loud enough for him to doubt he heard it.

Down the block, under the Apollo marquee, the crowd from the early show eddied out to the sidewalk on Main Street. Men with girls on their arms paused in mid-stride to light up. Couples swirled out the doors around the obedient row of patrons waiting entry to the next double feature. Clusters of moviegoers slowed him. He pushed his way through. He saw a man in a gold gabardine sport shirt. He accidentally on purpose bumped into him. The man said, "Watch it, kid!" Overhead two bulbs had burnt out in the marquee. They broke the illusion of the long running line of light.

No one ever noticed that he walked into people he needed to touch. Bumping was his only intimacy. Since his mother had disappeared into the kitchen of the Bee Hive, no one had come up the stairs above the Pour House to their small room with the single sink, the In-a-Door bed, and the old horsehair sofa where he had slept before she had vanished. No one touched him but the barber at the Barber College where he sat high in a chair every Saturday, between mirrors curving off to infinity, watching his hair clippings fall onto the sheet pinned tight around his neck and draped over his shoulders and arms and knees like a tent hiding his hands in his lap. So he had settled for bumps, as if could nudge off anonymous elbows and backs atoms and energy, as if he could learn through a bump, which strangers thought the accident of a clumsy boy, how it felt with someone else. His eye was a camera snapping fantasy people for footage he projected in his head late at night, laid flat out and alone between the sheets of the Murphy bed, listening to the shouts and singing downstairs in the Pour House, holding his private self hard in hand.

But this night he purposely touched no one. He darted through the doors of the Apollo, waved to the doorman, and headed straight up the stairs to the balcony. He folded himself into the last row of seats. He slouched down on the middle of his back and hooked the indentation in each kneecap onto the curved back rim of the seat in front of him. The empty screen reflected the soft glow of the intermission houselights. Every ten feet down both side walls hung amber globes, each with a hand-painted lady, bathing identically, her towel draped like bunting across her torso.

He had never seen the balcony so empty. A good double bill kept the few Monday night moviegoers on the main floor. He heard them settling into their seats. The murmur of their conversation climbed up the moorish lattice stenciled on the walls. Their voices gathered to a vast hum under the domed ceiling where violet light hidden indirectly behind the lip of the lower circumference of the dome mixed their human voices into a breathy whisper. He fixed his eyes on the hypnotic purple light that grew iridescent as the other house lights dimmed. The sharp light from the projection booth cut over his head, but the movie that night held no interest. He did not even take his eyes off the violet dome to look down at the screen as the violet and purple dome melted to lavender.

Some sense in his body told him he was about to defy gravity.

Only the crick in his neck and the pressure from the inner-spring cushion under his back seemed to hold him in his seat.

He wrapped his arms through the arms of the seat.

Staring up at the soft lavender light, he lost time and direction.

A moment of panic swept through him followed by ineffable pleasure.

He imagined himself falling up, up, up into the pool of violet light, floating unnoticed above the moviegoers, lazy and dreamy, until the intimate unseen hand, inflating and then letting go the neck of a balloon, reddened the violet, shocking the audience who craned their necks and pointed to see him ricocheting insanely off the ceiling and walls, growing smaller and smaller until he disappeared.

He had never been chloroformed but he felt it was much like this.

The unseen hand lifted, and a dark mass next to him, almost invisible to his eyes blinded with the dome's lavender brightness, rose softly and moved, he could not be bothered in his swoon to remember, either up or down the aisle. He woke from what he had recognized as not sleep. Like a man who starts suddenly during a sermon, he looked left and right to see if anyone had noticed.

He did not know how much time had passed or even the difference between what might have happened and what he might have
imagined. The balcony was still nearly empty. He untangled his arms
and sat up straight in his seat. The second feature had begun, and
he felt with little curiosity that the sticky wet on his undershorts
was growing chill near the open zipper that he had not opened. Ten
rows ahead of him sat the nearest patron. It was the lady who usually
tipped him the ten cents. Five seats from her he spied Crystal and,
he guessed, her friend Angela. In the first row, his feet propped up
on the balcony railing, he was sure he saw Mr. Coates sitting in a
blue halo of cigarette smoke. When had these people arrived? Then
he remembered the door at the top of the aisle opening and closing
during his doze, and he thought no more about it, because he was
used to the way people appeared and disappeared.

REEL THREE
Some nights you wake up screaming

After he graduated from school and his job at the Apollo, he found
other theaters, other cities. He moved upstate to Chicago. The movies widened from 35mm to 70mm Cinemascope. They left him
breathless. He panicked the first time he noticed it. He panicked
and gulped in a quart of air. He had sat through a feature and a half
before he realized that he was forgetting to breathe. He had thought
everyone breathed automatically, but somehow he was forgetting
and he panicked. He stood up in his balcony seat and walked up
the steps of the long carpeted aisle. He felt he would never make it.
He vowed he must stop going up to the balconies. He pushed open
the doors to the lobby with a great effort and brushed the arm of a
blonde woman carrying a medium popcorn and a large Coke. His
gasping lungs filled with her raggy scent. He felt sick. How could
he forget to breathe? He had sloshed her Coke. He left her damn-
ing him in his wake. Outside, down the street from the running
lights of the marquee, he leaned against a mailbox and looked up
at the cold moon rising over Lake Michigan. He wanted ten deep
breaths, but he counted only six before the freezing night air hurt

his throat. An elevated train rattled past overhead. He shivered and turned from the moon to the marquee.

An usher had climbed up a tall wooden ladder with a box full of large plastic letters. One week's bill gave way to another as the usher slid the letters around on their wire tracks. While the usher struggled with the film titles, gibberish hung on the Bryn Mawr Theater's glowing marquee. He remembered that a couple years before it had been himself up on such a ladder, spelling and spacing words for everyone to read. The flush of altitude sickness from the balcony burned in his gut and he turned, on that barricaded edge of not-knowing that is the edge of self-revelation, and walked away.

"Moonlight," he wrote on a scrap of paper in his pocket, "has the same believability as black-and-white film. The moon washes the color from everything. Landscapes and faces lose their tint. Everything becomes believable within the range of gray."

Even one's self.

As a part-time projectionist, living on popcorn, he had worked his way through college and into graduate school and had taken to writing while he walked, insomniac through lonely nights, hanging out in tiled coffee shops with fluorescent waitresses. Sometimes when there was snow blanketing and silencing the Near North Side of Chicago, the night waitresses would have mercy on him and for his dime pour him bottomless cups of coffee and call him Shakespeare because of his books and his glasses, but he would not really think of them as real until later when he thanked them ever-so because the air was cold on his shivering hand as he emptied his bladder under the El, signing his melting yellow autograph into banks of pure white snow. What he wrote on paper was secret and wonderful. He kept it, at the coffee-shop counters, covered with one hand and only read it himself when back in his rented room that was not unlike the room that his mother the waitress had so long before abandoned.

He could no longer remember her face and it disturbed him slightly, because the face of anyone named Helen should have launched a thousand ships. He could identify the profile of a long-since-dead Hollywood star at a glance, but her face had given way to his last shot of the back of her head disappearing in the kitchen steam of the Bee Hive.

"Movies," he wrote thinking of his life and her, "are spun out of talking heads. The way the physiological eye prefers light to darkness, the psychological eye selects face over scenery when contained in the same frame." He tucked that note into the drawer with the layers of his random writings. "The camera-work provides the psychology of the movie."

He hoped someday he would start bolt upright in his balcony seat during an "Eyes and Ears of the World" newsreel when he would recognize her face modeling clothes in a New York fashion show. Or maybe her face would come back to him as she straddled a horse diving into a tank at Atlantic City. She would surprise him that way and she would be immortal. He was sure she would remember that a living, and more than a living, could be arranged in the movies. She was out there among the stars.

REEL FOUR
Somehow between features he became a teacher

Time passed. Cinema was everything. He had touched no one and no one had touched him, not counting touches like that warm hand under the lavender light of that balcony. In his mind the fear had loomed large that he would live only to thirty, but he was five years overdue and no longer bothering to wonder why he hadn't been taken or why he had not made love. He seemed veined and delicate as a night-blooming orchid. His eyes, which in childhood had been a deep blue, had faded into the uncanny washed-out hue usually found in beach people and ranchers exposed to constant brightness. Light from the silver screen had burned like radiation into his sockets.

Voices told him, advised him, "You can always teach," so for years he taught literature and creative writing. In his lectures, *Leaves of Grass* was a shooting script and Whitman's montage esthetic anticipated Edison's technology; Dickens' editing style generated Eisenstein's; and his punchline for *Ulysses* explained the novel's fluid complexities by revealing that while writing his masterwork, Joyce worked in Dublin as a projectionist. In his writing classes he argued his hippie peacenik students out of turgid undergraduate melodramas about stolen sex and repentant suicide and death in Vietnam. He tutored them into screenplays personal in matter and disciplined in technique. His colleagues regarded him indulgently, urging him over an occasional sherry to invent courses with titles like "Film Interpretation," "Novels into Film," or "Movies and the Liberal Arts." But always he shook his head.

"Why not?" they always asked. "Is the novel any less pleasurable when read as a class assignment?"

Always he smiled pleasantly and excused himself from the hearty company of them and their cheery wives. He was an alien they tried to corral. If he would not invent their courses, then they would have him married, and when married, they would have him father children. Somehow he had given no hostages to fortune; no wife begged him, for the sake of the family food and shelter, to capitulate his secret cinema pleasures to their university schedule. He was a private person and his privacy kept him free. No one could exploit what they did not know. His privacy was, before all, his right.

"Perhaps," one faculty wife whispered, "he abstains from the sexual revolution entirely. There is that rarity called chastity, I believe."

She had glimpsed something of the ideal fire deep in him that gave color to his cheeks.

The wife of his Department Chairman took his arm and pulled him aside. "My husband," she said, "finds you amazingly droll. We're so happy you joined our little group of eccentrics. I mean, that's what teaching is all about, isn't it?"

He watched her tilt her glass to her lips. Her drink was gone but for the ice which stuck for a moment to the bottom of the upturned cylinder. Her braceleted wrist jarred the glass sharply to break the wet freeze. The cold avalanche of cubes slid toward her lips which parted and bit off the advancing ice.

"You know," she said, "you are the still water that runs deep."

So he became water and flowed away from her, in flight from all the pursuers of his life.

REEL FIVE
In mummy movies, every diamond has a curse

Waiting in the box-office line of the Campus Theater, he worried about himself. He was older, not suddenly, but slowly as in a series of dissolves, conscious that the youth culture, wild in the streets, trusted no one over thirty; but he hardly looked middle-aged, he was sure of it. His hair had thinned a bit, but nothing that some artful combing and men's hairspray wouldn't fix, unless he got caught in a headwind; and the skin around his eyes had wrinkled no more than to a moviegoer's permanent squint. His boyish weight had maintained under the discipline of popcorn, no butter and no salt. He was vainly prideful he had not gotten fat. Perhaps he was, like Monty Clift, one of those neurasthenic cases he had read about.

He no longer climbed up to the balconies. With each paid admission in newer and stranger theaters, he sat closer and closer to the silver screen, not trying to find once again, he told himself, the unseen hand in the lavender light. He sat absolutely alone always staring at the screen, never looking left or right, no matter who came and went in the seats around him. Sometime, he feared, he would walk into a theatre, glide to the front rows, and be sucked up into the screen, lost forever in the 2000-watt glow of the Cinemascope feature presentation. Only his notes, theory on cinema scrawled in the dark, would remain strewn between the seats. No one, not even the janitor, would be curious enough to read them or wonder where the man in the first row had disappeared. He panicked and felt his breath go shallow. He shed his coat and retreated back into the lobby.

The small Campus Theatre was an art house co-featuring foreign films with experimental underground films. The hippie audience was intense, even reverential in the lobby, intoning the names of drugs and directors, congregating around the pot of free coffee. He waited behind a petite young woman who blocked his way to the cups. A wreath of flowers crowned her long blonde hair so straight it looked ironed. She was all bracelets and beads and madras. With her middle finger she dabbed repeatedly at the surface of her steaming cup. He grew impatient. The next feature, Bertolucci's *Last Tango in Paris,* was about to begin. He cleared his throat. He coughed.

"Something's floating in my coffee," she said, turning to him. "Like wax or oil or something."

She was really quite lovely in her motley layers of scarves and beads.

He smiled coolly and placed his own cup in its plastic holder and held it under the tap. He pulled the spigot down and the coffee bubbled black in the cone-bottom of the cup. He teased it to the rim. His hand was steady as he raised the steaming cup to his lips.

"It's wax," she said. "Definitely wax from the cup. It won't hurt you."

He looked at her. He was embarrassed. They seemed to be standing together as much as the other couples in the lobby. Three of his literature students passed by. "Good evening, Professor," one of them said. The other two smiled. He moved away from the woman, who was hardly more than a girl, and nodded to his students over his coffee. She moved with him. He moved again. She followed. They seemed to be dancing in the middle of the lobby. The students pretended not to notice.

"I'm NanSea SunStream. It's a mantra. I'm an Aries. I chant. Enchanted, I'm sure." She extended her hand, reaching for his which he did not offer. She recouped with so gracefully circular a gesture she seemed always to have intended to pull her lustrous blonde hair back behind her ear. "Something tells me you're a Gemini. With a moon in Leo. And, maybe, a Scorpio rising sign."

Music from the screen sounded the Main Title. He turned nervously toward the door, turned back to her, shrugged and smiled and left her standing. He found his way down the aisle to the front. This was his fourth viewing of the movie unreeling on the screen. He knew exactly what would happen from beginning to end and he found comfort in that. Occasionally a film might break or the reels become confused, but overall he enjoyed an order in cinema he did not feel with people. On the screen everything was arranged and directed.

"Here's some sugar," NanSea said, slipping into the seat beside him. "Better take one lump since you half-drank it."

Behind him someone shushed them.

She whispered. "How can you drink that varnish? I couldn't sit back there thinking of you drinking that. I couldn't keep my mind on the film. I've seen it before."

He set his coffee cup on the floor. He knew people like her added lysergic acid to sugar cubes.

"What's that?" She pointed to his notes. "I'll bet you're a movie critic. Wow! I should be quiet so you can concentrate. It's like I understand. I mean, one of the places I hang out is the campus. This is so far out!"

He tried to will her away, but her blonde presence shimmered luminous next to him. Her flawless young face glowed in reflections from the screen. She could have been in the film. He leaned to the opposite arm. He could not help studying her profile that was so like the winsome Gish sisters. She leaned forward, cupped her hand around the lighter she held to a half-smoked joint. "Want a hit?" she asked. He shook his head. "More for me then." She inhaled in short, sharp huffs, and exhaled in measured puffs. He, who had to remember to breathe, envied her even as she relaxed down to perfect silence.

He wished her gone and gathered his notes together. He long ago had ceased bumping into people to discover how it would be with them and he certainly had no recognizable desire to be with her.

"Hey," she said. "You going?"

He was already near the end of the row.

"What would a girl like me," she said loud enough for him to hear, "want with a square like you?"

As he neared the aisle seat, a large old woman sitting in a pile of shopping bags said, "Why don't you two fight at home!"

He escaped to the men's room and locked himself in the middle stall. No one could reach him or see him. He sat and lamented the broken sanctity of even this small neighborhood university theatre.

"Somehow," he jotted into his notes, "the shrines are all broken and my Lady Cinema is dead." For a long while he sat, not hearing the door banging open and closed, nor the sound of the urinals flushing. Finally he looked to the stall wall and saw his initials written on an earlier visit. It pleased him that proof remained that he had been there before and saddened him that he would never come there again. He wet his finger and rubbed hard on the ink of his signature. The rubbing made a squeaking sound and caused a shoe in the stall next to his to tap up and down, moving toward him.

He recognized the sexual Morse code. He gasped for air. He pulled himself together and escaped quickly up the stairs, through the lobby, pulling on his coat—Oh, Mr. Coates!—in the middle of the street. He was miles and cities and years away from the arrangements made for him at the Bee Hive and the Apollo and he could only go home for the night.

Behind him, he heard NanSea SunStream calling after him. "Hey! Wait! I didn't mean it. You're cool. You're different. You want to come over for some wine..."

He took a deep breath.

"...some music..."

He walked faster.

"...or something like whatever."

He ran.

REEL SIX
The man who loved movies

Why he wondered do people believe that a man who is not married is available to anyone? No one understands vocation anymore. No one accepts dedication. No one believes in chastity.

He sat upstairs in the old house he had bought, locked safely behind the door of a closet large enough to be a small study. Snippets and yards of film footage clipped on fine wires were strung the length of the room: movie millimeters of eight and super-eight and sixteen and thirty-five and wide-screen seventy. The air was acrid with acetone editing glue. Its smell intoxicated him. A twelve-yard sequence of a Technicolor musical-comedy was wrapped around his neck, its ends trailing down his front like a priest's ritual stole. The hot light of his hand-editor had dried the moisture in his nostrils, chapped his lips, and wrinkled his forehead. Its glare threw his shadow huge against the wall-size screen that pulled down over the only door to the hidden room. Nightly he illuminated his celluloid strips the way monks once lovingly tooled manuscripts in lonely cells. He had only to arrange the sequences snipped from this movie and that movie into his own unreeling vision of what a film should be. Life, his waitress had told him was to be had in the movies, so he had waited, waited his whole life, for the return of the unseen hand in the lavender light.

REEL SEVEN
The transfiguration of the spieler

In his own time and by his own decision, he approached his colleagues. He smiled and was almost deferential as he made appointment to lecture in their Departmental Colloquium. Late nights he brooded in the very auditorium where in no time at all his much anticipated talk would be given. As the hour approached, he gathered his reels about him and taxied to the university theater. The seats and aisles and stairs were jammed. Students mixed with faculty. Even people from the local Town-and-Gown society arrived to hear him speak.

When he walked to the podium, the audience hushed expectantly. A slight murmur washed through the balcony and died. He raised his hand. The projectionist dimmed the lights and rolled the silent film.

His movie, ten-years-in-the-editing, was a montage, no, a barrage of hot light, choice sequences, brilliant frames, subliminal images, and remix snippets of found footage he had carefully scratched with pins, streaked with bleach, and hand-colored with multi-hued dyes.

Facing his audience, he stood in the center of the silent screen, looked, in fact, to be part of the screen as the images reflected off his pale skin and white clothing. The audience shifted and whispered in their seats. They expected from him something new, *avant garde*, possibly weird, maybe shocking, and hopefully wonderful. Somewhere an undergraduate girl giggled nervously.

"The silents," he began to speak into his lavaliere mike, "were never silent. Prosperous theatres featured orchestras. Small theatres had pianos and the clack of the projectors. Ethnic theatres hired monologuists to translate the written English titles for the neighborhood. The spielers, as they were called, freely ad-libbed, very freely ad-libbed, many a dull title and plot into gracious wit and good humor. They added dimension to the flat screen."

Only the shadow cast by his body on the screen helped differentiate him among the fast flash of images from Edison, Lumiere, Melies, Lange, Von Sternberg, and Riefenstahl to Brakhage, Anger, Deren, Warhol, Lean, Wilder, Hitchcock, and Bergman.

"In sixty minutes of film," his voice boomed through the theatre, "you actually watch twenty-seven minutes of total darkness. But the mind chooses to see only the remaining thirty-three minutes of light. I want to know what is between those frames, what is in that twenty-seven-minute darkness, what secret of life lies just out of reach in the flickers between those frames."

He began to pelt the audience with data.

"The very form of cinema is absurd. No picture moves. Still frame connects to still frame. The eye cancels the darkness, cancels the stasis. The brain aches for motion. The body aches for life."

He no longer heard the doors of the theatre auditorium opening and closing.

"The first movie audiences in Paris screamed and stampeded as Lumiere's train rushed toward them."

He dropped his arms to his sides and stared up directly into the projector light beaming down hard as grace upon him.

"We each," he said, "make our own movie."

He no longer turned his head. He panned it left and right. He no longer walked toward the stage edge. He tracked. The blink of his eyes became the click of a single frame. He blinked them quickly and the audience became a flicker. His talking became a whirr and his tongue turned to film feeding out of his face.

The gallery of his colleagues and the audience of his students rose to their feet cheering his passion. The applause continued at the reception arranged by his department.

"Very nice," the chairman's wife said, "very nice indeed. You really should develop that film course my husband wants so much. But come," she said, arranging the knot of his tie, "you simply must meet everyone."

The Barber of
18th and Castro

On the last day of spring, June 20, 1973, at high noon, at the corner of 18th and Castro in San Francisco, Robert Place found the Face of God in a pornographic photograph. Not that he was given to dirty pictures. Rather, he had been drawn, by some—what?—thing to this neighborhood, by some thing he had vaguely heard or read or sensed, that had nothing to do with the corner barber shop where he had sought refuge, but had everything to do with whatever was intersecting the intersection which was inventing its flamboyant self even as he watched.

He had parked his 1957 Chevy BelAire with the candy-apple red body, tuck-and-roll upholstery, and the white "Says-who? Says-me!" top, and then he had walked all four of the single-block arms reaching out like a cross from the main intersection which was more like ground zero than anything he'd expected even in California. Everything rushed oingo-boingo right up at him: the omelet-brunch cafes with cake made out of, go figure, carrots; the dandy little flower shop near the corner kiosk where a one-legged ancient eye, maybe the world's oldest newsboy, hawked the call, "*Chronicle!*" like the last screech of a dying species, selling headlines, "Nixon bombs Saigon"; the loud beer bars with slender young men in white tanktops and baseball caps posing and partying in windows open to the street; the chic boutiques selling nothing anybody would ever need after a nuclear attack.

All of it was alien to him. Or he was alien to it. He had entered foreign territory. Fear—not so much the fear of the unknown, but more like the human animal's fear of his own kind—bristled the shorthairs on the nape of his neck. The unexpected thrill of temptation put him on edge. Seeking sanctuary, he spied a revolving

red-and-white barber pole. He bolted past the blue arrow pointing
up the stairs. On the landing outside the barber's door, he stopped,
catching his breath. He was a young man in need of something familiar, and what was more solid than a good old-fashioned barber shop?

Until that bone-bright noon hour when Robert Place actually
witnessed what looked like the campus of the world's most flamboyant boys' college, he had little more than a tourist's curious Kodak
hope that there, at that world-famous intersection, he'd see people
unlike any of the people back home in southern Illinois, people
stranger and more festive even than the hippies he'd seen on TV
in the Haight, people, who, rumors persisted, had always existed,
the way bohemians and gypsies and magicians, all of them outlaws,
had always existed, even before the Druids, but had never been seen
before, at least not in broad daylight, in such visible numbers. So he
had come to see for himself.

Because of his uneasy feeling that he already recognized these new
people even if he did not know them, Robert Place immediately af-
fected toward them a distanced attitude which he knew camouflaged
his ground-glass fear he might, in fact, be one of them, whatever
they really were. After a grueling four-day cross-country marathon
in his car, he had come to California for what? A trim? Yeah. Sure.
That was it. A little trim and some talk. A simple visit to a quiet
barbershop. The best place for some local gossip. Some shaving cream
hot around his ears. The scrape of the straight-edge razor across the
thin skin over the hard bone of his skull. That was all.

Only a few days and many miles before, he had been driving
aimlessly through his small town where he knew every street and
every house and everyone who lived, or who had ever lived, in those
houses, when one of those almost religious, certainly reckless, trans-
figuring impulses no one can ever deny had possessed him. He had
thrown one suitcase into his Chevy, left a rose on his mother's fresh
grave, and headed west. He had driven from Canterberry, in Green
County, in southern Illinois to the San Francisco crosshairs of 18th
and Castro where, in the heart of lightness, of the California sun at
high noon in June, almost the solstice, the day of the year's longest

light, the most familiar thing to him, the only thing he understood, man-to-man, as his father always said, was the gold leaf spelling out FLOYD'S BARBER SHOP. His hair was not long and he had not even felt in need of a haircut; yet why else had he pulled his Chevy to the curb in front of the shop, traipsed back and forth three or four dizzying blocks, and then run from his car up the flight of stairs leading to the door of Floyd's Barber Shop that looked down directly on the corner of 18th and Castro?

Floyd sat customerless in his single green barber chair. He wore a white puckered nylon barber's smock. Across his lap were spread the guts of a player piano he was working over with a screwdriver. He looked up at Robert Place. "Come on in," he said. "I have to do it, otherwise I spend all day looking out the window. Take a look. You'll see. What a parade. It looks like half of Noah's ark. The stag half if you catch my drift. The neighborhood's changed."

Robert wanted to ask, from exactly what to exactly what, and was it good, or bad, or neither; but he kept silent, not wanting to tip his hand, because he figured it didn't matter where he'd played before: California was a brand new game.

"I'll be with you in a minute," Floyd said. "Hope you're in no hurry."

Robert checked his watch against the clock on the wall. One of them was ten minutes fast. Inside himself, the clock of his body, the only clock that really mattered, began to slow. He felt the speed built up on the I-80 freeway descent from Reno and Truckee down to San Francisco slowly recede from himself. Time zones like tide in the Bay ebbed from him. He jingled loose change in his pocket. Nickels and dimes from back home mixed through his nervous fingers with quarters and Kennedy half-dollars he won in less than an hour playing the slots at a filling station somewhere in Nevada.

"I hope you're not in a hurry," Floyd repeated.

Robert remembered his appointment book on the front seat of his unlocked car. Never had he ever left his car unlocked. He peered through Floyd's gilt-lettered window. At the parking meter he had forgotten to feed, a white-helmeted metermaid ticketed his windshield. She turned slowly from the Chevy toward Robert as if she could feel him watching her every move. The noon sun glinted from her helmet. Robert could not see her face. He did not want to. He did not need to. Back home he could drop a deer at a hundred yards. She was a dead bitch in his book.

"No," he said, "I'm in no hurry. I was late for the last appointments I made four days ago. I sell, I mean, I used to sell Fuller Brushes door to door." He was warming up, trying to feel like himself again. "I can tell you more than you'd ever want to know about natural bristle brushes for your hair and your bottles and your carpets and your drapes and your dog and your cat."

"That a fact?" Floyd said. More than once he'd been told his droll roll of a phrase reminded the teller of W. C. Fields, which only encouraged him, despite his efforts to speak naturally.

"And the women!" Robert presumed that Floyd, same as all barbers, liked to talk about women, when he should have known only most of them like to talk about women, but they all love to talk about sex, except the Seventh Day Adventist ones who were always closed on a Saturday when a man was most likely to get his hair barbered. "Let me tell you," Robert said, "about those little housewives. Those lonely ladies sure do want to talk, talk, talk. Always saying, 'Well, Robert, enough me talking about me. What do you think about me?' Do you believe the utter conceit of women?"

"Much, much less than I believe," Floyd said, "in the unutterable conceits of men."

"Those girls were always giving me coffee till I thought I was going to drown. Always asking me if the coffee was sweet enough and how they could make it sweeter, shaking their hair down, trying out the sample brushes, teasing me, asking me how I thought they looked. I tell you. More than once before I left, I had to comb my teeth. It was murder. Door-to-door can kill you."

"That so?" Floyd fielded like W. C. "I'm what you might say interested in hair brushes too. Being a barber and all, it's natural."

"I bet you've heard everything too," Robert, doing his best Holden Caulfield, said. "At least twice."

"Frankly, I never hear the half of it. In one ear. Out the other. I'd go crazy if I really listened. We're all maniacs except when we're not. I must confess music's my mania."

"Is that right?"

"Right as rain."

"What kind of music? Grateful Dead? Judy Collins? Lawrence Welk? What?"

"Piano. I play the piano. But not with these hands. These are the hands of a barber. I always play piano with my feet." He surveyed Robert's puzzled face and grinned. "I catch me a rube everytime with that," he said. "Player piano, of course."

"I knew that," Robert said.

Floyd gestured to the plaster-of-paris busts sitting awry on a shelf over Robert's head. He had saved and bought each one of them from Silvestri's statuary company in South San Francisco. "There you see them." He pointed with his screwdriver. "Bach. Mozart. Schubert. Beethoven. Liszt."

"A whole shooting gallery." Robert stared straight at the barber. Floyd was a man dragging age forty-five like it was sixty. He combed his graying hair into the stiff part and pomp he had learned as a boy thirty years before. His glasses were as thick as binoculars. Robert liked that. He liked the way some older men and older women kept on with the styles they got locked into when they were young, like they were fixed in some time warp, instead of changing with the fashions and looking ridiculous in clothes that were too young for them, or too modern, or too ugly, like the new uniform for the old, polyester leisure suits for the men and polyester pant suits for the ladies, topped off with a frizzy reddish short perm, or worse, one of those Dynel wigs that catch the sun like orange copper wire. If he got old, which he doubted, that's what he planned to do. Sort of stay just like he was. Not change a thing.

"Turn around and look," Floyd said. "Bach and Liszt. I like them best."

Robert panned his head to the figurines. They were each ten

inches of white plaster with the names chiseled into the bases. "Nice," he said. "Really nice." He surveyed the rest of the room.

This was not the first barber shop, waiting room, or bookstore that Robert Place had cased. In fact, it was a matter of police record that Robert Steven Vincent Place had been found guilty of at least one misdemeanor: slicing articles and smuggling magazines from the Green County Public Library. His mother had paid his hundred-dollar fine, but his year's probation was not half up, and he was on the run.

He had confessed to the judge that he had started with laundromats, that one day he had ripped one article from one magazine in one laundromat. The judge didn't bother to ask his motive, and Robert could hardly have volunteered one. He didn't know exactly why he coveted certain pictures like the first ones he had ever stolen, photographs of blond bodybuilders on Venice Beach hoisting even blonder starlets high as the American Dream onto their broad shoulders in the brilliant California sunshine.

From stray magazines in laundromats and doctors' offices, he had moved on to stealing the neighbors' mailed magazine subscriptions, and from there on to harder stuff, to the *pieces de resistance*, the photo-books on reserve at the public library. He had moved from a noisy tearing the pages to a quieter slicing them with a single-edge razor blade, and he had cut out for himself quite a collection of classical Greek athletes. His most prized theft was from a portfolio of reproductions of Lumiere's 1903 photos of the legendary strongman Eugene Sandow in an appealing variety of masculine, but modest, figleaf poses.

His satisfaction with his secret addiction had given him a false confidence that he figured out later had made him greedy and all too careless. He constantly needed more pictures to satisfy himself. Sometimes the actual tearing felt better, bolder than slicing.

Pleasant little dangers thrilled him.

It was his own fault when Miss Ollie Thomas, the head librarian, and his mother's cousin, had herself pinched him red-handed and called the sheriff. She had caught on to him, because he never coughed except when he was in the library, which, as his second cousin once-removed in a family inclined to TB, she thought was worrisome, but then she divined that he only coughed when he was, of all things, tearing out pages, and the louder he coughed the more pages he was tearing out at a pull. She was, of course, incensed, even when she apologized to his mother for calling the law.

The week after his sentencing Robert had returned to one of the two laundromats he frequented with a half-filled basket of clothes. He disliked washing his laundry in machines which he suspected harbored the curlicue hairs of strangers. He added his soap and extra bleach, dropped in his quarter, and settled back to pass the time reading.

Unexpectedly, as he leafed through an old 1964 issue of *Life* magazine, he came across the ragged seams of the pages he had ripped out the week before. The photospread had featured what they termed a man's-man kind of motorcycle bar called The Tool Box in San Francisco. Oh, he'd ripped that one out right away! Yessir! He liked cars and motorcycles both! And now he had the same gutted issue in his hands again. He looked neither to the right or left in the laundromat. He grinned at touching the ragged tear, the evidence that he had once before been in this place. Getting caught once was thrill enough, but better was the thrill of returning to the scene of an undetected crime.

In his switch of his clothes from washer to dryer, he stuffed the evidence, the rest of *Life*, unnoticed by the hawk-eyed manager, into the bottom of the basket on whose canvas he had carefully marked with a red felt-tip pen: "If found, return to R. S. V. Place." He didn't need to put his street address, not in Canterberry where everybody knew him.

"I don't really play piano," Floyd said. "I'm not a pianist. I'm a mechanic of the piano."

"I don't really sell Fuller Brushes," Robert said. "But I did. People like to meet me. I like to meet people." He reached for a small stack of magazines that lay next to him on the burgundy leatherette seat.

"Why don't you flip through a few of those," Floyd said. "Being from back East, you might never have seen those kind of pictures."

"I'm not from back East. I'm from the Midwest. The southern part of the Midwest. New York and New England's back East."

"It's all back East here in San Francisco which has nothing to do with California which has nothing to do with the rest of the country, if you catch my drift." Floyd adjusted a wire and a screw in the board across his lap. "Nossir," Floyd added, as if he were changing the subject to answer a question Robert had never asked. "I never get lonesome up here looking down on the boys and girls in Rainbow County."

"Is that a bar?" Robert asked.

"Nope," Floyd said. "It's the other foot of the rainbow arch from Oz. It's just a T-shirt I made up. It's a state of mind. What size do you wear? Maybe I should give you one."

"Hey, don't injure yourself doing me any favors," Robert said. "I can pay."

"I got a hundred of them," Floyd said. "A man has to be enterprising."

By the late Sixties, Floyd had nearly gone under. He had standards. He had tradition. He figured men and boys should be groomed a certain way. He hadn't been able to see himself as one of those fancy-nancy men's salons that other barbers changed to when nobody wanted Princetons or flat-tops or, his favorite, crewcuts anymore. He figured to ride out the long-hair fad. But here he was forty-five, with a one-chair shop and a steady but small clientele of older balding gentlemen of the sort people once kindly called "born bachelors" as opposed to "eligible bachelors." His trade kept him comfortable. The brisk pace that had once been Friday's and Saturday's had fallen off taking with it the strain from his eyes and the pressure from his varicose veins.

"I been closed for four months, yeah." Floyd said. "Just a second and I'll have all these wires tied up. Out for four months. Back for three."

"Vacation?" Robert asked. He was vaguely bored. The magazines were nothing to write home about.

"Operation," Floyd said. "Eyes. Yeah. Wouldn't be able to see today but for those two operations."

He smiled with such a general gratitude for his health that Robert, who in his own life was grateful for nothing, felt uncomfortable. Robert wished for another customer, preferably a mother with a small boy who would have to be hoisted to a kid's chair inside the big one. With commotion like that he could easily slip one or two of the crummy nudist magazines into the sleeve of his jacket.

"I always figured," Robert said, "that little boys always understand the world earlier and better than little girls."

"Why's that?"

"Because little boys get taken younger to barber shops. You sit them up on that little chair. You wrap that big cloth around them. All of a sudden they see what it's like to be a disembodied head caught between two mirrors. That's why little boys cry at the barber shop, because, all of a sudden, they're scared. They're face to face with the secret how we're all just curving off into infinity."

"I like that myself," Floyd said.

"Maybe that's why you barber."

"Could be." Floyd looked up at a hundred mirrored images of himself.

"To tell the truth," Robert said, "I think everybody ought to have two full-length mirrors facing each other in their house."

"Why's that?"

"So in case you ever need to escape for any reason, like, you know, to get away from whoever's after you, you can just stand yourself between the two mirrors and walk right out of space and time into some infinite dimension."

"That sure is another reason to be able to see," Floyd said. "If I was blind, I'd never know if you were telling me the truth about mirrors or not."

"You are so right," Robert said.

"Of course," Floyd continued, "more practically speaking, if I was blind, I couldn't barber. Whoever heard of a blind barber?" He thought a moment. "Guess it's possible to have, you know, the touch without the eye for it." He paused lost in the thought. "Me? I got the eye and the touch. Mmmm. Must be a blind barber somewhere."

"I figure," Robert said, "if the human mind can think of it, somebody somewhere is doing it. You should hear some of the things my human mind thinks about."

"Damn!" Floyd shifted his piano tools hand to hand. "That sure would take a trusting customer."

"What would?"

"A blind barber."

Robert began a careful roll of the magazine next to him.

"I can see now," Floyd said. "Good as you."

Floyd kept his eyes on the piano board, but Robert felt accused. He flipped the magazine away casually. The guilty flee, he thought, and he meant not from the barber but from back home. For crissakes, what am I doing here?

"It's funny," Robert said.

Floyd looked up with a vaguely cross expression.

"That I came up here, I mean. I came into your barber shop not wanting or really needing a haircut and I'm not getting one. I came into your shop and I'm not getting what I didn't want."

"Oh," Floyd said. He folded his tools into a felt bag. "I thought you meant that I could see was funny."

"Oh no," Robert said. "I guess I came up here looking for something else. Barbers always know what's going on around town."

"I mean," Floyd said, "it would be funny if I couldn't see and I was a barber. But it wouldn't be funny if I couldn't see and I was a pianist. You see them on the TV all the time. Pianists who can't see. They say it helps them play better. They feel it more. But you never see a barber who can't see cutting hair on TV."

"I guess not," Robert said. "Too bad for you that good old Ed Sullivan isn't on anymore. He eyed the morning's *Chronicle*. A sensational murder, one of a series of murders by the Zodiac Killer, spread across the front page; he was fascinated, but the paper itself was too bulky to smuggle under his clothes, and he was too shell-shocked from his arrest in the Green County Library to tear out the long article that continued to the last page of the first section. Instead, he tried to memorize the interesting, livid details of thirteen apparently connected murders and six other persons missing.

"Even if I couldn't see," Floyd said, "it wouldn't make me any better a pianist." He lifted the wired board off his lap. "This here's like I always rebuild." He carried it across the shop and drew back the curtain on an adjacent room. "You remember player pianos? I get them from all across the country. Bought one in Nebraska for twenty-five bucks. Sold it in Sausalito to Sally Stanford for you wouldn't guess how much." He pulled the curtain closed. "Nossir. Seeing or not seeing would be all the same to me pumping at one of my players with both feet."

Robert looked out the window. Down in the street the ticket left by the triumphant meter maid flapped in the ocean breeze sweeping down 18th Street to Castro where men, he never would have thought it, walked arm in arm. They were strangers, maybe dangerous strangers, but he recognized them all the same. "I should've locked my car." He thought of the .22 caliber handgun stashed under the seat and he laughed because it's impossible for someone on probation to get a permit for a handgun, but it's no way impossible for that same person to get a handgun, especially when that person's daddy dies and leaves it loaded in a bedroom drawer. "Damn," he said.

Floyd moved to the window, wiping his hands. "That your Chevy?"

He admired the Chevrolet gleaming all red and white with hardly a speck of any road grime Robert had wiped off every time he stopped to gas up. He had bought it, restored and cherry, the day he turned sixteen, paying for it with insurance money his mom had given him as his share of his dad's policy. Those had been the days! The draft had been lenient to neglectful. By 1973, the draft was carnivorous for red-blooded all-American boys. He told Louise Yavonovich, the gray-haired lady who ran the Green County Selective Service Board, that she couldn't draft him because he was leaving for California.

"For school?" she asked.

"Yes, a school" he said, "for becoming a minister, a Quaker minister," but his *yes* revealed itself for the lie it had always been before he had driven the first five hundred miles west. He knew he'd never sit in another school in all his life. He knew enough to get by in the world. And more. Even though he was no way, José, one of those spineless conscientious objectors, he vowed he'd never let anyone take him to some hellhole place like Vietnam, or even to prison for dodging the draft.

By no more than impetuous instinct, he had hopped into his car that day and worked out his plan about heading toward the coast, with its beaches and sex and drugs and rock 'n' roll, leaving fat old ugly Louise, no more the wiser, and a little the worse for wear, sitting on her cellulite in the sprawl of her manila alphabetical files. Even before the fierce rainstorm he had sat out in his car west of Omaha he had laughed. He was just another missing person out of millions. The old bitch would never catch up with him. He had no way of knowing that Louise had rather fancied him, and had let him make good his escape, because, in her heart she knew the war was a sad cause, and that Robert was all that was left of the Place family, his dad dead all those years, and his mother gone six weeks.

With Floyd looking down with him at his Chevy parked at 18th and Castro, he saw every mile of the 89,787.3 reflected back at him in the late sun of a thin Pacific afternoon. A wave of depression suddenly washed over him. It always did, right after he felt good about getting his own way. He wished to God he had been drafted. They'd have given him a uniform, an M-16 rifle, and his own chopper, and then turned him loose so he'd have had no choices to make about anything, but shoot it and screw it!

"Nice car," Floyd said. "And nice arms. You got real nice muscular arms."

"Thanks," Robert said.

"You work out a little?"

"Naw. I'm just naturally strong." Robert pulled up his sleeve and flexed his right arm, cocking his fist near his face. "You want to feel my bicep?"

Floyd rubbed his hands together and cupped his right palm over Robert's peaked arm and his left under it.

"Is that okay or is that okay?" Robert said.

"It's better than okay."

"You can let go now."

"So," Floyd said, "whyn't you drive your car over to my place? We can work us out a deal. You do something for me. I'll 'restore' it for you."

"Restore it?" Robert said. "You said you weren't blind! Are you crazy? That car doesn't need any restoring." He climbed into Floyd's barber chair. "Just trim it."

Floyd fastened the striped barber cloth tight around Robert's neck. He folded the tissue strip down neatly over the cloth. Wrapped and swaddled, Robert felt his body become subject to the barber. His mother had spent the entirety of his boyhood diapering and scarfing and lacing him in and out of clothes. One fall she had taken him after school to find a winter coat. She had wanted to shop at Penney's, but he had fast-talked her into a better buy at the Army-Navy Outlet. She had thought of her husband, a strict man Robert did not know was not his father, who had said the boy's last year's parka would fit well enough this season. Robert thought only of the brown leather bombardier's jacket he and his buddies had stared at through the plate glass window. They had pledged to form their own squadron. His blood-buddy Stoney named himself command pilot. Robert was to be head bombardier.

"This is the size," Robert had said, handing the jacket to his mother.

"That's too large, I'm sure."

"The boy's probably right." The clerk, whose name tag read *Nigel*, had spoken archly over the perfect knot of his stylish silk tie. "He really ought to know. He came in here several days ago with a gang of boys who disturbed the manager no end. I remember your boy especially. We caught him wearing this very jacket in the shoe department."

"I was trying it on."

"As a mother," Nigel the clerk had said, "you ought to know. We don't favor unattended young boys roving through our store."

His mother had been cowed. "Thank you," she had said. "I'll talk to his father."

Robert had ignored Nigel. He pulled the desired jacket down from the clerk's tight hand. He slipped in his arms and pulled the zipper. "I like it."

His mother had looked nervously at the clerk. "It does have windcuffs." Then making an unconvincing counterattack, for a moment she stared the clerk in the eye. "Well, Robert," she had said, "we'll take it. That's what we'll do. We'll buy it right now. No sense shopping around and then coming back right where we started." She looked Nigel the clerk dead on. "I think this will be fine," she had said. "Do you take charge cards? I'll have to put it on my charge card."

Back in the neighborhood, though the evening was warm, Robert wore the brown leather jacket out to show his buddies.

"Take it and shove it," Stoney had said. "Who needs a crummy leather jacket."

Robert Place could have taken them, maybe, one by one, but all of them together were too much. An older boy with light-blond down on his upper lip knocked Robert to the ground. Stoney picked up a piece of broken glass. He straddled the small of Robert's back and cut up the shoulders of the new leather jacket.

Robert escaped and ran and ran until he could run nowhere but to his mother's kitchen.

"I'm furious," she said. "After all I went through for you with that pansy clerk! Just you wait till your father gets home!"

Robert's father took one look at his bruised face and sent him to his room, shouting after him: "I'll be up to take care of you, sissy-boy!"

Robert sprawled across the bed. His head throbbed from the kicking. Angry voices rose and fell in the kitchen below. He dozed in pain and missed the tread of his father's boots up the stairs. He started when his door opened and light from the hall thrust an awkward rectangle across his bed.

"Take off the jacket," his father had said. "It goes back."

Robert wrapped his arms tight around his chest. The leather was warm.

"Take it off."

Robert glared up at the big man silhouetted in the doorway. "No," he said. He folded his arms tighter, holding on to himself as he had never held on to anything in his life.

"Then I'll take it off for you." His father pulled at the jacket.

Robert would not surrender.

His father pulled off his belt. He was a short, powerful man whose veins rose in anger as he twisted the buckled end of his belt around his fist. "Don't tell me *no*, you goddam kid." He lashed out. "No goddam pussy-boy is going to tell me *no*." His belt struck across Robert's chest and arms. The boy rolled defensively to his stomach. His father saw the scuffs and tears on the jacket. "Sonuvabitch!" he said. In fury he tore Robert's corduroy slacks down below his slim haunches. His left hand shredded his son's worn cotton shorts. The blows from his belt welted across Robert's flesh, until finally, his father, hardened in rage, fell across him. His breath had the copper tobacco smell of Camels. "You tell your ma any of this," he whispered close into Robert's ear, "and next time I'll kill you. Make it look like an accident and kill you. Just hang you up by your neck in the attic and kill you. Just knock over a chair like you did it yourself, and kill you, you little sissy suicide, just like all faggot suicides. Send you straight to hell!"

"My old man was a real bulldog lady-killer," Robert bragged to the barber. "Everytime I come into a barber shop it reminds me of him. The way he used to smell once a month of all that Fitch Hair Tonic and rosewater. Once a month I could smell him coming."

"You don't say," Floyd said.

"He got himself killed in a fight on an oil rig in Louisiana."

"That a fact." Floyd combed and clipped at Robert's head. "Getting kind of thin on the top."

"Yeah," Robert said. "So it goes."

Floyd clipped at one small hair growing in Robert's left ear. "Do you suppose," he said, "that they put out their eyes when they're kids?"

"Who?" Robert looked up from the magazine in his lap.

"Those pianists on TV. The ones that can't see because it makes them play better."

"I don't know," Robert said. "Most people'll do most anything."

"Sometimes in India they put out a kid's eyes so he can hustle more from tourists. Hear the Mex do that too."

"Sounds to me," Robert said, "something like the boys who sang soprano for the pope. I got an article I tore out of some magazine at home on that. They'd take these altar boys and, you know, sort of spay them, operate on them, you know, down there, so they'd keep their real high voices. Their families were happy. Even the kids were happy. A kid with a real high voice could make a fortune in those days."

"That a fact," Floyd said. "Maybe then that's why they do it. Just so 'Mr. and Mrs. America' can sit at home in front of their 'T and V' and watch those black boys who can't even see play the piano." He reached for the talcum. "Dagos really did that stuff, huh?"

"Lots of people do lots of things that sound cruel to us but not to them. Anybody who's not an orphan knows that." On the shelf, between Bach and Liszt, Robert spied a fresh half-eaten deli sandwich. He shifted nervously in the chair.

"Hold still," Floyd said. He reached for the shaving cream. "I'm finishing up around your ears."

On the end-table next to the chromium-and-leatherette couch lay a second half-eaten sandwich. Blood sausage, the same color as the burgundy couch, hung bitten out of the white bread. In a Coke with no more than two swigs out of it, small bubbles fizzed noiselessly to the top.

"One of your customers left his lunch."

"Some customers leave stuff. Some take it. There's losers and there's claimers. You want it?" He arced his razor in a smooth crescent above and behind Robert's ear. The downstroke scrape flourished into a fast, thrilling swoop down his neck.

"I feel like my life is in your hands," Robert said.

"It is," Floyd said.

"I don't know if I like that." Robert hated the nervous laugh in his own voice. "I only started back to barbers about two months ago. Before that it was nearly five years, being a hippie and all, I had hair down below my shoulders. Then something, nothing really, happened, and this guy, this judge, made me cut it. When I was a kid, barber shops always gave me a headache.

"So. Just a little scrape with the law," Floyd, W. C. Fields, said. He swooped his razor over and around Robert's other ear.

"I never liked anybody fussing over me that much. Besides, this barber shop my old man took me to had pin-up pictures of really big girls and I wasn't a very big boy. I mean now it wouldn't matter."

"The bigger the better, huh?" Floyd rinsed his razor. He knew enough to humor his customers ambiguously. He met all kinds at the corner of 18th and Castro. "Never kid a kidder," he said.

"I kid you not," Robert said.

For years Robert had been titanic cruising among icebergs of females in his hometown. At the age of four, innocent of all need for cover, in the driveway between their homes, he had compared himself to the lower half of a giggling little Judy Esterbank. One month later, a modern doctor, new to small-town practice, had sold his mother an introductory twofer on the latest big-city hygiene and had wheeled him through white double doors to pull out his tonsils and slice off his foreskin.

He never really trusted her ever again.

At the age of ten, playing Lewis and Clark, he had tripped over a tent peg catching the strapless halter of twelve-year-old Joyce Gillette. One flawless white breast popped pert and eager into view. He stared and she smiled. He stepped forward and she stepped back tucking herself away as neatly as she packed her camping equipment. He stared at the veil of her halter. She stepped to him and cupped his groin in her hand. It felt good. "I ought to kill you," she had said.

But her hand felt warm through his jeans. Three years later she kissed him there. Repeatedly. Up and down.

"Indeed I do love the little ladies," Robert said to Floyd. Screw Judy and screw Joyce. He hated himself for continuing the elaborate lie he had intended to leave back in the Midwest.

"And that's why you moved to San Francisco." Floyd dusted Robert's neck with clouds of talcum. "That's why everybody moves to San Francisco. They say it's the weather. They say it's the restaurants. But it's the sex that brings them. San Francisco's the place where when you go there you get laid."

"I'm interested in that Coke," Robert said. Brown air bubbles rose in slow chains up through the mocha cola.

"It's second-hand and half-dead," Floyd said. He handed Robert the bottle. "Just wipe the cooties off the top."

Robert toasted Bach and Liszt. He wished Floyd's magazines were better. Even a *National Geographic* with naked natives would help him swallow the dying Coke and the whole afternoon a lot easier. "You know," Robert said to distract his train of thought, "that a '57 Chevy is the best car GM ever put out. That's why I got it. That's why I still drive it."

"That a fact," Floyd said. He unwrapped Robert's neck, took two swipes with the talcum brush, and flapped the green-striped cloth with a whipcrack. "Being's we're finished, let me show you something."

Robert remained seated in Floyd's chair. Now maybe he would find what it was that had caused him to pull the Chevy to the curb, forget his meter, and endure a haircut and a Coca-Cola he had not desired. Floyd disappeared into the piano repair room. Two single swipes zithered across a dusty piano harp behind the Fifties' floral-print curtain.

Robert waited for Floyd as he had waited beside his mother's hospital bed. Her name was Isabel and his father always kidded her, saying like it was the first time, "Is a bell necessary on a bicycle? Is a bell necessary at all?" And she always laughed even though she hated him making fun of her.

For months she had lain wasting away with cancer in the depths of white sheets. He looked down at her remembering how all through his youth she had sized him up and encouraged him saying, "At least you're tall." She warned him that no girl likes a short man. "Short men," she had said, "are impossible to deal with." She should have known. Robert's father was short. But Robert had felt tall, standing next to her shrinking form. For an hour at the beginning of her last week, he had stood by her bed with the plastic tube of the intravenous fluid pinched tight between his thumb and forefinger. Mercy or no mercy, he had hoped to kill her, but his hand had cramped even before the nurse almost caught him.

In Floyd's piano room a large cardboard box grated heavily across the gritty floor. Robert heard Floyd say, "Ah, there it is."

"I suppose they do," Robert called to Floyd who was dragging the huge box into the shop itself.

"You suppose who does what?" Floyd panted with the exertion, but his face was triumphant.

"I suppose they do put out their own kids' eyes." Robert had read more than he even wanted hanging out in libraries, slicing pages out of magazines. "There's all those operas about Greek plays where the kids get turned into mincemeat. Some parents kill their young. Maybe they're no more cruel than nature is cruel. People wouldn't pay good money to go see that sort of thing if they weren't naturally interested."

Floyd began to dig into his box. "Now, don't you laugh at me," Floyd said. He was matter-of-fact. "I have these treasures I don't share with everyone."

"I understand," Robert said. But he did not understand as much as he thought he did, and he was about to understand a whole lot more.

The box was neatly packed with magazines, picture albums, and loose photos of the kind most adult men keep to themselves. At first glance, Robert Place knew, almost faster in his groin than his head, what kind of illustrations these were. They were the kind Robert had tried all his life to avoid, but could not. They were the kind who called to him, from the flat pages of magazines, to breathe into them his life. They were seductive, attractive, flowers of evil. They were, somehow, an occasion of sin. They were young men more stripped than dressed who posed as sailors and athletes and construction workers. They were the kind of pictures of men Robert had sliced from certain physique atlases in St. Louis bookstores to take home to lay with him on his bed, until he blacked out, saying, "Whoever you are, I want to spend eternity with you," waking up as if coming to, jumping from his bed, furiously destroying the evidence of his love for this kind of thing. He would crush the sticky pictures into tiny paper balls and burn them and flush their ashes down the toilet. They were bad boys and worse men and he was not one of them.

"Take a look at this," Floyd said. He offered a magazine to Robert.

"Very nice," Robert said. He fanned the pages from the back cover forward and made bits and pieces of bodies flip in crazy motion from the last page to the first. Couples began in orgasm and ended in foreplay.

"You know," Floyd said, "when it comes right down to it, your Chevy and my pianos show up for what they aren't." He scooped up a stack of magazines.

"What do you mean?" Robert asked.

"It's a lie what everyone says. That there's other things in life besides sex and money. Your car and my pianos aren't a hill of beans when it comes to getting laid. Down there at that intersection it's all bodies and sex. You could have the hottest car in town, and I could have the grandest grand piano, but unless you have a face and a body, which you at your age certainly do, and unless I have some extra cash, which at my age I have a little, no one's going to touch us."

Robert studied Floyd's pinched face. "What about love?"

"What's love got to do with it?"

"Hell if I know," Robert said. "I don't even care. I never loved anybody and nobody ever loved me. I'm not even looking for love. I got no expectations except of the worst kind."

"I'm a realist," Floyd said. "The only thing to be in life is twenty-one. Forever. After that, it's all hustlers. Everyone who comes through my door is selling something. Don't ever grow old."

"I've always looked young for my age," Robert said.

"So you don't know yet what I'm talking about."

"Yes I do."

"The devil you say!"

Floyd thrust a dozen magazines named *Young Adonis* and *Mars* and *Physique Pictorial* at Robert who immediately judged their covers. They made him covetous. He wanted three or four of the magazines, contents sight unseen.

"I'd really like one of these," he said, holding a copy of *Tomorrow's Man*.

"Money can't buy them. Some of these I've had for fifteen or sixteen years. When I page through them, it's like with dear friends. When I'm eighty, they'll still be the same age, the same dear friends, and I'll still have them and they'll be a comfort."

"They're a comfort right now," Robert said. As he paged the magazines, he felt his spirit rise inside him. He was in the room but he was not part of the room. He sat between the mirrors. The men in the magazines sucked his very essence into themselves, coming alive to him, whispering secret words he could not make out. He gasped for breath like a man being dragged down a drain.

Floyd pulled the yellow shade down over the glass door. Two years before he had painted in orange hippie Day-Glo the words SORRY CLOSED on the shade, and the paint had not faded at all. He had some rising hope that his strange customer was hinting, the way first-timers so often hint, that he wanted to become dear friends with him.

Robert, in fact, sat helpless in Floyd's barber chair. He made small gurgling noises as he turned the pages. Back in Canterberry, he had only imagined what he would find out west. But he had not found it; it had found him. His hand clutched his throat as his breath finally, totally, slid out of him. He suddenly saw how life was going to be with him. Really be with him. Really in control of him. The thought took root like mandrake in his heart. He had never considered until that minute that everything he was about, had always been about, had masked the slow flowering fact that he was not different from all those men and boys cruising arm in arm in the street below. The same wild lemming call that had summoned them from everywhere had summoned him from the south-midlands to them, to this city, to this very intersection, to this catbird seat in Floyd's Barber Shop looking down on something that was totally new to him, but also totally known.

He was not sure he liked the convergence.

What the fuck was Rainbow County?

The summer before, when he had fled south on a trial-run from Canterberry to St. Louis, Cleo Walker, with her brilly bush of flaming red hair, had walked right up and taken control of him. She had spied him sitting at a small table in an outdoor cafe in Gaslight Square and after she had scooped him up, she stripped him down in her sun-splashed studio on Delmar Avenue near Forest Park. He had not felt awkward standing nude before her. For years, naked exposure had been his urge, so he had slipped, a true exhibitionist, easy and erect from his clothes. Without meaning his words, he apologized for his thing, his *thing*, standing at attention. Cleo refused to dignify his apology with the benefit of a real reply, so he had stepped toward her, reaching for her breasts. That was the script, wasn't it? But Cleo had refused his advance for reasons he could not fathom. Wasn't painting only a high-toned excuse for getting naked and looking at nudes?

"I want," he stammered low, "I want...I want...."

"Don't reach for something," Cleo said, "you don't know you want."

"What do you mean?" he asked.

"You're a virgin, aren't you?"

He said nothing.

"I'm not a virgin," she said. "So I know things."

"You mean it shows?" he said. "I'm a book with blank pages?"

"You're a book with no pages," she said.

"I like the way you talk."

"Fuck!" Cleo said the word he had never heard a woman say.

"You have an excellent body and an interesting face. You have a sexual energy I don't care to release. I only want to paint you."

He was crestfallen. "You can see faces like mine hanging in the post office."

She felt a sudden sorrow for him. "Look, *Roberto, caro Roberto,* there's nothing wrong with you. I'm a painter. I want to paint you. I don't want to have sex with you."

Yet, in Cleo's studio, he stood insistent, his pouting mouth silent, his lower part as straight and to the point as a declarative sentence. "I'm sorry," he apologized again, this time half-meaning it. "It doesn't have anything to do with you."

"I didn't think so," she said.

"This always happens when I take off my clothes, or think about taking off my clothes."

"It's no big deal," Cleo said. "I'm a painter. I look at you. I don't see your precious dick. I see light. I see shadow."

"Light and shadow," Robert said. He tried to concentrate on a pile of littered art magazines; but even they, so far across the studio, could not slow the excited flow of his blood. He had never shown himself naked to anyone, and he was embarrassed at how much he liked it.

Cleo ignored his excitement. She poured him a small glass of blood-red wine, and squeezed white and tan and browns across her glass palette. "I'm in my sepia period," she laughed. "I'm glad I'm no devotee of Freud, who I wish had been otherwise employed. Who said that?"

"Mrs. Freud?"

"Lean against the wall, Robert. Relax. Move your head to the left. Fine. Hold it. Just relax. I'm brushing in your basic line today. Later on I'll work in the tension."

He had leaned motionless against the doorway and then, finally, leaned against her for the next two months, because, one rainy August afternoon, when she had lost the light, and poured them both some more wine, she had said, "When I told you I didn't want to have sex with you, you silly goose, I didn't mean I didn't want to fuck you. At least once."

Go figure, he thought.

Their love-making confused him. All love-making confused him.

"Was I okay?" he asked. He had not been able to keep from asking that question even he knew was ridiculous.

"Who were you thinking about?" Cleo asked.

"You," he said.

"Liar!"

He could have cheerfully killed her. She had him pegged. She polarized him the way all women did. She was all women. He knew he was supposed to desire them, but he had no feeling for why. They filled him with an empty want they could not slake. They took his coloration and line the way Cleo's sidelong look, her brush-hand resting on her mahlstick, had day-by-day transferred his face from his head to her canvas. He was the primitive and she was the sorceress capturing his spirit. Transfixed, he could not move from the pose into which she had enchanted him. His naked body trembled visibly.

"Get it together," Cleo had said. "Take a break."

She handed him a book of prints and text. Absently he leafed through page after page of what seemed to be the *Life and Hard Times of Andrew Wyeth*. Not one of the reproductions tempted him to pull his single-edge razor blade from his wallet and start slicing.

"That's why I like to paint you," Cleo said.

"Why?"

"Your face hides nothing. You're bored. You're light years away. From here. From me. From everybody."

"I don't care for cartooning." He tossed the Wyeth book to the floor and resumed his pose.

Cleo strode across the studio and retrieved the book. "Wyeth isn't exactly Norman Rockwell," she said.

"Same school." Robert hated the nasty sound in his voice, but he didn't care.

"What would you know about art anyway," Cleo said. "It's about order. You're all chaos."

"Is that so? I know plenty. I've read articles."

"So don't throw Wyeth down. Read it," Cleo said. She shoved the book hard against his naked belly. "And you better not tear a goddam page out of it."

"I confess my secrets and you refuse to forgive me?"

"Fuck you and your sins." She said it flatly and marched back to her life-size canvas. "Tilt your head to the left."

Robert obeyed. The Wyeth book hung in his right hand. It felt cool against his thigh. Holding his pose, he raised it and fanned once more through the pages. Print after print of paint-brushed faces peopled Wyeth's decaying afternoons. One painting, an immense field, contained a solitary male figure. Everything was brown and dead and spun out of sorrow. Wyeth had painted it the winter of his own father's death. The editor's note explained the painting as an exorcism of sadness. Robert stirred slightly from his pose. He caught the sense of the painting, but he could hardly see the face of the man in the field. Somehow Wyeth had lost his own face along with the lost face of his father. The canvas was full of nothing so much as his own grief.

Deep inside Robert that thin tensile strand of generations snapped. In a moment of his own infinite sadness he realized that he too had lost the face of his father. In the stead of the man who pretended to sire him, and had really abused him, stood only shadow images and half-remembered sounds of the sweet times: the wet-lipped kiss from that unshaved face in the dark over his bed. It was all reduced to that: the memory of his father, home from the late shift, leaning over to kiss him goodnight. As if he were again half-asleep in his little boy's sleep, Robert could feel his father's ghostly kiss on his face. He could not forget his father's love, but he could not forgive that one night of his father's drunkenness.

Robert realized that he had been losing everything despite his desperate collecting of folders of stolen clippings and magazines purloined from under the eyes of cheery dental receptionists. In the glory days of the large magazines, he had tried to save the images of the week by swallowing up the sleeves of his school jacket whole issues of

Look and *Life*. Finally, when he had been caught with his single-edge razor blade in the Green County Public Library, his mother had said, "I hope you're satisfied. You now owe me a hundred dollars more." Her face looked screwed with pain that he thought was no more than her embarrassment at his conviction. "Bobby, Bobby, Bobby. What do you expect me to live on? When will you ever grow up and settle down?" Six months later, she was dead and he had fled to San Francisco. He was fed up to his eyeballs with personal relationships. He had a need for a city of strangers.

Floyd, like most barbers, could hold a one-sided conversation with a corpse and was finishing up his long monologue when Robert remembered where he was. "Old Sammy Davis, Jr.," Floyd said, "only got one of his eyes put out. That's because his folks wanted him to dance. Be kind of hard to poke out both your eyes and dance too. Might fall off the stage. But before long, you'll see, someone'll show up and try it big as life on network TV." He handed Robert another magazine.

"And they'll be tapping out something in code, those dancers will." Robert took the magazine and laid his line on Floyd. "That blind guy you say'll be dancing on CBS will be tapping out in code something everybody ought to hear. Something like SOS." Robert considered his words. "Just like SOS," he repeated, and he wanted to cry out, not for help, but for something else, "because we're all in danger and we have to save our souls."

"That a fact," Floyd said. He passed a perplexed look up through his thick glasses. Should he make his move? Was this guy wanting it, or was he all talk and no action? Were the magazines, dragged out to arouse him, missing their mark?

"But not everyone will understand it." Robert slowly turned the pages of the last magazine.

"Maybe you shouldn't bother trying to understand what you do. Just do it," Floyd insinuated.

Robert looked up straight into Floyd's eyes through his thick glasses. "I have a gun," he announced. "A .22 caliber handgun."

"You don't say." Floyd backed off.

"Does that make you scared of me?"

"Do you have it on you?"

"No."

"Then you don't scare me. Your gun scares me. I don't like guns."

"Sometimes you have to scare people. Terror's the only thing they respect. If you scare them, you get their undivided attention."

"Whyn't you finish up," Floyd was changing the subject, "reading that magazine."

"Sure," Robert said. "So far I like it fine. It's your best one yet."

Floyd took a last few snips here and there around Robert's ears, then tried to gentle him down, and sidle on in, seductively rubbing Robert's neck with an electric massager. He was surprised to find very little tension in Robert's neck and shoulders. "You're a cool customer," he said, "as cool as a cucumber."

Suddenly, Robert sat bolt upright in Floyd's barber chair. He held it in his hands: a black-and-white photograph on an unnumbered magazine page. It was the picture he had spent his life looking for: magazines in one hand, razor blade in the other. The photo was of a man seated alone. On either side of the photo were separate single shots of athletic women. The one on the left held a golf club. She was set to putt and her breasts hung down between her stiffened arms. The naked woman on the right held a jaunty tennis racquet. But it was the naked athlete in the middle photo who mesmerized him as much as if he'd found a snapshot of his real father, the original missing person, whom he had never seen.

He was seated, stretched slightly back straddling a locker-room bench. He was a little older than Robert, and bigger, very blond, with a fully developed chest over his washboard abdomen. His thick wrists connected his athlete's hands to his powerful arms. He wore football pads across his broad shoulders, and a football helmet, and, between his casually spread legs, he was erect. His eyes looked directly from the helmet into the camera and directly out of the page into Robert's face. The face-guard on the helmet covered his mouth. No New Testament word of mercy could spring from those Old Testament lips that Robert knew were set, mean and hard and without mercy. He looked directly out at Robert. He was erect and Robert knew he faced the powerful, inevitable Face of God.

"I must," he said to Floyd, "have this." He rose out of the barber chair. "Ask any amount, anything. Only let me buy this from you."

Floyd thought to press the trade for sex, but the young man seemed too volatile. Besides, a quick flash of looking down the barrel of a handgun made him think better of it. "That one you can have," he said.

"I can't just take it. I learned my lesson about that the hard way."

"Then trade me something, anything," Floyd said. "I won't take your money." He stared into Robert's ecstatic wild eyes and suddenly, more than he wanted him, he wanted him gone.

"I don't have anything," Robert said.

Floyd laughed nervously at him. "Everybody's got something."

Robert mentally searched his car. He had his clothes. He had the loaded handgun. "Nothing," he said.

In the room, he seemed volatile.

In the mirrors, he looked vulnerable.

Floyd, fighting his rising lust, chided himself for being a cautious old fool. He threw risk against the wind. The boy was right. Danger was aphrodisiac. He put his hand on Robert's knee and slowly smoothed his palm up the inside of his thigh.

"Not that!" Robert watched the hand slowly advance up his leg like a giant spider. "Not that!" Robert said.

Floyd's heart jumped with a rush of adrenaline. "Then what?" Floyd stood straight up. "You said I could have anything for the picture."

"Not that. Not here. Not now. Not you."

"See what I told you about your car and my pianos?" Floyd worked the only logic he knew in situations like this. "What if I pay you?"

"For what?"

He thought to say for sex, but he said, "To take the picture. I'll give you money to take the picture," Floyd said, "and then you can leave."

"Don't go inverting everything."

Invert? Invert. Floyd had psychology books from twenty years before when *invert* meant only one thing.

"Then take the picture for godsake and get a move on."

"I told you, man! I can't take it for nothing."

"As far as I'm concerned, you can," Floyd said. "This is getting old. I want to close up shop."

"Wait," Robert said. "I got it." He pulled out his wallet and reached inside. He handed the folded-up paper to Floyd.

"What's this?" Floyd asked. "The number of your Swiss bank account?"

"No, you asshole," Robert said. "It's the combination to my gym locker."

"I'll bet."

"Go on. Read it!"

Floyd unfolded the smudged slip of paper. "I need my reading glasses."

Robert stared down at the picture of the blond athlete, but he barked his order at Floyd, "Read it."

Floyd hooked his half-lens bifocals over his ears and read the word "Postmark."

"That's the title," Robert said. "It's a poem. A short poem."

"Good," Floyd said. "Short and sweet." The afternoon had not gone the seductive way he had hoped and he regretted missing lunch as much as he missed lunching on Robert. "I have low blood sugar."

"Read it, please. No one else has ever seen it. I wrote it on my way out here. To send back home. To everyone back home."

"'Postmark,'" Floyd read. "'Dear God: You created me, then you hated me....Dear Folks: You conceived me, then deceived me.... Dear Teacher: You taught me, then you fought me....Dear Boss: You hired me, then you fired me....Dear Lover: You painted me, then you tainted me....Dear Death: You embraced me, then erased me.'"

"Well?" Robert asked.

"It's not...bad."

"Not bad?"

"It's pretty good."

"You think so?"

"Yeah," Floyd said. "I like it like really a whole lot."

"Good," Robert said. "We just made a trade. My poem for your photograph. Strange, isn't it? I came in here not knowing why I came in here. I didn't want a haircut and you cut my hair. I got a parking ticket. You handed me a magazine and I found a picture of the face that's always been in the back of my head."

"What's that?" Floyd said.

"Never you mind. You wouldn't understand."

"That's three bucks for the trim," Floyd said.

"Here's four," Robert said. "Keep the change."

"Don't insult me," Floyd said. "You never tip the owner."

"I do."

"Suit yourself."

"I'm leaving," Robert said. "It's been real."

Floyd slipped full into his W. C. Fields routine. "Never give a sucker an even break. Here's your hat. What's your hurry? Don't let the door hit you on your way out."

"You calling me a sucker?"

"No," Floyd said. "Take it easy. Where you headed?"

"To the beach," Robert said. "Land's end at Land's End." He walked to Floyd's cash register counter.

"It's been a slow day moneywise," Floyd said nervously.

"Hasn't exactly been a stampede, I'd say." Robert pulled the single-edge razor blade from his wallet and expertly sliced the magazine page so that the athletic girls disappeared, leaving only the 5x7 of the handsome football player. "Tonight's the full moon and the summer solstice. I've never seen the Pacific. I'm taking this picture and I'm going to watch the sunset and the moonrise."

"You want maybe instead to use my john?" Floyd slipped the four bills directly into his white nylon pocket.

"What for?"

"What all little boys use it for when they've stolen daddy's dirty magazines."

"I never did anything like that."

"No one ever does, according to them, when it's always the thing they do most," Floyd said. "Do you have anyplace to stay for the night?"

"What's it to you?"

"Nothing." Floyd backed off. He slept single in a double bed. "It's nothing to me."

"I'm going to the ocean. I'll roll up my jeans and I'll walk in the surf and I'll listen."

"To what?

Robert held up the photograph. "To him," he said.

"To him?"

"To him. I'm old enough to see if he'll ever speak to me."

Floyd wanted to roll his strained eyes back in his head. All these people, all these immigrants to San Francisco were getting stranger than strange. "So," he said. "What if he doesn't speak to you."

"He'll speak to me alright."

"But what if he doesn't?"

"Either way it makes no difference since he never has anyway."

"So if it doesn't make any difference, why you so hot to go?"

"Because that picture is the Face of God."

Floyd stopped W. C. Fields from cackling: "The Face of God. You don't say." He didn't say it; instead he said: "You got to be kidding."

"He'll tell me, if he wants to, everything I need to know."

"What's that?"

"Ways to keep me out of hell. Ways to get me into heaven."

"What ways?"

"Ways you could sell like Salvation Coupons the night before Judgment Day. Ways those men and boys down in the street probably know. Old ways. Ancient ways. Ways so secret only a few men, and maybe a few women, know them. But there's more of them out here that know than back home, or anywhere else ever before in one place on this whole earth, right here, I figure, in your Rainbow County. They know the ways. I know they know the ways."

"You mean sex," Floyd said.

"Sex?" Robert said. "Sure, why not? Sex must be one of the saving ways, but the way has to be right. Just right. Or else sex is just like everyone says, the way to damnation." He bored his stare hard through Floyd's thick glasses. "And guess what else?"

Floyd guessed what else was he had himself another one of those religious sex nuts trying to break out of his shell. He wanted to take a step back, but he was too proud to show Robert any fear; he remembered Robert bragging that terror was the only thing most people respected once it got their attention.

"Besides sex," Robert said, "guess what else."

"I can't guess."

"Damage."

"Damage?"

"Just a little damage."

"Why damage?" Floyd said. "What damage? What to? Who to?"

"To you," Robert said. "To me. To everybody."

"What kind of damage?"

"Big damages," Robert said, "and little damages."

"I could call the police."

"By the time they got here, my razor blade could cut your face. I could make you blind so you could go on TV. By the time they got here, I could cut my throat. Slice right through my jugular. None of it would make any difference to anybody but you. I don't care. I might die or I might go to jail, but you'd still be blind, trying to cut hair and play your pianos."

"I get the picture," Floyd said.

"No," Robert said. "I got the picture." He held the photograph up and out at arm's length. "He'll tell me what to do. In my life I know life does damage to you." He looked down at the swarming men in the street. He had his looks. He had his car. He had his gun. "So I figure I might as well inflict a little of the damage myself."

"I never quite thought of life that way."

"Well, you sure are the slow one. Everybody else thinks so. Doesn't that explain the evil that people do to themselves, smoking and drinking and whoring and taking drugs and driving fast and fighting and killing and raping and molesting, because that's the only way they can make the world that damages them everyday make any sense is if they do some of the damage themselves. Everybody but a fool knows when you can't beat it, you join it."

"You expect him, the guy in the picture..."

"God."

"...God...to speak to you and tell you what to do?"

"I expect he'll tell me if I should do any damage for him and if I should, to who. Maybe to you. Maybe to me. Maybe to anybody he tells me to. Nobody ever went to hell for that." Robert smiled and took a step forward. "Take it easy, Floyd. Relax."

Floyd pasted a smile on his face but his heart was racing.

"See what I mean about a little scare getting your attention?" Robert broke into guffaws of snorting laughter.

"You were putting me on?"

"I bet I had you so scared you had a bone on."

"You were putting me on!"

"If you think so, Floyd, ol' buddy! You should've seen your face, a hundred times over, scared sure as hell, curving off in those mirrors, which, by the way, could stand a bit of washing. Shoot, I was just kidding you, wasn't I? 'Don't kid a kidder,' you told me, but I did and you took it hook, line, and sinker. You wait awhile and you'll get to know I got a real killer sense of humor."

"Never mention killing."

"Hey!" Robert said. "That's a figure of speech. Nothing is what it seems. It's all mirrors. One thing's always meaning some other thing besides what a person thinks it means. You know that, being a barber, standing between your mirrors in all those parallel universes. I'm not dumb, you know. I've spent most of my life in recent years reading all kinds of the strangest things so the inside of my head's like an encyclopedia. My second-cousin, Ollie Thomas, who's madam librarian back home told me so."

"Perhaps you have," Floyd said, "low blood sugar. I myself often experience strange mood swings."

"Naw. My blood's fine and my sugar's better." Robert winked the way his father always winked. "If you catch my drift."

"Sounds like," Floyd pulled his ear, charading, working Robert toward the door, "like we've circled back to sex."

"Have you noticed that too? How everything sooner or later always comes back around to sex?"

"You are sure going to have a good time down there on 18th and Castro," Floyd said. "That intersection is laying on its back with its legs in the air just waiting for you."

"I ain't done it." Robert's face reddened with anger. "I told you I ain't done it! I ain't never done it when it was my will. But when I'm good and ready, I just might, and I just might be the best at it."

Something, some *thing*, in the room ground suddenly to a halt between them.

"What?"

It could only be one thing. Floyd wished he'd carried a little hand fan, something petite and operatic from the eighteenth century, to hide the smirk on his lips.

"I ain't done it. Not yet."

"Done what?" Floyd was intent on forcing Robert to say it. I love it, Floyd thought, all this talk and no action has been the braggadocio of a male virgin with very blue balls. "Done what?"

"You're going to make me say it, aren't you?"

"Robert, I bet no one could ever make you do anything."

"My mother always said that." Robert's eyes kind of crossed in his head.

"You haven't done what?"

"I haven't had sex. Okay? So laugh."

"And risk another wrinkle? Never. My God, as it is, look at my face. If wrinkles hurt, I'd be screaming."

"I'm serious, goddam it. I haven't had sex. Not really. Not ever. Not unless you count the time I didn't want to, and the time I thought I had to, but I never count those two times and I never talk about them."

"Some experiences are too painful to recall," Floyd said, "but I can't recall any."

"Shut the judas-priest up. I'm not dumb. I can do sex. I know what goes on out there on those streets. I told you I've read and forgot more stuff than you ever even thought of." He held up the picture of the blond athlete. "I know what he's going to tell me, but I want to hear it from his own lips, me lying in the dunes at twilight feeling the warm breeze from the ocean."

"This is summer in Northern California," Floyd said. "What warm breeze? You'll die of exposure."

"He'll tell me. And they'll tell me."

"Who?"

"The fellows down there in that intersection. One at a time. And I'll listen. One secret at a time. That's how to make sense of it. One after another of the men who know the secret ways. One after the other. They'll all whisper to me and when I've heard them all, I'll know all about life and damage and death and the ways to stay out of hell."

"Are you sure, really sure, that's what he wants?"

"I don't know what he wants. That's why I'm taking his face with me to the beach. So maybe he will talk to me first the way the others will talk to me later."

"Maybe you should forget him and them and figure out what you want."

"I just want one SOB and one SOS one right after the other. I want some of the pleasure of all of the danger if I'm going to suffer the damage anyway."

"You're talking crazy," Floyd said. "You're going to fit right in with all the fruits and flakes. You're a nut."

"No, I ain't," Robert Place said, "but so what if I am?" He held up the picture like a holy icon. "Only he can tell me."

"Sure," Floyd said, "you've got that pornographic picture."

"It's the Face of God!"

"I've seen London," Floyd, W. C. Fields, said, "and I've seen France. I've seen the queen in her underpants."

"Are you making fun of me?" Robert said.

"I wouldn't dare make fun of you," Floyd said. "My blood sugar's too low to keep this up. My prescription for you is to get laid twice before bedtime, and don't call me in the morning."

"What does all that mean? Everything means something."

"It means," Floyd said, "you've come to the right place. It means, Welcome to San Francisco. Welcome to Rainbow County."

"That's better," Robert Place said. "I like that attitude much better."

"Have you ever thought," Floyd said, raising his SORRY CLOSED shade and opening the door, "about maybe swallowing something you can buy on the street to lay yourself back some, about letting your hair grow long again?"

"Why, Floyd," Robert said, halfway down to the first landing, "You surprise me. I would never have figured you to be one to turn away business. I'm going out and I'm staying out..."

"You're coming out."

"...until he talks to me. So you'll see me again. A real regular. Plan on it. I intend to show your Rainbow County a thing or two. I intend to stay a close-cropped soldier until all of them down there in that intersection talk to me, and you're going to keep me ready for him and for them, barbered and groomed like I just stepped out of a bandbox."

The Story Knife

The Priest, the Alaska Cruise,
and the Cabin Boy from Genoa

After Skagway in Alaska, in the long Arctic light of the summer solstice, Brian Kelly, heading north, heading toward true north, realized the twilight of the gods must not be desperate. On his American cruise ship docked against the granite mountains of the North Pacific, he had caught Himself catching the eye of a cabin boy from Genoa.

The boy was, in fact, freshly tipped over the cusp of adolescence, a young man, the Italian kind who gives occasion to sonnets, whose innocence beguiles, whose dark curls and darker eyes and supple-shouldered body cause notes of invitation, of assignation, accompanied by a cabin number and a hundred dollar bill, to be written in hope and then crumpled and thrown away in confusion.

Sex was not the quest. Beauty was. Love was on dangerous times. To touch a stranger put life at risk, but the need to touch beauty, to trace the curling hair of the head and thigh and foot bit into his fifty-year-old heart. He Himself had always worshiped beauty. Sex was the perfect hook to distract beauties in their tracks long enough to savor beauty itself incarnate in them. Brian Kelly, Chicago-born out of a Dublin Dempsey come over to marry a Boston Kelly, was not some feckless rover traveling ignorant through the world. He was a priest who knew what people are for. The young man from Genoa may have hired on as ship's crew. But he was not for that. His beauty was his true vocation.

The cruise ship flying flags and streamers had put to sea from Vancouver and headed north up the calm waters of the scenic Inland Passage, passing fjords and forests, washing away the anxiety that had become his habit at home. He traveled alone for a week's retreat. He was happy keeping to Himself, that third-person High Irish pronoun of importance that helped him bear his otherness and his soul's alienation from his body. In San Francisco, days before, at the jammed "Bloomsday Fleadh Festival 1989" in Golden Gate Park, he had stood separate from the sunburnt crowd cheering Van Morrison and Elvis Costello singing out the anthem of the "thousand miles of the long journey home." On the cruise ship, he skirted the wine-tastings, the karaoke, and the whale-watchers playing canasta in the fitness salon. He made Himself invisible. As the ship cruised northwards, he walked the wooden decks, sometimes warm with June sun, sometimes cold with pelting Arctic rain, purposely neither smoking his cigarettes nor saying his rosary, leaving his senses open to what flow of smell or thought or feeling might come from the sea, the passing blue ice, the mountains.

Always his *Daybook*, full of scribbled notes, was in the pocket of his long Australian duster that flapped like a priest's cassock around his ankles. Always he carried his camcorder, shooting with exotic angles the wake of the ship, the rain dripping on the decks, and the empty chairs and empty tables of the piano salon in the last hour before dawn.

The Reverend Father Brian Kelly purposely kept people out of his rectangular video frame. His footage, viewed and re-viewed alone on his monitor in his cabin, made the ship, built in 1957 and never done up for disco, look empty of the present, and so reminiscent of romance he wondered that no Hollywood location scout had exploited its varnished wood decks and steep stairs and long corridors. He brooded that the rental movies he viewed late nights alone in his bedroom in the parish rectory were no longer musical comedies and dramas about shipboard love affairs to remember. The way of the world had turned Hollywood to crash-and-burn action scripts with no use for the nostalgia of the vintage ship but to blow it up.

His camera eye zoomed in across the decks and cubbyholes and doors and brass handrails, and tracked down the upper-deck gangways with an aching need for the years he had wasted on purity that taught him nothing but denial. His blazing blue eyes searched the shadows for ghosts of shipboard romance from times past when, long ago, as a young priest sitting in the dark confessional, whispered sin had once been interesting, even tempting in the Sixties and Seventies before the fundamentalist whining of neurotics seeking reconciliation face-to-face had caused him to laugh out loud because he was only a priest and not a therapist.

Other passengers nodded to his head of red hair haloed gold by the bright summer sun, nearing solstice, but could not penetrate his aura of privacy. He protected Himself from the presumptuous privilege of strangers thrown together for a week, eager to unload their life stories on new acquaintances, unsuspecting lone travelers wishing to God there were boundaries sailing over the bounding main.

His cabin stewardess, a worldly little blonde from Strathchyde, Scotland, hardly surprised him with her openness. At first he had been uncomfortable with her constant attentions, making up his room, turning down his bed. He felt the visceral class distinctions of the world. He had never felt comfortable around the faithful old parish housekeeper because he always took to heart workers hired to do what people could but won't do for themselves. But his stewardess put him at ease. She too knew what people were for.

He figured she knew what he was for.

She was fluent in gaydar, earning his confidence, kidding him that the Roman priest collar in his closet was the très perfect costume for the Captain's party. She told him what no one else would tell. She told him how some passengers boarded to die. Some knowing they might; some planning they would. How one or two a month died; how they were rolled away to refrigeration below deck. Old people, ancient ones, and sickly people, terminal ones, and young ones, viral ones, sometimes in their beds, sometimes slipping overboard silently into the icy water, the quick icy water, unseen in the twilight of the midnight sun, unmissed by the crowds of robust breeders and feeders. That was not what the cruise ship's festive television commercials had promised.

Father Brian Kelly after sitting twenty-five years in the

confessional was not surprised at her tale. But he had not expected the dark surprise of the cabin boy from Genoa.

He'd thought he was beyond temptation.

The young man slept below the passenger decks with the crew. His stewardess told him of their small rooms with no windows. "We sleep below sea level. This is a prison for us, it is," she said. His own cabin had a porthole with three brass bolts he had unscrewed to let in the cool North Pacific air. Small icebergs flowed south past his porthole north of Ketchikan in the Inland Passage. He kept to his cabin surrounded by his books and papers and cameras.

The other passengers were swanning through a catered week above their station, foraging for croissants and custards and cocktails from breakfast to midnight buffets, feasting through Roman banquets, soup to nuts, each day appearing in new clothes unpacked in expanding sizes as they boozed their way northward intent on getting their money's worth from the all-inclusive cruise which did not, he rued, include the boy from Genoa. The wives of businessmen and contractors and doctors were ice queens unto themselves: plump, pink, junk-jeweled members of the wannabe classes, women in cruise-ship fashions towing what was left of their conquered husbands, impatient wives waiting for the man of the house to keel over leaving them free at last to enjoy the life insurance benefits footing the bill of the real merry widows on board.

None of them, old or young, husband or wife, bothered him. He tried to be charitable and tolerant, because, between the fat and the dead, he found the silent thin thread of his own solo gay life so unlike their noisy endurance of each other. Anyone who thought priests should marry could be cured by listening to the confessions of married people. Yet somehow their lively eating and drinking lifted and changed his condescending heart because their binging was so opposite the slim disease of plague. They seemed so ordinary, so harmless, so nice, he wondered if sins any longer existed, because God could hardly take offense from such poor creatures. If all the old traditions and taboos were fading away, was he Himself as a priest irrelevant? When everything's all-inclusive, can you do anything you want?

The cruise was a mercy ship carrying him away from his daily life, his daily things, his daily routines of Mass and prayer and counseling. No priests of his acquaintance could telephone him from the Cardinal Archbishop's office with gossipy updates rattling beads about who was doing what to whom, or who was drunk or dying of you-know-what, or dead. He read no news. He watched no television. He attended no films, and the less he saw and heard, the more visible he became to Himself.

Writing in his *Daybook*, he mused about the magical thinking of priests forgiving sins, exorcising devils, and conjuring the white magic of the Seven Sacraments. His Jesuit spiritual director counseled him he could never read or write too much for his own good. His ordination made him a Catholic priest standing daily at the altar casting spells transforming bread and wine into the flesh and blood of the handsome young Christ with the ritual words "Hoc est enim corpus meum." He understood why non-Catholics called such literal dogma "hocus-pocus." Cognitive dissonance, his poetic Jesuit said, especially for a priest born under the sign of Gemini, was the blessing of the road that rose up to meet him on the long journey of his Irish soul. He believed in the sacred and the profane. He was a priest, fully a priest, and more than a priest. His reading made him feel like a pagan magus, writing in his *Daybook*, spelling the twenty-six runes of the alphabet into erotic words raising the living flesh and blood of divine young men.

He stood naked in his cabin with the sea breeze from the porthole cooling his body, and his camcorder taping his solo movements. He danced the exotic slow-motion choreography gay men do when stoned alone, heads spinning with ballet and mimes and Judy jazz hands and the man that got away. After a port-of-call at a lake where he had helped row a long Tlingit canoe with twenty other male passengers who meant more to him than they knew talking baseball over included reindeer sandwiches, he returned to his cabin and danced for his camera, a slow undulating male dance to ancient music no one but he Himself could hear. The ship's engines hummed white noise under the rhythmic slap of waves against the hull.

He was more than naked. He was not his telephone ringing. He was not his car driving. He was not his Roman collar. Not his sermons. Not his books. Not his face smiling at the sick, blessing children, comforting widows, telling gays quivering inside the confessional box they were not sinners, telling the priests who confessed to him they were forgiven. He was stripped clean by sea and sky and ship, simply becoming Himself behind his smile, behind his Irish eyes, behind what breezy conversation he sometimes felt obliged to make as a reality check to keep himself grounded, behind his gentlemanly stroll rubbing shoulders with cordial strangers who did not perceive him as clergy to see if he was, behind the priestliness that isolated him, still a human man.

He was Himself in his cabin. Despite his abiding grief that his priestly life had turned into a disaster movie because no one needed priests anymore, he was overflowing with energy, imagining the ship taking the sick and the old, and the dying from his tribe, sailing toward the cold comfort of ice floes. He admired their courage. They no longer bothered to ask priests for Last Rites.

Love and death. The death of love. The love of death. He had fled everything familiar at home because his Rolodex of priests who were friends read like the Tibetan Book of the Dead. He could no longer cry when a classmate from the old seminary died. His grieving had run out of tears. So many priests, some of them great beauties, faded so quickly, died so young, with death certificates forged against the final stigma of AIDS. His own suspicious blood coursed through his veins hiding what horror? He had bought passage on the cruise to be alone for healing his head. He had to think over his Jewish doctor's advice. Was it cynical or not?

"Father Brian," Dr. Bernie Wiegand had said. "If your test comes out negative and you play safe, the plague is over for you. Keep your act together."

What act he had was driven by beauty more than lust, but driven all the same. "What do I know?" he wrote in his *Daybook*, "I'm a burnt-out case."

The third night, his stewardess pulled him aside. "A man must

have jumped overboard. One of the thin ones. A lad. A grown boy."
He was as horrified to listen to her as she was insistent to prove what
she had said was true. Her trilling Strathclyde burr chilled her voice
opposite his Dublin-born mother's warm brogue that still entertained
him during their late-night telephone conversations. "He's nowhere
on board. The crew's looked everywhere. Jumping is better, better
for me, better than finding them in the morning lying there cold
in their beds. I leave them till last. The dead ones. Clean the other
rooms first, I do."

She was progressive enough, and Protestant to boot, a Calvinist,
not caring a fig for priests, but he could not bring Himself to ask her
about the cabin boy from Genoa who smiled knowing full well what
was wanted and what he was for. Remembering their first exchange
of looks, that first look, Brian could not deny the rush in Himself.
He had no poker face. He knew the boy recognized the look. The
boy knew what the man was for.

Brian could only hint to the stewardess about the looks men
exchange with the gay cast in the eye that identifies them to each
other. He was confused, unfamiliar with shipboard etiquette, uncomfortable, yet turned on by the pinch of class distinction that
made the boy and him inaccessible to each other. Was the boy's look
really beauty smiling back? Did the boy really know what he was
for? Was he an innocent at sea, a stammering naive Billy Budd, or
was his the come-on of a Mediterranean rent boy hustling trade in
the North Pacific?

On the fourth morning, the ship docked at Skagway. The other
passengers flocked to the curio shops that were the same as all the
other curio shops in all the other ports. Brian stood quietly in the
center of the village to listen for the sound of hammers, following
the sound, finding the local men, talking with them, telling lies,
pretending he was a teacher, saying his principal had made him
promise to bring back to his students some documentary truth about
the people of Alaska. The men, tuned to humor all the quirky cruise-
ship characters who brought money to town, kept nailing up fence

boards as the priest knelt before them worshiping their natural male grandeur with his camcorder.

Only minutes before returning to the ship, he approached a mountain man sitting in a beat-up van with a canoe strapped on top, a stove pipe jutting through the rear roof, and a large Husky with one blue eye and one brown panting on the passenger seat. The mountain man talked utopian anger about big government and oil companies and clear-cutting and how stupid the voters of Ketchikan had been to allow a nuclear warship to home port in their fishing waters.

His camcorder worked like a magic confessional. The lens sucked in people eager to spill their opinions and their secrets. Everyone wanted to be on television. The mountain man, smooth-talking into the camcorder, showed him, through the driver's window, objects he had crafted while snowed in till the May thaw.

Brian was fascinated by a small knife, its tiny blade an ancient striated mammoth tooth polished flat as an arrowhead, its six-inch handle a burnished willow twig, honey-colored, with dark wood knots. He instantly liked the delicate object held like a talisman in the mountain man's hand.

"It's a story knife," the mountain man said. "When the Tlingit or the Eskimo elders tell a story, they use this knife. They smooth out the snow. They draw a rectangle with the knife. The kids watch the knife draw the story in the snow. The knife draws the stick figures of one or two images inside the rectangle. The story unfolds when the storyteller wipes out the drawing, smoothing the snow, drawing a new rectangle for the next part of the story."

Brian turned his camcorder off, hung it from his shoulder, and reached into the pocket of his duster where he kept mad money in the flap of his *Daybook*. "I'd like to buy it."

"You want to know how much?"

"You made it. You tell me."

"At those shops over there? Cost you twice as much. Me? I don't have any overhead. I can let you have it for a hundred."

Brian wondered how people arrived at a price for beauty. "I'll take it," he said.

"No haggling?"

"I don't know how to haggle. I don't usually shop at all."

"I should've said two hundred."

"Okay. I'll haggle. Here's a hundred."

That easily he bought the story knife which he planned to keep next to the white screen of his new laptop computer. He imagined Himself teaching Bible stories and Catechism and the Lives of the Saints to children in a whole new way. He'd tried everything else.

The fourth night at sea, after the morning at Skagway, he stood aside in the lobby outside the main dining room, purposely leaving the table a bit hungry, holding his camcorder and watching a scrum of a dozen young Aussie doctors clowning, glad-handing, offering cigars, inviting everyone to come hear the infectious-disease papers they were presenting in the Jack London lounge. They waved an invitation at him across the room. He gave a thumbs-up, smiled, pointed at his camera, raised the viewfinder to his eye, and slowly zoomed his telephoto lens into their exhibitionist antics and the laughing stream of passengers ducking the quacks, looking at their watches, and running away.

"We'll give any other health professionals on board a letter saying you attended our seminar. For tax purposes."

Videotaping their horseplay in that carpeted lobby on the main deck outside the Purser's Office, surrounded by the tax-dodgers and their cheerio wives, he saw, suddenly, walking into the frame of his long lens, the cabin boy, all innocence, so dark and young, coming toward him, flesh and blood conjured through blue swirls of cigar smoke, his angel's face smiling a smile more genuine than the smiles of crew cadging tips for doing almost nothing. Brian held the shot steady on the boy who in a growing close-up in his viewfinder came cutting courteously through the doctors straight toward him. Brian lowered his camera. Face to face, neither having spoken to the other, the young man crossed all bounds. He placed his left hand on Brian's left shoulder in a quick glamouring pass noticed by no one but Brian Himself who said nothing in his flush of surprise. It was the boy who spoke. He used his baritone lightly, as if the upper register would promise more than threaten. "Come stai questa sera? How are you this evening, signore?"

Brian Kelly, born with the gift of gab, could say nothing. His fair skin blushed red as his hair. As fast as he had appeared, the boy was gone down the stairs. In years past, before the world was scared sexless, Brian might have dared follow the boy down the stairs to some private place.

Pacific whales would have spouted in the northern sea.

Brian, that night, could not, would not, by a conscious act of will, follow. Assignation required discussion. The boy was pretty, but was he pretty poison? A thousand doubts of language and reason and vexed passion sent him careening down the long tunnel of sloping passageway to his cabin.

In the bygone dream time before the viral horror, on one of his trips to the monastery hotels of the Amalfi Coast or the blue-domed churches of the Greek isles or that guided Von Gloeden photo tour to Taormina, this boy could have made his heart sing. He threw his porthole open to the velvet gloaming of the midnight sun. He braced Himself against the force of the wind. Desire beat his brain with lust for the boy's beauty. He had been careful so long, he would be safe if he continued his care, but the only care he knew for Himself, because he had taken a vow of chastity he had only rarely broken, was abstinence. Life wasn't a cabaret; it was a conundrum. He loathed the discipline of purity. He hated the contagion of plague.

He sat at his desk writing in his *Daybook*. His face hard with desire. He slammed the book shut and wrote three notes, throwing all three away, not knowing how to navigate access to the young man. He walked from his desk to the open porthole. The solstice wind below the Arctic Circle blew silken and silent around him. The Alaska midnight, at this longest daylight, was the constant twilight his life had become. He slept fitfully.

The ship cruised northward fast under the strengthening aurora borealis of the Northern Lights.

He rose early for the docking at the village of Sitka. A Russian church filled with gold icons sat in the town center. He hadn't fled one church to tour another. Not this time. Not this trip. He pulled away from the crowd of passengers flocking into the little wooden cathedral and headed to the combustion-engine sounds of a hundred small fishing boats bobbing at mooring. The crews of one or two men in rubber deck-boots, yellow slickers, and watch caps, smoking and talking, drinking their coffee from steaming paper cups, paid him no attention as he shot them, men whose hands and labor he envied, close-up with his telephoto lens.

He could look and long for everything through the gazing crystal of his viewfinder, but he could not touch anyone. He could only look at them re-run at night, saved and safe on his video screen. How had he become so dead? He was beside Himself. He became Himself watching Himself. How had fear made him a voyeur of his own life?

At Juneau, Brian boarded a helicopter tour which set him down twelve miles away on top the windswept ice desert of the Mendenhall Glacier. The tiny chopper lifted off leaving him and three strangers alone to wander for an hour. He set out on his own, away from them and their voices, finding solitude behind a tall palisade of ice. He set his camcorder down steady on the glacier, his wide-angle lens recording in the distance, the mountains, and, in close up at the bottom of the rectangular frame, the ancient ice running rivulets of topaz blue water.

He walked into focus in front of his own camera. He knelt down. He was his own best director. Who else would bother shooting his private dances? Who else would shoot his private rituals? He was a lone pilgrim kneeling on the ice-cap at the top of the world. He reached into his pockets for the dozen crystal rosaries he had bought as therapeutic souvenirs when he took his arthritic mother on pilgrimage to the Shrine of Our Lady of Knock in Ireland. He laid the rosary chains down flat into the freezing blue trickles where the crystal beads became one with the glacier ice. If his priest friends believed in miracles, then his dunking the rosaries into the mystic Arctic ice, steeping them in the clear water in the bright light, might empower all the more the gifts he was taking back to the silent ones desperate for any hope.

Later, in his cabin, reviewing his glacier footage on his monitor, he thought his anointed hands looked very young for a man his age who, if he could dare work sacramental magic, could certainly dare write a mash note to the divine boy from Genoa.

After Juneau on the fifth night heading from the smooth flow of the Inland Passage out to the open sea of the Gulf of Alaska, northwest, hundreds of nautical miles towards Anchorage, he realized the cruise was passing him by. Only two nights remained. He had to decide. He wrote lists in his *Daybook*.

If the young man found him a fool wanting to discuss safety, he would not have too long on board to be embarrassed. He felt unreasonable being safer than safe. Was his life reduced to a search for safety? What was living without risk? He had always, almost always, disciplined his passion with absolute purity. Had he no trust in his reason to govern his lust? If alone with the young man, would abstinence turn to abandon? It would be simpler to throw Himself overboard.

He was not afraid to die quickly. He was afraid to die slowly.

He felt sick. He was fasting. He had not eaten all day. He headed down the corridors toward the main dining room. He could not walk a straight line. He pitched from wall to wall. The choppy open sea of the North Pacific was lifting and dropping the ship. The line at the buffet was short. Nausea was turning the Roman banquet into a vomitorium. He fled back down the stairs to his deck. He skirted around two passengers with gasping faces. He noticed white paper bags had appeared, stuck every ten feet into the railings along the passageways going to all the cabins. He had will power. He willed he would not be sick. He slammed his door behind him. His *Daybook* slid from the desk to the floor. The story knife flew through the air. The room was hot as a furnace. He pressed his hands to his temples. He was wet with sweat.

He opened his door to let the cold air blow through.

He was not prepared for the sudden spectacle.

There stood his stewardess. Her face wide-eyed in astonishment.

An overstuffed woman, supported by two other graces, had just, as he opened the door to his cabin, thrown up on his stewardess's shoes.

"You bitch!" the stewardess screamed.

He ran past the four women, hitting first one wall, being tossed against the other wall, down the stairs to the Infirmary where the good ship's Doctor Marcello told him, "I've just the thing. A shot of Promethezine. Fix you in minutes."

He rolled up his shirt sleeve as three new patients arrived tossing at the tiny Infirmary door. He watched with his gay eye to make sure the straight doctor knew enough to snap open a new syringe with a new needle because what kind of decent doctor becomes a ship's doctor. Calmed almost instantly by the injection, he felt suddenly superior to the rough seas. He lay on the gurney smiling, relaxed, freed, his blue eyes staring up into the bright light, feeling thoroughly Himself, slowly calming, balancing, finding his sea legs again as he had once before with his mother on that trans-Atlantic cruise to Ireland. Always in his life he had decided what he would do; and what he had decided to do, he decided he could undo.

He returned through the deserted passageways to his cabin. He was no longer at sea. He was on the sea, happy he was high on the high seas. The desperate self he had felt the first days alone on board seemed anemic to the sense of giddy self-purpose throbbing in his veins. He stripped off all his clothes. He paused once to consider if the Promethezine might be affecting his judgment. He opened his porthole and thrust his slender upper body out into the bright evening air, a pink human torso with flaming red hair sticking out the port side of the white ship. The waves made by the cutwater prow spread out on the running sea of topaz water like foaming chevrons under the midnight sun. He trembled remembering it was Midsummer's Eve, the twentieth of June, his fiftieth birthday, the solstice, the year's longest day when a person can, his mother always said, be gifted with wisdom or madness or death or be spirited away by mischievous faeries. He felt chilled by the wind. He could not afford to catch a cold. He pulled Himself back into his cabin. His teeth chattered. He had never intended to jump, not really, but he laughed at how easily he could have flung Himself, live on camera, into the freezing sea when he realized the siren call of the open porthole. The scenario offered so perfect an exit it was ridiculous. He was getting pleased with Himself. That was a good sign. He had the luck, he did. His mother and father both told him so.

The throb of white noise from the ship's engine excited his senses soothed by the injection. The Arctic swells rocked the rising tide of pagan Irish blood flushing his baptized body. An ashtray slid across his desk to his laptop whose white screen lit the cabin. The story knife rolled into his lap. At that moment, so abrupt, so crystal clear, it surprised him that he suddenly knew what he would do and how he would make the best of bad times. It was not the twilight of the gods. It was the call of the wild. He congratulated Himself that he and his kind, sacred and profane, were always so goddam clever. He sat down at his desk and wrote in his *Daybook* that he who had told a mountain man he could not haggle had actually perfected haggling into a lifestyle. He had to take action to escape his scrupulous conscience of outmoded prohibitions. He took the story knife into his consecrated hands and invoked the power of its nature. He set it down intentionally next to his fountain pen and spelled a decisive message on a white sheet of ship's stationery: "Se tu per favore. If you wish. E il mio compleanno. It's my birthday. 11 PM, Cabin 336," and stuck a precious hundred dollar bill with the note inside the envelope. He rang for his stewardess.

"Did you see what that pig did to my shoes? Now she's off early to the midnight buffet!"

He was glad she was madly distracted. She took the envelope, glanced at the name of the young man from Genoa, and smiled. It was not her first billet-doux. He gave her ten dollars, left the door unlocked, and carefully placed the crystal rosaries in his Dopp kit on the table next to the bed. He set up his tripod and aimed his camcorder into the soft light, framing the bed, framing the waiting rectangle of cold white sheet like a Tlingit elder smoothing snow for a story about to be told. He sat in his chair, contemplating the delicate story knife, and waited. There were safe ways, clever new ways, as good if not better than the old ways, for worshiping beauty live in person and forever on screen.

"Ah, signore," came the knock, came the boy, came the envelope, came the hundred dollar bill. "Buona sera."

Mrs. Dalloway
Went That-A-Way!

Mrs. Dalloway each night decides to buy the flowers herself, on the *Mrs. Dalloway* channel on satellite dish. All *Mrs. Dalloway*. All the time. Twenty-four hours, reliable as a clock ticking up in the sky aiming down signal digital bits of *Mrs. Dalloway*, of Vanessa Redgrave being, acting, Mrs. Dalloway-being-Virginia-Woolf, she of the abiding presence, all the Mrs. Dalloways deciding to buy the flowers themselves.

In the last month of summer in the last year of the last decade of the last century of the second millennium, Mrs. Dalloway, the person, the novel, the film, the myth, not yet the play and not yet *Mrs. Dalloway! The Musical*, hanging the way she does in the framed film poster, (cadged from the cute gayish couple who own the arty Rialto Cinema), smiling, umbrella, promises of a life flown by, imaged with an airbrush on the cover of the paperback novel, *Mrs. Dalloway*, meaning Vanessa, her head, omniscient goddess, smiling down on two lovers; her younger self, as a remembered girl, holding a bouquet of flowers she picked herself, speaking as she does the lines in *Scenario* magazine printing the film script of *Mrs. Dalloway*, realized, written, by Eileen Atkins, wondering about La Atkins and La Redgrave, who have played Virginia Woolf and Vita Sackville-West on stage in Atkins' play, *Vita and Virginia*, holding a copy of a yet another parallax parallel Mrs. D in that prize-winning novel of Mrs. Dalloway impersonators, *The Hours*.

"My head is swimming. I can't keep up with them all," Huxted Daly said to his lover, Riley Daly-Thomas, mixing his media, widening his experience through page and screen, (Huxted Daly was a writer known for capturing *pastness*, his sketches of *pastness*), and dealing with Mrs. Daly, Virginia Daly, his mother, Mrs. D, or rather what was left of his mother, Virginia, realizing at the party, the party itself wobbling, the party for her eightieth birthday, born when Virginia Woolf was thirty-seven, born in 1919 during those five years, 1918 to 1923, that Virginia Woolf thought changed people's very look, surrounded by thirty-one of her ancient friends, (31x80 equals 2,480 human years), laughing at the party, or smiling through the pastness lostness of their glory years in the early mid-century; talking around monuments of old men, husbands really of the women who were the actual friends, the tissue of women the actual human connection through the years, not the men who early on had evaporated in their shoes, the way his father had evaporated, *poof*, long before he died, leaving him, Huxted, dallying his own way with his father's wife, Virginia, his mother, his own Mrs. Daly, the talker, the social gadfly, the conqueror, who was a Virginia not at all tremulous the way Vanessa made Clarissa Dalloway as fragile as, well, he presumed Virginia Woolf herself, given all the goods, jot and tittle, her anal-retentive nephew, Quentin Bell, had spilled about his famous family who could not stop writing diaries and essays and novels about one another, publishing one another, binding the books, entrepreneurs working at home in Bloomsbury.

At Mrs. Daley's party, of the thirty-one guests, twenty-four were senior women, 24x80 equals 1,920 female years, two female millennia, of wisdom he was himself trying to understand, because the male god, *oh, and it grieved him so*, this message, that this male god, the former god, God the Father, God the Son, God the Holy Ghost, the God of the Creed, "*Credo in Unum Deum, Patrem omnipotentem.* I believe in one God, the Father Almighty," was the avowed god of all these women, but not really the one they worshiped silently secretly.

Huxted could not, without shaking, think of the gender shift, the quake of one tectonic plate scraping over, under, another, theologically, feeling, mid-gender, a bit himself like Septimus, the red-haired man, Mr. Septimus Warren Smith, whom Virginia, pen in hand, had walked through the streets of London, parallel to Mrs. Dalloway, all day, on the day of the grand party seamed up seamlessly by Mrs. Dalloway who had bought the flowers for her party herself, richer, better flowers in the mind's eye, on the page, than in the film, squeezed, *oh yes*, "budgeted," Eileen Atkins told Todd Pruzan, so that although expensive ravishing sweet peas were called for in the flower-shop scene, less delicate chrysanthemums had to do, and what was to be done about it, about the low budget, in that movie, marginal, independent, a film by Marleen Gorris, but to go on, like life itself, to completion, shooting frame after frame.

So Huxted agreed, shaking his head, *oh, yes*, affirmatively over the texts of Ms. Woolf and Ms. Atkins and Mr. Cunningham and even Mr. Bell as well as the visual text of Ms. Gorris and the *gravitas* of Vanessa Redgrave's acting. All so sad, every night on the satellite dish that had fallen in love with endless running of *Mrs. Dalloway*, so sad that at the same time, 65:57 minutes into the film, (22:22 minutes into DVD Chapter 4), Rupert Graves jumps from the window, and, *oh, yes*, wasn't Eileen clever to have imagined him, Rupert, his face, all of Britain in his face, before even starting writing her screenplay, because even his pretty teeth act in his pretty face, waking on a couch, dreaming a dream, a nightmare of a soldier, calling the name of "Evans! Evans!" the way a man calls a lover, lost, or a god slipped away into the past, who cannot return, despite the promise of a Second Coming. "Ha, not on this millennium," Huxted said, arranging gorgeous roses he could well afford even on his writer's budget, because he had vowed, right before his father evaporated, to live seamlessly the way people live in movies.

Quite so sad, all this Woolfian loss, lost pastness, and every night, like a ritual play, over and over, Sunday through Saturday, and around again, Septimus, shaken, shell-shocked by the way the world, the century, life itself shifted under his feet in the trenches of the war, the first war, fleeing the doctor, feeling the power of others; (all humans are dangerous humans); what happens when others gain power over one? Not suicidal. Panicked. Poor Septimus, saying his last words, "You want my life?" Septimus jumping, falling, flying out the window, impaled below, *oh*, that sound of guts on the soundtrack, guts impaled, smackdab in the middle of what should have been a Merchant-Ivory film, but wasn't, and why not, the way his mother,

Mrs. Daly, was not supposed to have fallen, kept falling, one time after another, that first night outside the Rialto Cinema where he and Riley had taken her to see *Mrs. Dalloway* on New Year's Day night, January 1, 1999.

In the dark, seventy-nine she was then, that first day of the first month of the last year of the millennium, Mrs. D had roared on ahead of him, leaving go of his arm, surged toward the box office, the warm light of the ticket window glowing in the dark January night, and she had roared, so much competition for such a tiny little shrinking body, denying it was growing tiny little shrinking, as if her body were not herself, falling flat down in the dark, on the pavement, crashing next to Huxted, at his feet, him looking up at the marquee letters spelling *Mrs. Dalloway*, and the posters declaring Vanessa Redgrave and Rupert Graves and Natascha McElhone and that adorable Michael Kitchen, directed by Marleen Gorris who seemed Sapphonic, roaring not shrinking, not falling flat, coming off winning the Oscar for *Antonia's Line*.

Why had his mother, Virginia, Mrs. D, actually always to roar and shove ahead, competing with everyone male and female, people standing in line waiting to buy tickets, why, and why him, since his father driven to death no doubt by competition, by losing, and by Mrs. D. He thought of her as she fell past him, always saying, as she fell past him toward the pavement, always saying, in the looped dialog of widowed mothers dependent on gay sons, "I'll never surrender," and he answered, "I'll never surrender," and she had repeated, quite primly, "I'll never surrender," more than once in her little porcelain Mrs. Dalloway house, a house of her own, covered in modern aluminum siding, with windows sealed closed and so barred against intruders no Septimus, not even he himself, Huxted, had he wanted to, could have thrown himself out of his mother's windows. His whole life he had resisted any waterlogged, slow, sinking of his will into hers. He would not snap the "snap" in Virginia Woolf or in Edward Albee. "Snap, Martha!"

Mrs. Virginia Daly said she would buy the movie tickets herself. Then she flew through the New Year's dark, toward *Mrs. Dalloway*, pushing around all the happy filmgoers shivering in line, and fell past him toward the pavement, making a little sound, *oh, Oh, OH*, crashing down in the dark; her wrist was broken and her chin was cut; blood; why blood on New Year's night, the first night of the New Year. *How dare bring blood into my year!* He knelt on the cold pavement and held her, his mother; a doctor came from the line of moviegoers; and a nurse; and the handsome young gay couple who owned the theatre, so young they gave Huxted (who thought *he* cultivated *them*), because he was an older gay gentleman, free movie posters, "*Mrs. Dalloway*, A Motion Picture Starring Vanessa Redgrave, Adapted for the Screen by Eileen Atkins."

His mother eliciting a child's greatest fear, a parent making a public spectacle of weakness, a what? A lapse of taste, a fall, *no, No, NO!* The instant guilt in his heart at her fall. Into their cell phones, a dozen moviegoers punched 911. The ambulance; the flashing lights; the cold from the pavement sucking the warmth from Huxted's kneeling legs. All the paramedics, handsome, efficient, no time for giving Huxted the mouth-to-mouth resuscitation, resurrection, he so desperately wanted, needed, taking her pulse, Mrs. D's tiny wrist; she was not on a fainting couch; she was not Ms. Redgrave acting. She was his mother. The 35-degree night temperature, her age, *Mom!*, the fall life-threatening.

"Where do you hurt?" the handsome paramedic asked.

"All over," she said, so typical, quite like her, hers not being the breathy voice of Vanessa Redgrave husking dialogue in a voice-over; real; panicked.

Familiar with long kneeling, from church as a child, from bed-rooms as a man, Huxted knelt on the pavement with his bare hands under her back, holding her fragile old body up off the cold, feeling himself, them, his mother and him, and Riley, his lover, the man who won him, who loved him, handsome blond Riley who was really the prize, kneeling there together, the three of them, a gay couple and the mother/mother-in-law, surrounded by paramedics and flashing lights, like some spectacle, some urban tableau of violence, as if someone had been shot; but not; the anger and competition exploding from within themselves; feeling themselves, a family tripped up, being stared at like something dysfunctional by the voyeur line of filmgoers finally shuffling off to admittance into the theater lobby, into the seats, to watch the screen, the opening credits rolling over the explosions of World War I montaged over the gorgeous face of Rupert Graves so ripe, so endearing, so unforgettable in movie-memory as the stableboy in *Maurice*.

"No," the paramedic insisted, "Don't tell me you hurt all over. Be specific."

Thank you, Huxted thought; the paramedic insisted his mother focus; finally; *thankyouthankyouthankyou*. The paramedic was a man, so handsome; *"Evans! Evans!"*; easy to imagine frontal, a male from central casting whom no one dared tell that the male gods were on the way out, as Huxted had been informed at rallies; headlines: "Extra! Extra! Read all about it! Rising goddesses oust male gods! Extra!" He still saw those male gods, knelt to them, especially when he looked at Riley, kneeling with him on the pavement beside Mrs. D, crying, being brave, blood running from her chin, her glasses askew, her white cloth coat reddening at the collar.

He knew that all their life together, his and Riley's, that in those twenty-five years he had seen the male god rise and rise and rise again triumphant, in himself, in Riley, in a thousand men, until this New Year's, this last pre-millennial New Year's the two of them, coupled, longing for marriage in Hawaii or Vermont or wherever a civil union might be recognized in a ceremony for which they would buy the flowers themselves, in a house of their own, brought down to the pavement by a woman falling, nude descending staircase, shouting, "I will never surrender."

A policeman came up, walked up, sidled up, himself, a frontal male god attending on the female deities that had fallen, temporarily, for the evening, like Mrs. D who did not drink, *not ever, no sir*, and, *if I were the IRA,* his mother had said to Huxted, had challenged him, two minutes before her fall, *and if you were England, I'd never let you win.* Win what, he wondered. What is the nature of resistance?

What is it that people, women, resist, like Clarissa Dalloway resisting herself?

At least, he knew, Mrs. Dalloway had a past, savory with choices. Riley had the novel, Virginia Woolf's novel, *Mrs. Dalloway*, in his jacket pocket the way Virginia Woolf carried rocks in her coat pockets. They both, Huxted and Riley, not Mrs. D, had read it; and Huxted had moved on to *that novel that won the prize by that handsome writer, whose name I can't remember, who is on the best-seller list with that book whose title I can't remember,* Huxted had said in the bookstore, trying to buy the book from a half-remembered review, *that is not about Virginia Woolf but is sort of a spin on Virginia Woolf, you know,* but the bookstore clerk did not know, kept typing on the keyboard of his computer, hitting *search*, and kept insisting that they had *five copies of Virginia Woolf in the store, sir, "Orlando," "A Room of One's Own,"* and, and, and Huxted, frustrated, had kept insisting that Virginia Woolf hadn't written the book, but, *oh*, then, as part of his ritual abasement before the rising goddesses, so they would not be correct about one more angry male, he had apologized to the clerk recently graduated from MacDonald's saying, *I should have written the title down, everything whirls by so fast, the holidays, the internet, the satellite dish, I'm not sure where I am in time and space, in California, I know, but I mean where in time, memory and all that, yes, of course, but more, where exactly in time on the big clock, actual clock, to the theater-wide TV screen, virtual clock, which knows all time the same, because,* he laughed, *ha ha ha,* his voice like bright water rushing fresh over stones, at himself, *ha ha,* and Riley, his constant and true lover, had agreed, that *the speed of light doesn't seem as fast anymore,* when insomniac in bed at 2 AM in California they were seeing the future *simultaneously* in the early-morning *live* 5 AM wake-up news in New York, *live* 7 PM traffic reports from Tokyo, *live* 10 PM jumpers from windows in New Zealand, and *live* 10 AM stocks from England where over the head of the news anchor on location for the London weather in Regent's Park buzzed an airplane, noisy, flying over Bloomsbury, spelling out something in skywriting. "Nothing is more evanescent than skywriting which all writing is," Huxted wrote in one of his streaming critical essays which grew even more evanescent when his editor, at Riley's insistence, published them on the worldwide web and they went in digital bits of one's and zero's God knows where. Huxted adored the manifesto of the Swedish filmmakers of Dogma 95, proclaiming the way they composed film, handheld from the hip, budget zip, improvisational actors, shooting with available light, available props, freeing themselves of studio constraints, almost the way Ms. Redgrave/Mrs. Dalloway, night after night on one channel after another, stands in her own window contemplating her life in a monolog voice-over, almost the way Huxted himself folded time and place and words beyond convention: "There exists a future time when we are already dead."

Riley, the truly good son-in-law, had said, making conversation in the hospital emergency room, holding Mrs. D's hand on her unbroken wrist, how sad magazines and media, *All Diana All the Time*, had become since Princess Diana had been driven into that tunnel that August night in Paris, much like the August night when Huxted and Riley realized they were watching the *All Mrs. Dalloway Network, All Night, Every Night*, living through the slow-motion single-frame advance of the last August of the last summer of the century ticking toward the anticipated millennium midnight.

In fact, *Mrs. Dalloway* began reappearing on satellite television the exact last night of the last August, almost two years after Diana sped off from the Ritz not wearing a seat belt, and French doctors massaged her heart, her poor broken heart, as the ambulance, with her in it, moved (slowly) through the Paris night, *live* (as she died) (slowly) on satellite feed, as they watched the orange glow of Paris lights glow *live* on CNN, and wreckers hoist *live* the twisted Mercedes from the Alma tunnel and haul the car away *live* on a truck, while paparazzi sat *live* under arrest, having hunted Diana the Goddess of the Hunt to death, under suspicion, in a van while cameras *live* photographed *flashflashflash* them for a change.

We all make ourselves up; we make our own selves up, Mrs. Dalloway said on Virginia Woolf's pages. Diana had made herself up. Mrs. D had made Riley up insisting Riley, his beautiful fresh color, resembled her fair family more than the dark Huxted himself. Huxted had to laugh when the paramedic said to him, with his own hands freezing on the pavement under his ancient mother's back, and Huxted not as young as he once was, or ever as young as Riley still was, *oh, my, yes*, he had to laugh, when the paramedic asked him, "Who are you?"

The policeman asked him, "Why do you have your hands under that woman?"

The pair of man-gods, authorized by their uniforms, looked, demanding an answer, and Huxted said, weakly, trying not to sound weak, "I'm her son," as if that should have been enough to keep her from falling, and the cop flashed his light into Huxted's face, momentarily, just momentarily, but long enough, long enough to see Huxted's eyes had the intense stem-cell quality of gay; the key to the gene was in the eyes; the straight beam of light bright enough to hurt Huxted's eyes, as if he'd turned and looked directly into the bright light of the movie projector right that moment inside the Rialto Cinema where *Mrs. Dalloway* was unreeling, the younger Clarissa running and the mature Clarissa walking, two Mrs. Dalloways, two for the price of one, through the hallways of what Riley called a "furniture movie," trying to decide, she was, Clarissa was, Mrs. Dalloway was, (Virginia Woolf had been) whom to marry to be safe, secure, not perhaps to the one who loved her best, but to the one who made her safe, because, perhaps love was wonderful, but safety was better.

Huxted never thought safety was better than the risks of love.

Michael Cunningham knew that when out of his own hands he let his own draggy Mrs. D, Richard, sitting in a windowsill, exactly like Septimus, let him let go, spilling him, not letting him fall exactly, letting him fly down, full of HIV (neither love nor passion were safe), down three stories inside the window well.

"It was a window well, wasn't it," Riley had asked after they had finally found the prize-winning book, (bought it actually over the web, their first net purchase, searching Amazon.com for "Virginia Woolf" which led to "Michael Cunningham," a real writer winning real awards in the real world, not the velvet gay world), and read it the week of Huxted's mother's eightieth birthday party, and *The Hours* kept them excited, hearing the writer's voice. Dreaming of the strapping athletic author, Michael Cunningham, gorgeous as a Hurrell film star on the cover of *Poets and Writers*, working out his chiseled Los Angeles cheekbones in Manhattan, sweaty, buffed in a gym in Chelsea, kept them sane visiting in Mrs. D's aluminum-covered house where they tried to invent themselves (*re-invent* themselves, everyone was saying in the so clichéd new small talk).

In that dollhouse, Huxted had invented himself as a boy; then, coming back, returning for the party, as a man in longtime domesticity with another man. All of Virginia D's friends knowing what it was, but never saying what it was, as if, how dare you boys bring this into our party that you have paid for, but you haven't bought us, you *must* not say what we *must* not know.

You must do this! You must do that! Huxted's parents had told him that. Riley's parents had told him, also, *You must!*

Must? Must? They both had grown up saying, *Must? Must?* What is this *must*? You *must* marry. *Must* marry. *Must. Must. Must.* So like Virginia Woolf herself, *must* marry, *must* marry, *must* marry whom? Lytton! Marry Lytton! Lytton who said the word, "Semen." Unbuttoning Bloomsbury. How could you; you can't; he won't; he might propose, but he *must* run. Lytton *must* run. Marry then, not passion, but safety. Marry whom? Leonard? Leonard Woolf? So very Mrs. Dalloway. Marry Peter? Marry Richard? Mrs. Peter Walsh. Mrs. Walsh. No. Mrs. Richard Dalloway. God, Huxted's mother, Virginia, Mrs. Daly, Mrs. D, who knew when she was fifteen whom she would marry, delivered by ambulance to the hospital's bright lights; the cold air of the emergency room; left waiting, waiting, waiting.

"Is my face cut? How is my face? Huxted? Riley? How bad?"

Mrs. D, a madonna; rosary, novenas; she was their lucky charm, praying for them, her two sons, one by birth, one by luck. Sweet old girl, not vanity; her face the only part of the old seventy-nine-year-old body turning eighty that still in its features looked like the girl who at twelve, when planes were young, had defied her mother and flown up in the air, bi-planing, once, thirty minutes for a dollar she had earned herself, with a skywriter who for an extra quarter wrote her name in the blue. *How fast we are all growing old*; Huxted looked at his mother in the emergency-room glare, shied away from his own face in a mirror, looked at Riley; even Vanessa Redgrave could no longer play her younger self in films. There exists a future time....

Eileen Atkins was right lamenting the slow progress of films directed by women or written by women and, *oh, my, yes*, beyond all that doggerel and dogma, saying people, agents, send her women's books to adapt, figuring she must like them, because she's a woman—a cause-and-effect presumption which she can't bear; and she was right, but it was true for men too, at least for men who were stem-cell men the way Huxted and Riley existed in the genome of males, resisting especially even other men like themselves, too gay, ("straight-acting, straight-appearing" was the desire of all the Gay Personals ever printed), acquiescing only to frontal males. They had a *must* to marry, each other, and daily the news was about same-sex marriage, *pro* and *con*, but finally, thankfully, at last, a daily part of the national discussion in the press, on the internet, over the satellite dish. There was no old boys club for old boys like them, and no old girls club for the girls to get together, have a bake sale, and raise the money for shooting their little film about Virginia Woolf who was the original-recipe Mrs. Dalloway. How dare a budget interfere? How dare a budget enter art and politics; how dare a budget come into any grand little party and jar the music and make the flowers a bit less than grand, and make people stretch and say ridiculous things like "less is more," (when every gay man knows in his twist of XY chromosomes only more is more), when the budget causes the lighting to be too bright, to flood the screen to almost burn up the incandescent Redgrave.

Oh, God, Huxted and Riley, reassuring Mrs. D her face was fine, her chin was cut, (stitches), her wrist was broken, (a cast), but her face was fine, and, during the long wait on the gurney for the emergency-room doctor, Huxted could only imagine where in the unreeling *Mrs. Dalloway* at the Rialto the plot might be. This was the first showing of the first night of the New Year. Only 364 days to count down. Signs and omens were everywhere. How dare blood! Was this to be their luck for the last twelve months of the millennium?

During their last stay in London, in Kensington, Huxted and Riley had watched in awe as Princess Diana surged by on the sidewalk, in sweat clothes, running to her gym in the hot August, so humid, that Huxted's face had wept sweat as he shot video of the full moon over Kensingston from the window of their small apartment hotel at 7 Trebovir Street, (Earl's Court Station), not far from 22 Hyde Park Gate, in Kensington where Virginia Woolf had been born; the last full moon Diana would ever see, he had shot on video tape.

In London, a few years before that last visit, the way time was relative, quantum, folded, the hours before, seconds before in memory, they sent a note backstage saying they were friends of a British actor in Los Angeles, Peter Bromilow, who had been young in stock with Vanessa Redgrave. She had, herself, the Redgrave, invited them backstage after her performance in *When She Danced*, (a color photograph of the blue marquee of the Globe Theater lit with billboards and red-and-yellow neon letters spelling out *"When She Danced*, Vanessa Redgrave, with Frances de la Tour, A Play by Martin Sherman"* was the screen-saver on Huxted's laptop), greeting them on the stairs of the Globe lobby with her right hand extended, "Exactly," Riley said, "exactly the way she extends her arms at the end of *Mrs. Dalloway* to dance with Peter Walsh the man she loved but was afraid to marry," and *oh*, the two of them, Huxted and Riley, had lived on that (touched by Vanessa Redgrave) for years, going off to her party, swept off to a party by Vanessa Redgrave, a party in London, a lovely party.

"Save me," she said, "we're trying to raise money" for a play, a movie, something, (perhaps even for *Mrs. Dalloway* itself, or *Vita and Virginia*) and she, Ms. Redgrave, had signed her autobiography, new out that week, (the index alone a "www" meta-data *Who's Who*), and handed the book to them, wishing that they were, perhaps what she hoped them to be, angels, producers from the States, backers with money, when they were just theater queens died and gone to heaven watching Vanessa dancing Isadora Duncan, folding time, in the quantum writing of the script, making the older Isadora dance the younger Isadora by simply standing stage-front center, still, still as a still life, still as a human can stand, her shadow cast up enormous on the back wall of the bare stage by a light, the kind of low-budget light which theatre can make magic—and movies, which are light, cannot. "I have just spoken with Vanessa Redgrave," Tennessee Williams said. "She is the greatest actress of our time."

Spinning, Huxted and Riley had spent the Friday evening with Vanessa Redgrave playing Isadora, three nights before the Monday Princess Diana handed Vanessa the 1991 Olivier Award for Best Actress in a play, six nights before the Thursday Vanessa Redgrave, once Vanessa Redgrave Richardson, left the stage dark, because her former husband, director Tony Richardson, the father of her two daughters, was dying in Los Angeles, died November 14 in Los Angeles of the viral plague, leaving them, leaving the stage empty as a window from which someone wonderful has lifted floated flown away, run off in the loneliness of the long-distance runner. "You want my life?" What does the brain matter compared with the heart? Tony was to direct Vanessa in *The Cherry Orchard*. Virginia wrote through Septimus: "How the dead sing."

"I hope you slept with him," Vanessa Redgrave said to Huxted, meaning her old friend, Peter Bromilow, with whom Huxted had a short affair and a longer friendship, until Peter, so elegant with cigars and leather and T-cells, died and *Variety* printed his obituary, "... played Sir Sagramore in *Camelot* to Vanessa Redgrave's Guenevere." Vanessa and Glenda Jackson, both in full queen costumes, (posed together for *Mary, Queen of Scots*, in a huge black-and-white photograph), had hung, framed, in Peter's entry hall in Los Angeles, signed by both actresses, "From a pair of queens to a truly Big Queen."

Gods and civilizations rise and fall, plagues come and go, plays open and close, but what matters any of it, all night, every night, when the quantum clock of a 97-minute movie lights the wide-screen TV, lights the faces of Huxted and Riley, ticks out the digital bits of the satellite dish and *Mrs. Dalloway Mrs. Dalloway Mrs. Dalloway*—is the title, so insistently *wifely*, ironic?—repeats over and over, Septimus falls, yes, again, and yes, again, to bits in one's and zero's, and they read on in books, reading through the stunning, endless, bibliography of Virginia Woolf, reading *Orlando* out loud to the eighty-year-old Mrs. D who smiles her smile of "no surrender," seeming to more than understand a story of how a woman becomes a man becomes a woman becomes a being. Watching Tilda Swinton swing in DVD from Derek Jarman's *Edward II* to Sally Potter's, *Orlando*, Virginia Daly, asking, "Is that the woman, that actress, you met? I can't keep your friends straight."

"Vanessa Redgrave," Huxted said. "Not friends, actually; we met just once."

"Don't you criticize my senses; my memory."

"Why become so defensive, mother," Huxted asked, "why go on the defensive, all I answered was your question, why do you think everything is an attack, why do you think everything is a competition, how did I become the enemy, how does someone gain the power over another one, and you will not, mother, no one will be, the rock in my pocket. I'm your son, an adult, not your husband. If you want a yes-man, get married. I don't want your life."

Huxted only imagined saying little cruelties like that, spurred on by snipey magazine rhetoric. He was rereading Janet Malcolm's tasty article, "Bloomsbury, live" in *The New Yorker*, the same issue that Peter Conrad, paraphrasing others—others who had paraphrased Huxted, to sound informed in their own personal right—wrote about Robert Mapplethorpe, (who had once been part of Huxted's own private Bloomsbury), calling Mapplethorpe "The Devil's Disciple" and making bad puns, calling Huxted's dear, dead Robert, the "Prince of darkrooms" who died, throwing his life away, without knowing his own self; which was not true. Indeed, Robert had thrown his life away; Huxted, in fact, years before, when they were young together had predicted that Robert would throw his life away; but Robert, his own kind of Septimus Warren Smith, always knew his own self, and when he would jump.

Huxted knew Virginia Woolf's Bloomsbury had not all been

sweetness and light; the Woolfs, censorious, frightened, bourgeois bohemians, refused to publish *Ulysses*; their strained relations with the painter Dora Carrington who ended up living with the writer Lytton Strachey who had proposed to Virginia then ran for his life. Huxted knew gay life was the same or worse; was, in fact, Bloomsbury; Bloomsbury, the very model for gay life, especially the gay literary life, where East Coast writers, *indifferent* and *hostile* VW would have called them, sniffed at West Coast writers, as if the geography of fags were literature, and in Manhattan, the Gay Mafia, the Gay Reich, friends publishing friends, reviewing each other, all living together in the same apartment building, giving each other awards at circle-jerk ceremonies, canonizing themselves, plowing pertinent academics, writing blurbs that caused *ha ha ha* in the country house which Huxted was pleased one day to hear Riley name their own "Monastery of Art."

Their house, their domesticity of twenty-five years, was a retreat from the violet Mafia Reich, because Huxted was a writer not comfortable in the purple company of other lavender writers who pontificated into their Cosmopolitans that AIDS writing was a genre, and gay writing was political correction, as if politics were literature, and social climbing, and money, and publishing contracts reserved for viral twenty-one-year-olds, and queenly expatriation to London (for twee unsuckable kveens) and to Tuscany (for young feckless fucks). They all seemed fundamentalist, very Miss Kilman, as righteous about lilac "literature" as VW's Miss Kilman about strict "religion," sectarian, carrying their violet violent grudges intravenously against each other, perhaps because the straight world marginalized gay writing into genre writing, reduced alongside "westerns" and "mysteries."

It was not them personally he disliked, it was the platonic ideal of art from which they had fallen, petulant, inbred, drunken, impotent, imperiously entitled. Huxted tried to liberate himself from competition and cliché. He was comfortable with readers who thought writing was sexual magic. A hard cock was the best review. Still, one wondered, really, "Why after all does one do it?"

With clarity, free of tree-based books, Riley was an internet biographer. He wrote, "The way Mapplethorpe was an artist who was a photographer, Huxted Daly is an artist who is a writer in his own private Bloomsbury, www.virtualgayliterature.com." They laughed together, poking fun privately, like married couples, which was their abiding dream. "Happiness is this, is this," Riley said.

They could not be separated against their wills.

Lone Woolf-like they manufactured biographical narrative, Huxted of others, Riley of Huxted, all tapped out on the internet, sent directly to satellite, by Riley himself, from a laptop in a room in a house in a vineyard in a valley in the country where at dusk the peacocks screamed. *"Evans! Evans!"*

Yet, Huxted found a certain esthetic incest agreeable. He took delight that in the international circle of Vanessa Redgrave's power, that she herself could star with her brother, Corin Redgrave, and his wife, her sister-in-law, Kika Markham, at the Gielgud Theatre in the revival, *Song at Twilight*, a play written by Noel Coward, once her own father's lover, with whom her father, according to her mother, had chosen to spend his last night prior to his enlistment in World War II. On eBay, the on-line auction house, Huxted had bid on, and won, a letter handwritten by Vanessa Redgrave to her father, and signed, age sixteen, and a first edition of *Mrs. Dalloway*, published 1925, on May 14, Riley's birthday, twenty-five years before his birth year.

Huxted wondered if in the long pastness in the Noel Coward clique of London *artistes*, the ever-widening pools of Bloomsbury, Vanessa Redgrave herself had been named by her father, Sir Michael, and her mother, the actress, Rachel Kempson, Lady Redgrave, after the fifty-eight-year-old painter, Vanessa Bell, Virginia Woolf's sister, and the mother of Quentin Bell. His head was swimming, which was the way he liked it, because he had no choice, born the way he was with gay stem cells and a queer genome spinning analysis on feeling. On a sudden entrepreneurial inspiration, with his laptop on his lap, he typed in the correct "www" to buy a website. What fun, he thought, to own www.VirginiaWoolf.com. For ninety-eight dollars, he might buy a piece of virtual real estate and sign it over to Vanessa Redgrave Enterprises Ltd. in perpetuity, with $5,000, to do with as she and Eileen Atkins might see fit to build a budget for a film whose rolling end credits would acknowledge Huxted Daly and Riley Daly-Thomas.

"It says here," Riley said, pointing at the DVD's "Interactive Menus," "Scene Access," and "Letterbox Format" showing *Mrs. Dalloway* on their theater-wide screen, "that Virginia Woolf in 1941, having experimented with suicide previously, knew enough, at fifty-nine, that on her final walkabout to the river, to the water, to pick up a stone, a big stone, to put in her coat pocket, so she could not fight the tide, the river's tide, and the will to live, which she no longer had, or wanted, but could not trust would not roar up in self-preservation at the last moment, except by loading her pockets with rocks to drown herself. Fifty-nine then was old. The new fifty-nine is the old thirty-nine."

"So the new eighty..."

"Is really the old sixty."

"Huxted! Riley!" His own Mrs. Dalloway, his own Mrs. D, his own Virginia, over eighty, grown stronger once she entered her new decade, came in the door, wrist healed, flushed from driving her own car, happy in her independence, ("I forgive you, Huxted."), she of the abiding presence, ("I forgive you, mother."), much happier and less angry with a knee replacement and two hearing aids which finally she admitted she needed after five years of telling everyone around her to speak up and stop mumbling. "Huxted, I bought these flowers myself. They're for tonight, for you, and for you, Riley, dear, for your party, for your engagement party...after all these years."

Why, and how escape? His own Mrs. D taught him the will to survive. Would they all live forever on stem cells, cloned parts, and gene therapy? Huxted's talent for pastness made him hungry for the futurity, the futurity, the futurity of the new millennium, standing at the window of the new millennium, the way Vanessa/Clarissa stood at windows, white curtains rising softly in the evening summer breeze, thinking his own voice-over. "Is death the only way? No. I won't go. Not falling, not calling, 'Evans! Evans! Riley! Riley!' Not the cliché of exit, at least not that exit cliché, not that very gay cliché, the *must,*

must, must of suicide, *The Children's Hour* fate of every mid-century gay character—'You want my life?'—in every gay play or movie, not jumping out some window, not like Septimus Warren Smith, not like my father, best, bested, who's afraid of Virginia Woolf, who's afraid of Virginia Daly, not with rocks in my pocket into a river, not like Dora Carrington shooting a hunting rifle into her own heart, not like Diana flying arabesque unbuckled into a Paris tunnel.

"Why would I try to escape such sweetness as union with Riley? What matters if a future time exists when we are already dead, if we are alive this moment. I shall live, and some day die, a happy man, a groom, a man who has had a wedding, happier than Clarissa Dalloway, no Sapphonic suicide like that Virginia Woolf, peacefully in my lover's arms in our legally licensed marriage bed in a new world in a new century with digital bits of *Mrs. Dalloway* written in the air like skywriting from a plane over a park in June. I will not surrender. Why should the male gods surrender? Why should anyone surrender?"

He saw his reflection in the window glass.

"Here I am at last."

He heard Riley's voice, coming from another room, welcoming guests, "Here we are at last."

"This millennium," he voiced, rejuvenated, feeling that sixty was the new forty, toasting the new forty, "is a new age of stem cells, web sex at www.toughcustomers.com, compact discs of one's and zero's, and books printed on demand and on-line"; he voiced in his inner voice, saying nothing, greeting their incoming wedding-engagement party, hearing someone shout "so *Four Weddings*, darling!" and, he vowed, "We will neither live nor die the past deaths forced on our kind of tender genome people: *non exeunt*, like Diana and Dora and Virginia, pursued by a bear."

Together, at their party, with the flowers Mrs. D had bought, Huxted took Riley into his arms, and Riley took Huxted, and they danced close to "Moonglow and Theme from *Picnic*," closer even than Mrs. Dalloway (on the *All Mrs. Dalloway Network, All Night, Every Night*) dancing in the final scene with Peter, Peter Walsh, her one true love.

**There's a Summer Place
at Bear Lake
where the Lord of the Bears...
A breathless one-sentence romance.**

Three Bears in a Tub

Listen here, boy, there'll be no hibernatin till after I finish tellin you this bedtime story about Big Daddy when he was himself hardly more than a boy and how he turned into a six-foot-five man and what he done to earn that reputation he got that famous summer on Bear Lake when the canoe overturned late around midnight and Big Daddy on his thirty-fifth birthday saw them two young hairy fishermen floppin like bears in the water next to drownin with their rubber boots suckin them down to the clear rock bottom and them able to stand just barely with their chins on the surface of the moon-lit water cuz Bear Lake as you know ain't that deep but deep enough that Griz and Cub was standin so chin deep both their beards was floatin around their heads and all of Big Daddy's two hundred and fifty fucky pounds standin spread-legged on the dock thought even if it was the funniest gutbuster sight he ever saw he better climb on into his rowboat without so much as puttin on a stitch of clothes to cover his hide he was always so proud was so well upholstered that way with a coat of thick fur that grew out of his toes and wrapped up his foot to his ankle and grew up his calves like somethin you could curry with a brush especially near his pair of big thighs that made his powerful packed legs a sight to see especially if you caught a lordly eyeful of him come strollin butt naked out of the two-hole outhouse he had downwind from his log cabin up on Bear Lake which could happen since Big Daddy always walked around like a big built hairy man is God's gift which I suppose is true with no supposin after all us seein Big Daddy standin lathered up next to his cabin under that shower with the tub of hot rainwater he tied up on the roof where the sun could always shine so he could scrub up his hairy crack he said where the sun never shined except I know different but that's another story about harvestin dingleberries if you fudgin know what they are and I do appreciate Big Daddy's hairy butt cheeks and sweet sweaty hairy crack where there never was one of those little ingrown hairs cuz Big Daddy always rough-buffed his fur with a big ol towel which them two handsome boys Griz and Cub could have used while they was waitin still sinkin in the middle of Bear Lake next to drownin with the little waves lap-pin around their mouths and their beards and long hair floatin in the water cuz of Big Daddy sittin naked in his wood rowboat in the moonlight lookin down and laughin at the two heads floatin on the water and them yellin Keerist, Big Daddy cuz everybody always called Big Daddy Big Daddy ever since he done sired Griz when he was seventeen out of that sweet Kathleen Jones over the other side of Bear Lake and never bothered to marry cuz her father was one of them shaggy men who takes a sidewise shine at life and don't care if a young man rolls his daughter in the hay as long as he gets to roll the fucker himself the way he tried everyone knows to roll over on Big Daddy but Big Daddy rolled over on him and shagged him holdin him by his hair and forcin his mouth open and then his ass all the time shoutin that there was room on Bear Lake for only one Big Daddy and the cum was rollin down Kathleen's legs at the same time it was rollin out the hairy butt and down the hairy legs of her pa and they both was screamin for Big Daddy at first to stop fuckin them and then not to stop fuckin them and that night was a night everyone heard about and no one forgot mostly because nine months later little Griz popped out of Kathleen and some months later out popped Cub makin Big Daddy a real big daddy twice which he said was enough for him so he gave up screwin Kathleen and just kept on screwin her pa who by the way is famous for his moonshine still which he drinks from frequently always namin the praises of Big Daddy who he calls his son-in-law except no preacher hitched the unhitchable Big Daddy to anybody so Kathleen's pa who's less than a dozen years older than Big Daddy kept lit the torch Kathleen and just about everybody else carried at Bear Lake after they saw Big Daddy layin naked on those big rocks in the middle of Bear Lake where he always laid sunnin his big burly belly and butt and exhibi-

tin his famous foreskin dick right out there on the water in almost
the same spot Griz and Cub were sunk drunk as a skunk in their
rubber chest waders unable to move watchin Big Daddy five feet
away kickin back in his rowboat gettin a boner watchin them struggle in the bubbles burblin up their own hairy bellies and up their
fuzzball chests floatin in the cool dark water on a moonlit night so
bright people sat on their docks under the big trees around the lake
rockin in chairs and watchin out on the still water those two curly
heads spittin lakewater out of their mouths like fountains in the
middle of their beards and shoutin to their pa Big Daddy come on
and rescue us and under the moon like exposin himself to some
spotlight Big Daddy leaned back in the boat and rubbed his big
hands up his naked thighs fingercombin his fur and runnin his
palms into the dark swirls of fur on his big chest with wet nipples
that stood out lit by night stars in the clear night like a constellation
over the risin sine of Big Daddy's hardenin cock that made all the
voices on the shore go silent out of respect except for the crickets
and a loon or two whoopin at the powerful sight of two men caught
neck deep wantin for all the world to be saved by a bear god in a
rowboat rubbin his big wooly belly and scratchin his most beautiful
beard in all of Bear County him never shavin ever even as a growin
boy so that his wavy long beard was as full as ever a beard could be
and he could part it in two and wrap it around his starry nipples or
lean over as he did that famous night and wrap his beard around
his big uncut cock which if truth be known he could suck himself
better than anyone else includin Kathleen or her pa or even Griz or
little Cub who all had their turns by choice or by force which was
one of the stern ways Big Daddy had of makin sure everyone who
turned an admirin glance on his broad hairy shoulders and the
hams of his furry forearms and the baseballs of his downy biceps
got a taste of his dick first in the mouth and then sized up the ass
which impressed one and all becuz of the bristly bush surroundin
the root of Big Daddy's blue-veined ramdick with the uncut head
slidin out so big and shiny even that night drownin out in the
middle of Bear Lake Griz and Cub who was both themselves
famously endowed thanks to their pa had to comment at the size of
their Big Daddy's huge bear meat weighin itself maybe a pound or
two and tentin up like a big white pole out of the hills of his thighs

over his shaggy pair of bear balls bouncin against his sweet smellin butt crack and archin up the forest hills of his belly and mountains of his meaty chest all of him oiled with bear grease so he shined shined shined in the moonlight on the water while Cub started to sob in his curly beard floatin on the water cuz his big dick was gettin bigger and harder inside his rubber waders an he couldn't get at it and Griz was pleadin Come on Big Daddy we need rescuin and Big Daddy's only response was a big bellylaugh which growled like a roar echoin through the warm night makin all the busybody eyes watchin from shore all the more surprised when the two hundred and fifty fucky pounds of Big Daddy like the Lord of the Bears stood up in the rowboat stark naked and shinin with grizzly grease settin starlight tweakin off his nipples like lightnin rods takin a huge piss aimed right down into the mouths of first one and then the other of his two sons who opened their faces like two little bears hungry and thirsty for Big Daddy's big piss which was their regular drink anyway like I say about Big Daddy and the way he trained his two boys Griz and Cub to waste not and want not by learnin to drink his piss and lick his hair and toothcomb his beard and tongue-suck out the sweat from his armpits and big hairy balls and even when they was all drunk enough which was not as often as they pretended because pretendin to be drunk gave them huntin permits even Bear Lake was not used to when both Griz and Cub would wrestle naked and hairy at night on the cabin floor in front of the fire so the winner could be the first one to crawl up to Big Daddy's big hard butthole and suck wind from the cave when Big Daddy hung his buttcheeks and balls over the edge of the bunk showin his big cock standin up hard with excitement and strokin it himself in anticipation of leanin forward and suckin his own big knob while Griz and Cub took turns feastin on the just desserts of his big bear belly pushin peanut butter and jelly out of his hole and them goin shit for brains nuts suckin and jackin themselves and chewin out Big Daddy's gifts of nature which of course made them see stars and howl at the moon like they was doin that famous summer night the boys thought they'd nearly drown with Big Daddy standin over them pissin down on them with them drinkin every drop and beggin Big Daddy to do with them what he wanted because he was their Big Daddy and they loved him so much and that's what Big

Daddy wanted to hear so he saved them yes saved them both by cuttin them out of their rubber waders so they floated to the surface of Bear Lake and Big Daddy took ahold of them by their hair and beards and nipples and dicks and buttholes and pulled both them boys into his rowboat where they sat the rest of the night laughin and drinkin and shoutin through their beards at the moon while stars glistened between them nipple to nipple with comets shootin flume tails from their dicks and they floated ever so happy on the still surface of the water while the real constellation of the Bear rose and set over their heads and their fudgey fingers sticky from their buttholes were all entwined in the fur on their chests and the hair of their bellies and the carpet on their shoulders and the bush of their crotches and the hugeness of their beards and the curly sweep of the hair on their heads and they were all three of them so satisfied that the summer night smiled and half asleep in each other's big furry arms, Griz and Cub and Big Daddy drifted slowly across the mirror of stars to their dock on Bear Lake as if the rowboat knew their way home.

Sweet Embraceable You

Murder me," Ada said.

"The reception began at eight." Cameron set his second bourbon glass down on his newspaper blotting Herb Caen's Tuesday, August 15, 1972, column. "It's now eleven-thirty, precisely. Time is not your forté, my darling. Must you always run on your own clock?"

"Don't tick me off," Ada said. She was chilled from the San Francisco night. Her coat hung from her shoulders. "I hate when you play daddy. Next you'll be into spanking."

"We've never tried that."

"Keep it that way." She stood her ground across the tiny cocktail table.

He smiled under his thick black moustache. "Let me help with your coat."

Cameron Vicary rose to his full height. Ada watched him grow taller than she, and she was tall enough to be striking. Her coat rode like a cape across her shoulders. He lifted it and dropped its smartly tailored lines across the chair he intended for her.

She sat.

A waiter stepped from the piano bar. He looked up at Cameron who said something Ada could not hear. Cameron sat down.

"I asked you to murder me," she said.

"Don't change the subject." Cameron lit a cigarette. "I never do anything uncivilized." He handed it to her.

"I've stopped again."

"Start again," he said. "You prefer yourself with vices."

She took the fresh cigarette and held it. "God, I hate this place. All of San Francisco and here we sit." She tugged at the light fold of dark tricot falling down from her throat. "We come here so often.

I'm suffocating." She ground out the cigarette. "Must we always come here?"

"Where were you?" Cameron asked.

She looked at him.

He looked at her.

"I had a reception of my own to attend," she said. "Stop trying to make me obedient."

"Simple, isn't it?" He knocked down neat the last of his scotch.

"Simple? What is? For godsake, do you need such a big bush to beat around?"

The waiter hovered for a moment. He served Ada. He served Cameron. He disappeared.

"Cheers," Cameron said.

"To what." Ada said it flat. "Our one-thousandth visit to this bar?"

"Bistro. This bistro," Cameron said. "Remember? You picked me up here."

"Correction," Ada said, lifting her glass. "I met you here. I picked you up later."

"You love this place. We're old faces here."

"Being an old face anywhere is something I don't love."

Cameron lifted the single candle. His hands cupped the warm glassful of wax through the white plastic mesh. He lifted the wavering light to Ada's face. "An old face, Ada, you'll never be."

She began to melt in tenderness to him, but caught herself. Was he joking? "You could be fatal to me," she said. "So lay off the mood swings."

Cameron lowered the candle to the table. "Well?" he said.

"That's a deep subject."

"You're so sophisticated for a professor's wife."

She glared at him. She had her own degree, her own teaching certificate, her own car, what had been—before he moved in—her own Victorian flat. She bit her lower lip. From tables nearer the bar came brief applause as the pianist finished her set. Ada's ears rang in the sudden silence. Cameron stroked his chin, waiting. She knew the feel of his sharp clean face when his midnight stubble raised just enough to rasp her body raw. There was no part of her he had not scraped. Night by passing night the tiny bristles of his strong face were sanding her smooth. She felt she was losing herself to him.

"Don't be abrasive," she countermanded. Her word choice pleased her.

"Where-have-you-been is hardly an abrasive question. Not when a husband asks a wife who has stood him up publicly in front of his colleagues for two hours."

"You mean those goddam geologists actually noticed?"

"Yes."

"All eight of them?"

"And their eight wives. And the chairman. And the woman who was the guest of honor."

"You've never cared what they thought."

"So where were you, Ada?"

"I was having an affair with a rich man from China. A kinky little fellow. You know: whips and chains. *Spanking*. And a special little gadget that..."

"I don't care where you were." Cameron gulped down his drink.

"Then I'll tell you. We had a department reception of our own at the St. Francis."

"Why didn't you call?"

"Why didn't you?" She smiled at him. Things were always shifting tectonically between them. "Can this marriage be saved?" she asked.

"Why not?" Cameron reached for her hand.

"That'll cost you two-bits, buster." She stood up.

"What for?" He dug into his pocket for change.

Ada held out her hand and took his quarter. Leaving the table, she signaled the waiter for another round. "If my students could see me now," she called in the silence left by the stilled piano. "Hi, honey," she said, passing a young, balding ex-jock. He was all teeth and curly blond hair. She patted his butt the way she had seen players pat rump on the Bowl games Cameron insisted she watch with him. She made sure that Cameron saw her action. "What this joint needs," she said to Mr. Touchdown, "is some sounds." She headed to the jukebox.

Ada hated herself, taking a too-cute finger-in-the-mouth eternity deciding on her selections. She felt the ex-ballplayer heating up behind her.

Cameron watched her through his lifted glass. She rippled in the soft psychedelia of the jukebox. He knew her every trick and he liked watching her.

She fed the coin into the machine and danced onto the floor by herself. Her arms were slender and bare, silky against her rich mauve dress. The barkeep to amuse himself more than the patrons turned a flashing strobe on the lone and lovely woman. Her body flowed, flicked out in instants by the light. For half a lyric she was lost in her exhibition. Then with a fast move the blond jock joined her on the floor. Cameron watched her pull away with short, jerky motions. She left him, standing bewildered, alone in the middle of the floor. She made her way back to the table and stood: "He says he played a little ball in college."

Cameron smiled. "I bet he wanted to play ball with you." He leaned into the table, pulling her soft hand to his chin. The strobe caused Ada's eyes to divide his tender movements into rhythmic spasms, but the feel of him pulling her hand to him felt smooth. Between the appearance and the reality, she often lectured her classes, is the difference of what isn't and what is.

"Come on," he said. "Let's get out of here."

"I drove my car," she said.

"My bike's outside."

"On your motorcycle in this dress? I'll die."

"You wanted me to murder you." He took her by the arm. "Come on. We'll get the car in the morning." They both of them knew they were odd. Not so anyone else took notice. Just late-at-night odd: confessing, prevaricating, revealing to each other their apt match.

*

"I should have written a different thesis," Ada said. She turned on her side in the bed toward Cameron and ran her hand down his back.

"Lower," he said. He liked the feel of her hands. Her light touch floated across the dark hair downing his cheeks.

"My master's thesis," Ada said. "I should have written on Emily Dickinson."

"Lightly," Cameron said.

"An American woman poet." Ada sat up in bed.

"Don't stop," Cameron said into the pillow.

"Not a poetess," Ada said. "A poet." She hiked her nightgown above her knees. "A bit of tippler, Emily was." She straddled Cameron's thighs from behind. "A spinster like me." She massaged from the small of his back up the twin muscled ridges leading to his strong neck. She touched lightly the scar on his left shoulder. It was a bullet wound from the war that he had hated.

Cameron moaned in pleasure, his face buried in the pillow.

"What?" Ada said. She pushed hard on the base of his spine.

"You're no spinster. You're a married woman."

"Then I haven't been a spinster twice."

Cameron rolled over beneath her light straddle. "You're my first marriage," he said.

Ada laughed. "But hardly your first fuck!"

"I'm cold," he said. "Come here." He pulled Ada down, her face to his face. "You're beautiful," he said.

She kissed his ear. "Then there's a pair of us....Don't tell."

He began the familiar rocking motion, holding her. She was a little girl and a grown woman, in a boat, holding the sides, laughing and screaming, holding Cameron now, because years before Curtis had rocked her so wildly in the rowboat on Stow Lake lagoon that the Golden Gate Park attendant had called to them through a megaphone.

Cameron slipped her cotton nightshirt over her head and inside it she smiled remembering how she had been so embarrassed by Curtis, mortified, when at the end of their row, the attendant with the megaphone had helped her from the boat. She and Curtis had been married a week then. The attendant had reached for her hand. The marriage lasted into that winter. The attendant, throwing a quick look at Curtis, had apologized to her, as if he, and not Curtis, had frightened her nearly out of her wits in the middle of the wide lagoon. The week after Christmas she had, with justifiable anger, left her groom of five months.

The last of the nightshirt trailed off her arms. Cameron tossed it to the floor and Ada descended at her own speed full on to him. He was perfect. She knew he was perfect. But nothing, not even this, she had felt—long before she had nearly drowned in public embarrassment—was ever going to be enough. She could never forgive Curtis.

"Be here now," Cameron said. "Ada, be here now."

With his call, her mind came back into her head. "I love you," she managed and floated away again. This time to the porch glider. Cameron had spent the warm afternoon watering the lawn. He had worn white flannel trousers rescued from a resale shop. She had drowsed idly lying in the porch glider. Its gentle squeak had lulled her half to sleep, dreaming she lay aboard a gentle sloop rocking lazy at anchor. Through the white porch railing, she watched Cameron, all in white, wrap the dark green garden hose around his forearm, his thumb pressed hard into the water to fan the pressure into a wide spray.

He'll have arthritis when he is old, she mused. His thumb will grow stiff and gnarled because this one August afternoon he has meticulously watered every inch of grass.

She closed her eyes.

He was too bright. He was far brighter than Curtis. He was perhaps always too bright for her. Out there, white on the lawn, against the wet green, he soaked up the very heat of the sun. She was cool and he was too warm. At night he glowed, as if the sun had gifted him with dazzle. Sometimes she lay awake next to him and watched him sleep. Once she had awakened, cold as death. The old dream of Curtis clutched her throat. Her breath had been pressed out. She had wanted to wake him, to say, "Hold me." But then, as now, finished, he lay asleep, dark moustached and naked. She knew he would gladly hold her, but she said nothing. He was a good man and she rolled off him, reaching out her hands, chafing them together, holding them over his sleeping body, warming herself in his sweet animal heat. She watched him glow in the moonlight streaming down past Sutro Tower and in through the old Victorian windows.

He turned toward her on his side. She turned away and snuggled her back into his belly. It was their favorite way of sleeping.

The moon hung low and full outside the windows. The tower blinked a hundred tiny red lights on and off. Ada, her face in full moonlight, smiled.

*

In the morning, Ada smelled the coffee. In the kitchen, Cameron stirred his cup with a silver spoon. She pulled the blankets tighter around her. An ocean chill had crept over the City and into the room. Unusual even for August. A lock of her long black hair caught on her lip. Her tongue pulled in one of the hairs. Her teeth bit it lightly, nervously, careful not to cut it through. The hair had thickness and resiliency. It had sides, definable, as she turned it between her teeth. She had slept soundly, but she had not slept well. The blankets had weighed her down. She threw them back and shuddered as the cold air of the room sank into the warm sheets. She lay studying the ceiling. "Might as well," she said outloud, and she meant get up, which she did, pulling her terrycloth robe around her.

From the bathroom, she shouted to Cameron, "Good morning!"

"Coffee!" he shouted back.

She splashed water in her face and pulled a brush through the pleasant tangle of her hair.

She headed down the hall, past two photographs Cameron had taken of the City. Both showed the Golden Gate Bridge shrouded in fog. In the background of the second, the tip of the new TransAmerica Pyramid pierced the fog bank with the rising sun haloed directly behind it. "You ought to sell postcards," she shouted into the kitchen.

He looked at her framed in the doorway. "Lay off," he said quietly.

"That's not what you said last night." She swept into the kitchen and went straight for the coffee. "What are you reading?" she asked, stirring three teaspoons of sugar into the small cup.

"Nothing," he said. His forearm, peeled out of his rolled up flannel shirt, shielded the book.

"Come on!" She pulled at his big soft fist.

He relaxed.

"*Dickinson*," she said. "the *Collected Poems of.* Really, Cameron, I'm touched."

He took a long slow pull on his coffee. He said nothing. He was expressionless.

"Here's one for you," Ada said, turning the pages. "Pain has an element of blank."

"I'm cycling out to the park," Cameron said. He stood up.

"Someday you'll be killed on that motorcycle. Someday you'll leave me all alone."

"Maybe today," he said.

"And that will be my proof."

Cameron pulled on a light leather jacket. "What proof?"

"That we're alone."

"That you're off-balance, sweetheart." He kissed her. "And out-of-whack, out-of-synch." He touched her breasts lightly.

"And out-of-bounds," she said, pushing his hands away.

In his big silence he moved away from her. Something they both needed more than they recognized, something that had not quite melded together from their separate spiritual lives, sometimes hung unspoken between them. He turned at the door, and said, "Whatever," as if she, not he, held the mystery.

The ancient front door closed. Beneath her, the garage door of the old Victorian ratched open. Cameron kicked his bike into muffled life, paused on the lip of the drive, returned, pulled closed the garage door, and roared away into the sounds of the City.

Ada put both elbows on the table and interlaced her fingers across her forehead. She stared down into the steam rising from her coffee. She had papers to grade. Errands to run. And the telephone was ringing.

It was Cassiopeia.

*

Unhelmeted, Cameron cruised west out Fell Street, along the green boulevard of the Panhandle. The morning cool felt wet and good on his face. He angled his Harley Sportster smoothly into Golden Gate Park and roared loud down Kennedy Drive. The park lay emerald in the morning light: meadows, rose gardens, eucalyptus groves. Every stick and bush and tree transplanted into perfect place. He passed behind the DeYoung Museum and prowled the tarmac circle wrapped around the Stow Lake lagoon.

He laughed thinking of Curtis years before rocking Ada insanely in the rented rowboat. He gunned his bike. Hard. Fast. Breaking down curds of inertia inside his own flesh as the bike ate up the parkway. He turned right, in full shot of the ocean, roared past Point Lobos, Land's End, and out El Camino del Mar toward the Golden Gate Bridge.

*

Once he had taken Ada for the thrill of her life, speeding in an earlier dawn, in and out of the fogclouds, across the Golden Gate. She had held him tight as the lover she was then, tighter than when she made love to him now. Her raven hair had whipped around his face as she buried her head into his shoulders. He caught a mouthful and pulled on it. She clung tighter. He thought he heard her scream, "Balance!" as she dug her nails into the insides of his jeaned thighs.

They had ridden that Sunday to Tiburon. She was furious. "You're worse than Curtis," she said. "What is it with men? Don't ever scare me like that again."

"How should I scare you?"

"The usual way will be just fine," she said cupping his crotch.

"That's never scared you," he said. "Come on."

"Where?"

"Brunch, kiddo." He stooped down to chain up the big bike. The sunlight caught in his hair. It reddened his moustache. He hadn't shaved. He clamped the padlock shut and smiled up at her.

He grinned around the butt of a small burnt-out cigar in his perfect white teeth. "You're some looker," he said.

"You're no Bogart."

"Thank God," he said.

Ada followed him into the dark interior of the restaurant-bar. At the end of the hall, sunlight burnt bright enough to hurt her eyes. Cameron headed straight for it. She squinted as he pulled her out onto a floating deck with a hundred or so summer people brunching over eggs and gin fizzes. Three waiters and a busboy seemed to manage the whole affair for an invisible chef.

"There's no place to sit," Ada said. "It's too bright. I can't see a thing."

"I can." He took her gently by the hand.

"Must you always lead?" she said.

He pulled her through the maze of close tables. She bumped a chair, pushing a matron's leather-tanned face into the foam of her gin fizz. "Sorry," Ada said. The woman tried a smile, then napkined it away along with the ridiculous moustache of fizz beneath her nose.

"Sunday's House Specialty," Cameron said over his shoulder.

"What is?" Ada giggled.

"Gin fizzes. They're terrible, but they're In." He pulled her down to one of the two vacant tables. They leaned back against the railing. A yacht rose and fell at anchor twenty feet down a short gangway.

"This whole place is floating," Ada said. She panned the entire Sunday morning scene. "If I don't go blind, I'll get seasick. This better be good."

"Watch this," Cameron said. He pointed to a couple newly arrived into the glare. No one seemed to notice them. The woman's hair was lazily knotted on top her head. She wore big-rimmed shades. Her blouse and jeans looked comfortable enough to scrub floors in. She was warm. She walked a short-leashed mongrel dog. Ada liked her. But the man with her projected something: breeding, aristocracy, cool.

"That's California for you," Ada said. "That's pure San Francisco."

The couple headed straight for the empty table next to them.

"What do you mean?" Cameron said.

"The men are more chic than the women."

"Chic? No," Cameron said. "That's the wrong word."

The couple sat down. The woman excused herself as she bumped into Cameron's chair.

"That face!" Ada whispered. "Cameron, do you know who she is?

Cameron put the mock of his fist to his mouth. "And who do you think the guy with her is?"

"Don't let them know," Ada said.

"Don't let them know what?" Cameron whispered back. "You're acting like a groupie."

"Don't let them know we know who they are."

"Nobody seems to care," Cameron said.

"Nobody else recognizes them."

"They're off-camera," Cameron said. "Movie stars aren't what they used to pretend to be."

"Quiet," Ada said. She had this fan-madness about her. Cameron had witnessed it before. She had a passion for the fabulous, for fabled people. She collected fame the way a philatelist collects stamps. Once in Union Square, Clint Eastwood had smiled at her between takes in one of his films.

"Do you think he recognizes me?" Ada said.

"You're kidding."

Six months before, Ada had been in the right place at the right time, the corner of Broadway and Columbus, when the cast and crew of *The Streets of San Francisco* carried Edmund O'Brien costumed like a cop out of a little jeweler's shop on a stretcher. Ada had worked her way to the front of the crowd and planted herself smack between Karl Malden and Michael Douglas. Malden's line had been to the crowd: "Move back, everybody. Move back." And she had, frowning, but not too much, under-acting for the Panavision camera, determined not to end up on the cutting room floor. When the take was over, Michael Douglas, like Clint Eastwood, had smiled at her. She had been wearing a tight T-shirt of alternating blue and yellow stripes that she had then folded into her cedar chest as a souvenier.

"Ada," Cameron whispered. "I think he recognizes you."

"No, he doesn't. He couldn't." Ada looked for a menu. "Why do you think so?"

"By the way he keeps his back to you." He nudged her ribs.

A gull reconnoitered greedily overhead.

"Call a waiter, will you, Cameron? For godsake, I'm starving. I need a menu."

The woman with Michael Douglas turned around. "Here you go," she said. Her voice was husky. "We seem to have three." She handed the menu to Cameron.

"Thanks," he said.

Ada smiled. The woman turned back to her section of *The New York Times*. "Don't let her know," Ada said. Her eyes narrowed from more than the glare.

"Know what?"

"She's Brenda Vacarro."

"She probably knows that," Cameron said. "What are you doing with the menu?"

"I'm folding it up for my collection. It's not everyday a movie star hands you a menu."

"Ada, you're putting me on."

Ada's eyes narrowed even more in the Tiburon sunglare.

"Omigod," Cameron said. "You're not putting me on."

"Right," Ada said. "Indulge my little fantasy."

"You'll laugh about this when you have a saner moment," Cameron said. "Don't you dare ask for an autograph or I'll tell our future children."

"You hate children."

"I forgot."

A waiter took an order from Michael Douglas, who did not smoke, while Brenda Vacarro lit up a filter king, and tossed a breadcrust to a cruising gull. The waiter, oblivious to Ada and Cameron, spun his exit still scratching on his pad. Douglas returned to the "Arts" section of the *Times*, looking up only when Vacarro interrupted to show him a recipe which his father's wife, Mrs. Kirk Douglas, had been asked to supply to the "Gourmet Supplement" she was reading.

"What about our order?" Cameron said. "We were here first."

"We're not famous," Ada said.

The waiter returned with two gin fizzes and a Sanka for Brenda Vacarro. So close were the two tables, he kept his position and turned on point to Cameron and Ada. "Have you decided?" he asked politely.

"We'll have..." Cameron began.

"Whatever they're having," Ada interrupted, triumphant.

*

Cameron grinned as he sped north off the Bridge. Sausalito lay below him to the right, and that crazy Sunday in Tiburon lay even farther off in time and space. Ada should have written her thesis on Millay, he thought. With her little petulant hand an annotation of her greatly petulant life. He took the off-ramp from 101 and headed up the canyon roads, past the Muir Woods turnoff, shifting gears and climbing the snaking asphalt up the mountain, above the Pantoll Ranger Station, roaring beyond the natural Mountain Home Theater, to the top of Mount Tamalpais, the highest point in the Bay area, a forest and crest sacred to the old Miwok Indian gods.

Cameron loved the mountain.

It was worn and smoothed, twisted with trails as ancient as the fog that rolled through its pines. Hikers puffed up and down its paths, rediscovering traces of the old gravity-pulled Mt. Tamalpais Railway that before the San Francisco quake had pulled fashionable ladies and gentlemen up the steep grade for picnics of chicken and lemonade in the sun.

Cameron kicked up his bike in the asphalt parking lot below the peak. The ladies with the lemonade had vanished. A tie-dyed hippie replaced them, lounging in the mountain heat against the stainless-steel sides of a pickup truck fitted out to serve cellophaned sandwiches and coffee.

"Black or white?" the hippie asked.

"Black." Cameron took the styrofoam cup of coffee in his hand and flipped the kid a half-dollar.

"It's sixty cents, man." The boy hooked his long hair back behind his ears and dropped his hands to his hips. "Overhead," he said, looking up at the clear blue sky. "The cost of doing business, man."

"Yeah." Cameron flipped him the dime.

The kid caught it. "Have a nice day," he said.

Cameron headed back to his bike. "Whatever," he said over his shoulder. He set the coffee on the asphalt, zipped off his leather jacket, pulled off his flannel shirt, picked up the coffee, and lay back on his bike, head and shoulders padded with his rolled jacket against the handle bars, feet stretched back over the hot leather seat and rear fender, his torso exposed to the sun.

He sipped the coffee and watched the valley below the mountain. Brown grasses, dry with August, waved in heat shimmers between him and the water of the Bay. A road below, white and winding, wended its way up and down ridges and rises, leading toward, and then disappearing, before it reached the Golden Gate Bridge and the white City of Oz itself shimmering across the Bay in the translucent August sun.

He closed his eyes.

Be here now. He relaxed into his mantra. *Be here now. Three. Here.* Counting backwards. *Two. More here. One. Really here.* He breathed deep from within his center and through his eyelids saw not the Fire Watch Station at Tam's peak but the clear unspoiled way the mountain had been when holy men roamed its trails fasting and praying, dreaming visions for their hunting shields.

Cameron had dreamed once of a bull's head, horned and cocked left, nostrils flaring. A tattoo artist in Oakland had needled it deftly on the outside of his shoulder above his left bicep. He had never regretted the rite. He had opened his flesh to the ink and the needle like a burning razor blade. It had been his first willful and completely irretrievable freewill act.

"How terribly," Ada had drawled, mocking his machismo, "existential."

Behind his eyes, he smiled and opened his pores to the sun. Energy flowed into him. Sweat beaded on his chest, grew to a rivulet, and inched down his side. A fly buzzed, circled, landed, sampled. Cameron felt its feet gigantic on him, treading up and down in place, the way Ada's cat at night often stood atop the blankets padding its paws up and down on his chest as if he were so much dough to be kneaded. He relaxed into the fly, tried to become the fly, but finally the itch was too much. Eyes still closed he swatted, missed, and had only his own sweat to lick from his hand. The fly landed again. This time it marched strangely across his chest. A bead of sweat headed fast down his belly toward the pool in his navel. He opened his eyes.

"About time," said the figure silhouetted against the sun.

Cameron was momentarily blinded. Startled. The man had been tickling his belly with a stalk of mountain grass.

"Curtis!" Cameron said. "You're late."

Curtis brought the stem of grass to his mouth. He bit off the end and smiled. "I like to talk to people when they least expect it." He spit out the butt end of grass. "Guess you'd say I'm strange."

"Curtis," Cameron said putting his feet on the ground, "you're more than strange."

"Come with me," Curtis pointed partway down the slope. "We can talk better down at the old Tam Railway Station. My car is parked over by the lovely hippie." He climbed uninvited on the motorcycle. "You can drive us down," he said. The straw twitched between his teeth.

"So get off so I can start it," Cameron said pulling on his shirt.

Curtis obeyed.

Cameron kick-started the bike into roaring life. "Okay," he said. "Get on."

Curtis swung his leg across the machine. "Where do I hang on?" he asked.

"Sit on your hands," Cameron said. "Don't play so dumb."

"It's time we talked," Curtis said. "Really time."

"About what?"

"About Ada."

"What about Ada?"

"I married her before she married you."

"That makes you some kind of expert?"

"Exactly."

Cameron shifted the bike, angry, and peeled out of the parking lot with Curtis hanging on for dear life.

*

Ada sat naked on the marble floor of her shower watching the water sputter down the brass mouth of the drain. Once she had read of an elderly woman who had slipped in the tub and laid in five inches of water for six days before anyone found her. She was alive but wrinkled as a prune; she had kept warm by adding hot water every hour or so. Ada had filed that information away for her old age. "If there's going to be an old age," she said outloud. "I wonder if other grown-ups ever sit on the shower floor and play?" She laughed thinking of Cassiopeia sitting on the shower floor, if Cassiopeia ever showered, with the water pelting down, filtering through her hip Brillo-frizzy locks.

Cassiopeia had been Cameron's prior old lady. He had met her in the Haight, five years before, during the Summer of Love. Ada had visions of Cassiopeia leaning provocatively against the Haight-Ashbury street sign with her madras skirt up over her head and her mattress on her back. Or at least her sleeping bag.

The little lady's birth name, before she had rechristened herself Cassiopeia by taking an extra large hit of magic mushrooms and shouting "Here I go," had been simply Margaret Mary O'Hara. After her christening, she had felt the need for a lysergic communion service; she had renounced her Catholicism, but adored its sacramental choreography: her confirmation ceremony had been a strung-out drug-bang of chemical mysticism.

Cameron, at that time a mescaline novice overdosed on Alan Watts' books, had been certain that against the Hashbury street sign leaned his spiritual guide. Margaret Mary O'Hara was buying none of it. "St. Theresa of Avila, honey, I'm not." She raised her hands.

"With these," she said, cupping her 36-D breasts like a treasure, "I am Cassiopeia Star Child."

Ada knew Cameron had said something ridiculously trendy like: "Far out!" She shook her head violently under the shower spray, shimmying like a retriever run in from the rain. Her hair whipped water around her face. As far as Ada was concerned Cassiopeia was a burnt-out chick. Talking to her was harder than running on foot across a twelve-lane freeway.

She turned off the shower, splashed herself with baby oil, wiped down with a soft sponge, then wrapped her waist with one towel and turbaned her head with another. She stepped carefully from the shower and met her bare breasts in the medicine cabinet mirror. "Thank God," she said, "I'll never be as mystical as Cassiopeia."

She toweled herself dry in the bedroom. A few beads of water flipped onto the ungraded student papers stacked on her vanity. Her students hated papers. She hated papers. Still they wrote and she corrected. She tried to towel dry the top paper. A blot appeared across the title. It made no difference. The paper, twice as long as assigned, was from an ardent little feminist who always wrung political relevance into everything. Ada checked the blotted title, something about "'Women in Literature: Enter as Juliet; Exit as Ophelia' by Ms. Pat Leavitt for Ms. Ada Vicary, MA."

Ada grabbed a red felt-tip. "All these abbreviations," she wrote petulantly on the title page, "remind me of writer S. J. Perlman who wished he had become a Jesuit so he could have signed himself S. J. Perlman, S. J." Ada appreciated Perlman's chiastic sense of humor, knew that it would be lost on the intense Ms. Leavitt, and added, "Sorry about the blot." She threw the marking pen on top the stack; that was at least a start on the thirty-four research papers for English 252: Shakespeare.

Ada felt mean pulling on her jeans and knotting her blouse above her midriff. She had neglected to tell Cassiopeia that Cameron had roared off for the day. She blow-dried her hair and was almost finished when the doorbell rang. She grabbed her lipstick, drew a bit of color across her mouth, blotted her lips together, tossed the tube on top the "Juliet-Ophelia" paper, said, "Whoops! Sorry, Ms. Leavitt," and headed down the stairs to the door. Through the stained glass, she could see the dark silhouette of the one, the only, the original.

"Cassiopeia!" Ada said, opening the door. "How are you?"

"My nose hurts," Cassie said.

"I can see why," Ada said. "Come in."

Cassiopeia's nose had been pierced with a gold ring, or, more accurately, her left nostril had been.

Cassiopeia also had a Janis Joplin tattoo on her wrist and Bette Midler tweezed eyebrows. Her body was a map of fads in and out.

"Why have you done that?" Ada asked.

"Makes me think twice about Kung Fu fighting," Cassiopeia said.

"It would be hell to have someone grab your nose in a catfight," Ada said.

"Worse than pierced ears, but I'm a nuclear pacifist now. No fighting." Cassiopeia swooped into the Victorian parlor. "Far out!" she said.

"What a lovely saffron robe you're wearing," Ada said. "Sit down, please. Have you joined that dervish group? What are they called? The ones who shave their heads except for the ponytail and play drums for the tourists down at the Powell and Market Street cable-car turnaround?"

"Still the same old Ada," Cassiopeia said. She pulled a joint from her totebag.

"Still the same old Cassie." Ada threw her a box of footlong wooden fireplace matches.

Cassie toked up. "Where's Cam?" she asked, her voice whistling and high as she spoke on the inflowing blue air.

Ada settled back into a large wicker chair, one leg under the other. "Cameron's out," she said.

"Just us girls then, huh?" Cassie said, hitting her joint again. "Say," she said, "does Cam still leave the toilet seat up?"

Ada knew they were off and running.

"Cam always used to leave the toilet seat up," Cassie said. "More than once with that man I crawled out of bed at night and plopped my buns right down into the water."

"How refreshing," Ada said. "Did you have to change your jammies?"

Cassie was deep into her joint. "Do you have any peroxide?" she asked. "For my nose."

Ada shifted a cushion behind her back. "In the bathroom. Left side, second shelf."

"Thanks," Cassiopeia said. She billowed up from the couch like a saffron cloud.

Ada checked out her spreading size. "You want to go to aerobics class with me?"

"You've got to be joking," Cassie said. "Hold this, will you?" She handed the jay to Ada who sat holding the burning joint. Across the front bay of windows hung Ada's precious Boston ferns, four huge bushes with fronds bursting up and then down through the macrame hangers. She laid the joint in an ashtray, crossed to the windows, picked up her misting can and sprayed the jungle-sized plants.

"I can't find the peroxide." Cassiopeia's far-away voice whined a child's ploy.

Ada set down the misting can and headed down the long hall. "I'm coming," she said. She turned into the bathroom. "It would help," she said to the stoned Cassie, "if you opened the cabinet." Ada pointed. "What's this mess on the mirror?"

Cassiopeia grinned at Ada. She held up a bar of soap. "I was feeling inspired."

In the mirror both women were reflected. Over their reflections handwriting was scrawled with soap.

Ada attempted a smile. "When did you become a graffiti artist, dear."

"My latest poem," Cassie said. She began to read: "Chameleons are not furious. They color themselves to fit their world. Suddenly this long here...." She studied Ada's face. "What do you think so far?"

"Terrific," Ada said.

"Suddenly this long here," Cassie continued, "I no longer speed on the urgency of there. Chameleons are." She stopped. "That's all the farther I wrote when you came in."

"Too bad," Ada said. "You and Coleridge."

"Huh?" Cassie said. "I don't get it."

"He was a poet. Here let me squeeze this cotton over your nose. Someone interrupted him in the middle of a poem and he never could finish it. Hold still."

Cassiopeia gasped like a fish as the peroxide foamed in her nostril. "But I finished mine," she blubbered.

Ada capped the peroxide. "That figures." She tossed the soaked cotton into the wastebasket.

Cassiopeia stood between her and the door. "Chameleons are adaptable."

"Move aside," Ada said.

Cassie moved, still reciting: "Chameleons will be here long after the rest of life, extinct, has died of a mushroom ulcer." She smiled at Ada.

"That's it?" Ada asked.

"Far out, isn't it?" Cassie said.

"No wonder Cameron thought you were a muse lately sprung up in America."

"What's that supposed to mean?"

She led Cassie into the hall. "Care for some tea?" she asked.

"I have some ginseng in my tote," Cassie offered.

"Thanks, dear," Ada said, "I'd as soon not swallow anything in your bag."

"Don't be smart," Cassiopeia said. "Just because your toilet seat is down."

"You noticed."

"You've broken him, paper-trained him like a lap dog." Cassiopeia looked genuinely sorrowful.

"Don't be ridiculous," Ada said.

"No. Really," Cassiopeia said. "Signs and omens are everywhere."

"You've confused peace, love, and granola with life," Ada said.

"In the universe. In the cosmos. In the constellations of stars. It's all magical."

Ada busied herself with a pot of Mu tea.

Cassie rattled her costume bracelets across the old white-oak table. Silence stretched between them. Once, when she was eleven years old, Ada had connected a wire between two soup cans and had given one to her best girlfriend. They had been barely able to hear each other.

Cassiopeia stared vacantly at her fingers full of rings.

Ada switched on the 1932 Philco that Cameron had restored. KFOG crept around the aspidistra and wandering jew plants, filling the kitchen with guileless music. At least once an hour they played an instrumental version of "I Left My Heart in San Francisco."

"That station makes me feel like I'm in a dentist office," Cassiopeia said.

"It calms me," Ada said. "In the room," she clung for balance to her favorite line of poetry, "the women come and go, speaking... speaking..."

Cassiopeia was not listening. She nervously twisted her rings. "I think I'm leaving Frisco," she said.

It grated on Ada. "Never call San Francisco 'Frisco,'" she said. "What's the matter with you?"

"Nothing," she said. "It's all over here, unless you're gay. I just want to go away."

"Then go." Ada said it flat.

"You've never liked me." Cassiopeia looked about to cry.

"I could cheerfully murder you," Ada said. "Hand me your cup. The tea's ready."

"I tried to leave before."

"That was a happy day till you called us late that night." Ada poured the tea.

"Long distance."

"Collect," Ada said. "I accepted your call when Cameron refused." She poured her own tea. "Why should I like you? My husband's old...." Ada stopped pouring in mid-cup.

She felt reversed, turned around. It was the New World the liberated Ms. Leavitt loved: Ada, the princess, out defending, rescuing again, perhaps, her prince.

She set the tea-cosy down on a mirrored tray in which she saw the upside-down face of Cassiopeia. "Okay," Ada said, "take a sip of your tea."

"Thank you, Nurse Rat Shit," Cassiopeia said.

"Furious this may make you, my tired little hipster, but you're going to hear me out for once. Stoned or not. Try to focus your fried-out brain."

Cassiopeia rose up in her seat. "Nobody talks to me like that."

"Except me," Ada said. "And you look straight at me, Margaret Mary O'Hara. "Watch my face. Read my lips."

Cassiopeia bolted. Lectures frightened her. She stood straight up, knocking over her chair. "Dear, dear Abby," Cassie said, "I'm not one of your sophomores. Who needs this? I'm leaving."

"Good-bye, good luck, and good riddance."

Cassie grabbed her tote and ran down the hall, heading toward the front door. She stopped. She turned. "I'm pregnant," she screamed. "Tell Cam that!" She slung her tote over her shoulder. "From what I figure about you, Ada Tomato, that's more than you'll ever be able to tell him!"

Ada started for her, walking fast, then faster down the hall. "I'm going to tear your nose off your face," she screamed.

Cassie yanked open the front door. The afternoon sun hit her directly, exploding her into a ball of saffron light.

Ada was momentarily blinded. She stopped in her tracks. The door slammed. The hallway grew quiet, except for the tiny sniffle Ada stifled with the back of her hand. This wasn't what she had meant to happen. Not at all. "Oh damn," she said.

*

Curtis directed Cameron down the dirt fire-road to the old Mount Tamalpais train station. The sign on the stone-and-timber building read West Point Club. Cameron pulled the bike up under three shady pines. The dust ball that had followed the bike down the trail caught them and sifted into their clothes. Curtis hopped off, preening himself like a swan. Cameron wondered if Curtis, neat old Curtis, sportscar nut and terror of women, wasn't just a bit of a fag, even if he had married Ada who refused to rate Curtis' performance on a scale of one-to-ten. He kicked the stand under his bike. Why give fags a bad name, he thought. Curtis is Curtis.

"Hey, Mala!" A raspy voice called down from the porch. At first Cameron couldn't see to whom the man at the railing was shouting. Then a streak of gray flashed out of the bushes. Curtis moved quickly behind the bike as the gray Malamute loped her panting way up to the newcomers.

"Hey there, girl," Cameron said. The dog looked up at him and rolled over on her back. Cameron stooped down.

"That's it," the man on the porch said, "scratch her."

Cameron pulled the white hair on the dog's belly back and forth. Her back wriggled through the dusty gravel. Her eyes rolled ecstatic back into her head.

"Be careful," Curtis said. "She might bite."

"Come on, Mala," the man said coming down from the porch. "Don't be a pest." His chin was grizzled with whiskers. He was shirtless and wearing brown leather hiking shorts he had crafted himself. "She found a rattler this morning," he said, "curled up on the porch steps." He held out a hand to Cameron stooped over the dog. The tips of two fingers were missing. "Name's Jerry," he said. His grip was strong and he was so veined with muscle he easily pulled Cameron to his feet. "I killed it with a stick." He pointed to a nail on the porch railing. "Come on up. You can see the rattles."

The dog followed the three men up to the porch where she lay down possessively guarding the steps. Four hikers, two couples, in their late fifties, early sixties, sat at one of the many tables on the porch, one sipping hot tea, and three lemonade.

"What a view," Cameron said. "From down in these trees I didn't think you could see anything."

"Everything from out in the Pacific, in past the Golden Gate, all of San Francisco, Oakland, on around to Berserkley and the Richmond Bridge," Jerry said. "On a clear night, the ocean and Bay are black as the sky. You can hardly tell the constellations of stars from the constellations of city lights."

"A poet," Curtis said, "and you know it."

"Nope, the caretaker." Jerry spit over the railing. He liked most people, but already he disliked Curtis. "Lemonade?" he asked.

"Fresh squeezed?" Curtis sat in one of the heavy wooden porch chairs.

"Wyler's Brand," Jerry said. He toyed with a chain hanging heavy with keys at his left hip.

"Make it two, okay?" Cameron said. He shot a .22-caliber look at Curtis.

"Come on, Mala," Jerry said.

The dog rose, looked with dumb affection at Cameron, and passed on into the club rooms. Cameron looked in. The floors were rough and unfinished. The walls and ceiling were an ancient enamel yellow. Some of the leaded glass had fallen out of a built-in cupboard, and the fireplace had been converted to a gas burner. Even the globes hanging from the ceiling burnt gas. Directly opposite the door hung a portrait of John Muir.

"How long has this place been here?" Cameron asked.

"Forever," Curtis said. "Sit down. I want to talk to you."

"Yessir!" Cameron said and saluted smartly.

The woman with the tea took a quick look at Curtis and then whispered something to her husband with the lemonade. They both laughed.

Cameron sat down, back to the view. Curtis began talking. Cameron studied the map of trails that hung framed under glass over Curtis' head.

"Here's your lemonade," Jerry said. He set the tray down between the two men.

"Pay the man," Cameron said to Curtis. "It'll be good for your soul."

Curtis looked hurt. Ada always said money was Curtis' only friend. "How much?" he said.

"Fifty cents," Jerry said.

Curtis laid five dimes on the table. Jerry's stubbed fingers deftly flicked the change into the palm of his hand. "For the West Point kitty," he said.

The other hikers called him to sit with them.

Curtis drank the lemonade in one gulp. "Everything tastes like chemicals," he said. "Even if you could afford it, where could you find any quality to buy these days?"

"What makes you think you could ever buy it?" Cameron sipped his lemonade.

"As I was saying," Curtis said.

"What were you saying?"

"I was saying the trouble with Ada is..."

"There's no trouble with Ada," Cameron said.

"...is the same as the trouble with me." Curtis was relentless. "When we were married, such a short time, we both were very young. She was in school. We were both in school. We were peace activists in the streets, but we fought each other. All the time. About everything. We needed, well, a referee."

"Someone to count you out? 8-9-10?"

"I loved...no, love, Ada." Curtis looked about to whimper.

"That makes two of us," Cameron said. "But I have my doubts about you."

"No doubts," Curtis said.

Mala crept over next to Cameron's chair. Jerry was playing the harmonica, one of three he kept on a shelf inside the door, and the four hikers were singing a German song.

"So what do you want me to do?" Cameron asked. He scratched the dog behind the ears.

"I want...." Curtis hesitated.

"Go on," Cameron said. "Good girl, Mala. That's a good girl, Mala."

"I want," Curtis said, "to live with Ada."

"You're crazy," Cameron said. "She thinks you're a joke."

"No." Curtis leaned into the table. "I want...and this is really hard to verbalize."

"Try," Cameron said.

"I want to move in with Ada. And with you."

*

Ada lay prostrate on the couch with laughter. "Poor Curtis!" she said. "What did you say to him?"

Cameron fell across her, stretching down the length of her body. Her laughter was infectious. He laughed too. "What do you think I said?"

She roared. "Yes!" she screamed. "You said *yes*! We're no longer a marriage. We're a *menage*!"

"He wants us to be his mommy and daddy."

Ada's hilarity ignited her immense energy and she pushed Cameron off her to the floor. "You idiot," she said, gaining control of herself. "Of course, you didn't really!"

"You hurt my back," Cameron said. "Of course, I did. I couldn't help myself."

"You didn't!" She began to strike his shoulders with her small fists. "I'll hurt more than your back. I'm not ready to adopt. Anyone." She meant Cassiopeia especially.

"Watch your knee," he said. He rolled into a fetal position.

"Say you didn't," she said. "I'll positively murder you!"

Cameron was laughing, tickling her, teasing her, driving her crazy. She pounced across his butt, snatched a pillow from the couch, and pummeled his head.

"I didn't." He confessed, but he never surrendered. "I didn't. I really didn't."

"That's more like it." Ada stood up triumphant. "Curtis and Cassie are both children, and we agreed not to have children."

Cameron rolled over and unhitched the belt on his jeans. He held out his arms to her. "We can change our minds," he said.

"Is that all you care about?" Ada reached for the misting can and walked indignant toward the windows.

"Go drown your ferns," Cameron said.

She sprayed the ferns so heavily they began to drip on the hardwood floor. "That's all you care about," she said. "That tramp Cassie might have been your trampoline, but not me!"

He locked his hands together under his head. "I used to care about a lot of things."

"Here it comes," she said. "Whatever it is we never talk about." She pulled a red bandana from her back pocket and tried to wipe the wet floor.

"Yeah. Here it comes," he said. He leaned up on an elbow and stuck a cigarette between his teeth.

"You ought to trim that moustache before you burn yourself up."

"Here it comes," he said. He lit the cigarette and pulled the smoke down deep.

Ada took advantage of the pause. "First there were the Kennedys," she recited. She repeated his litany by heart. "Assassinations. Executions, you say. And second there was…"

"Nam," he said.

"Sometimes I think the only heart you have is purple."

"Smart-assing doesn't become you, Ada."

"Don't forget drugs," she said. "You and your sacred mushrooms."

"And drugs."

"And Cassiopeia, the human air-mattress."

"Lay off," Cameron said.

Ada rose from her knees waving the wet red kerchief. "Would the bull like a surprise?"

"What surprise?"

"She was here today."

"Cassie?"

"Yeah."

"What'd she want?" Cameron let the cigarette hang forgotten in his mouth.

"Same as Curtis I imagine." Ada folded the wet kerchief

deliberately into squares. "But you know Cassie. She always says the opposite of what she means. You have to read her in a mirror." Ada never believed in telling anyone everything. She decided not to lighten up with a joke about Cassie's chameleons.

"What'd she say?" Cameron rose and crossed to the bottle tucked away in the bookcase.

"She said she's leaving San Francisco. She said she stopped over to say good-bye. She said she'd never call us again. Not even collect. She said she was a chameleon. Her hints were as broad as her hips. I think she wants to live with us too. Fuck her!"

"Cut it, Ada," Cameron said. He was flashing on the night Cassie had called them long distance, desperate and sick on junk. "That poor kid," he had said. He had spent the night in the Greyhound Bus Depot waiting for her to get back from Santa Cruz.

Ada had been furious. "You can't really expect me to go down to that filthy bus station practically on our honeymoon to meet your whore," Ada had said. "What kind of woman do you think I am?"

"I don't know," he had said. "I suspect I'll find out. Sooner or later."

*

Even through that long night waiting for Cassiopeia, Cameron hadn't blamed Ada. Strangers in the station had surrounded him, deathly alive at 3:30 AM. They had breathed on him. Everyone smoked. Their blue exhalations had yellowed the air, thickening the pallid fluorescent light.

He hadn't blamed Ada and he hadn't blamed Cassie.

The longer he had waited that night the more he had needed the men's room. He had stalled leaving his seat in the crowded terminal, mainly because an old woman, a white choir robe folded over her arm, had stood sentinel, waiting, like God's Righteousness at the end of the full row of seats. She had tried to stare Cameron into relinquishing his chair. But he had sat, steadfast, bladder hurting, because her face, over the folded choir robe, because her face, over the righteous folds of her melting flesh, was so mean.

From the moment of Cassie's emergency call, Ada had given him no peace; and Cassie wasn't due till 6:47. Cameron had reached for a cigarette. Out. He had frisked his pockets for a stray pack.

Another predator had eyed his nervous movements. Seated in the row opposite, a young hooker, in shorts and leg-warmers, had been clipping her nails, licking each finger after each snip, rubbing each cuticle meticulously dry on her denim blouse. That night among desperate travelers going nowhere had been terrible.

Cameron took his drink and turned to Ada. "If nothing else," he mumbled, "here and now...."

"What?" she said.

"Nothing." He took a good slug of the whiskey. "There's too many people in the world to care anymore," he said.

That night in the bus station, too far away to hear, Cameron had watched a security cop hassle two men lounging without luggage. One, a young black, had produced a ticket. The cop had reached for his eyeglasses. He took the ticket, examined it, and handed it back. The other man, a wafer-thin Appalachian with red hair, had fumbled through his pockets, offering at last to the cop a shred of paper. Even at a distance, Cameron had felt the failure. Outside, a bus roared. The cop had jerked his fist, thumb extended, back over his shoulder. Obediently, the red-haired man had risen, defeated, cast out, and shuffled out towards Seventh Street and Market Street.

"How can anyone care anymore?" Cameron lay back on the couch. "There's just too many."

The depot had been a mess with people. Too many people always meant a mess. They had drained him of sympathy. All their patience. All their hurry. Their smell. Their sound. He knew he was the same to them. Just another body taking up the last available seat. If the security officer had shot the red-haired man in the face, Cameron would have felt no pity. No more sorry than watching an actor like Edmund O'Brien get shot in a TV series. Maybe the cleaning woman might have minded the red-haired Appalachian brains blown under the bus station seats about as much as she minded the hooker's snipped crescents of dead-white fingernail.

*

"Hello in there!" Ada rubbed Cameron's forehead with the cool wet bandana.

"Cassie's really gone then," he said.

"As much as Cassie ever goes," Ada said. "I wouldn't worry. She has her own ways of coping, weak as they are."

"She'll keel over out there, Ada." The hand with his drink sank to the floor beside the couch.

Ada lifted the glass to her lips and finished the burning whiskey. "Cassiopeia will be alright. So will Curtis," she soothed, climbing on top of Cameron's outstretched body. She kissed him. She loved him. "Everything's alright," she said. "Everybody drops people now and then." She kissed him again. "We're alright, Cameron. We're here now."

She cupped his head in her hands, nuzzling his lips, nose, eyes. "They're both gone," she said.

"They'll come back."

"And we'll send them away."

"We have no choice."

She kissed him. "We're all alone."

"We need to be alone together," he said. He brought his arms up around her, pulling her down on to him. "We two." He needed to hold her, just hold her.

She let him embrace her sweetly.

She relaxed across the full length of his body. She rose and fell with his breathing as he drifted off to sleep. She felt his unshaven face chafe against her cheek. Some things she sometimes accepted. She was not sleepy in her vigil, holding him, protecting him, but she could not afford to look too long at his face. Maybe he wasn't the best man in the world, but he was the best who had yet come along.

Everyone thought they were a great couple. They were charmed, emerging from the burden of their pasts. He was as handsome as she was attractive, and, lord knows, something in the very look of him warmed the cold Curtis had left deep inside her when his dose had killed her fertility. Someday when Cameron was ready, when she was ready, when she could afford the astonished look in his face, when she could chance his disappointment might not drive him away, she promised herself to tell him why, really why, she didn't want, couldn't have, children.

God! His radiant heat made her eyes burn. She closed them, in self-defense, closed them tight against his seductive, engaging brightness that was like the beautiful blinding brightness of San Francisco itself when tour boats pull away from the Embarcadero at noon into the windswept cross-currents of the Bay.

Coming Attractions
Kweenasheba

A Snappy San Francisco Comedy
1 Act in 2 Scenes

"Kweenasheba" was first produced by the Yonkers Production Company, San Francisco, premiering March 13, 1976, at the Society for Individual Rights SIR Center Theatre on a double bill with "The Madness of Lady Bright" by Lanford Wilson. The author adapted his 1975 play from his 1972 short story, "Sweet Embraceable You."

Time: Christmas, 1972
Setting: San Francisco, Castro Street, Soap-and-Floral Shop
Four Characters: two women, two men

Ada Vicary: 30, with an MA, teaching in a junior college; her own woman; sveltly attractive; first married to CURTIS, she is now divorced and living with JOHN; independent; clever; as a girl she bound her own books, hunted bugs, and invented animal nicknames for her relatives. In many ways, ADA is a compensatory swinger; owner of a restored Victorian on San Francisco's Castro Street.

John Stack: Early 30's; a craftsman-motorcyclist; dark and handsome and into an ironic trip as owner of a Soap-and-Floral Shop located in Ada's Victorian. JOHN, formerly the lover of KWEENASHEBA, is now ADA's lover. JOHN is the straight foil to both KWEENASHEBA and CURTIS.

Kweenasheba: 29, formerly named Mary Margaret Chase until her lysergic rechristening in the Haight-Ashbury. She is amply endowed as any Rubens nude; she fancies herself "the one and only reincarnation of the Queen of Sheba": Kweenasheba. Her body is a tracery of fads: a Janis Joplin tattoo, tote bags, saffron robes, and a pierced nose. Basically she's been around and she's winded. She is a photographer snapping her borrowed camera.

Curtis Boughner: 34, pansexual; even more masculine of body and voice than John; sometimes lilting in manner of delivery when he chooses; as handsome in his fair way as John is in his darkness; Curtis, formerly Ada's husband, is now KWEENASHEBA's lover.

This comedy should be played light, lively, and fast—midway between the madcap comic style of vintage Hollywood and fast-paced TV sitcoms.

TWO SCENES. ONE SET.
Playing time: 40 minutes

SCENE ONE

A morning before Christmas in the storefront Soap-and-Floral Shop of a restored Victorian on San Francisco's Castro Street. The calendar says December 1972. Two couples share this house: Ada Vicary and John Stack, upstairs; Kweenasheba and Curtis, downstairs behind the shop.

The single set is decorated for Christmas and divided by the service counter to the left of which stand the soap baskets, the green plants in white wicker, and the inevitable macrame-bilia. To the right of the counter is strewn a combination work and living area. To the left is the street entrance. Coming down at rear center stage is the last curve and landing of a stairs from the second floor.

To the right, behind the clippers and styrofoam frogs and 1940's couch is a door curtained with nostalgic floral draperies. An old coffee dripolator sits steaming on a hotplate. A vintage 'Forties radio, receiving a contemporary station, plays Christmas carols.

John: (Off-stage, singing with the radio)
"Tis the season to be jolly;

Fa La La La La La La La La!
Time to sell the goddam holly!"

JOHN ENTERS

The shop is his and he readies it for the day. His voice is big enough to sing his own lyrics over the radio.

John: "Don we now our gay apparel..."
Ada: (Entering, switches off radio) Not you!
John: (Rising from plants) What?
Ada: I smelled the coffee.
John: (Closing in to embrace ADA) Then good morning. (He kisses her lightly)
Ada: Thanks for the stroking. I'm beat.
John: Tired?
Ada: All last night I could hear them.
John: Curtis and Kweenasheba? They'll be here forever.
Ada: They giggle. Too much. What could they have in common?
John: Your Curtis? My Kweenie? Once upon a time, each one of them had each one of us.
Ada: Comparing notes, I suppose. Curtis always was one to kiss and tell. God! I loathe the smell of fried bologna. What are they cooking back there?
John: Roses.
Ada: Roses?
John: In these boxes are 20 dozen roses.
Ada: You're the only florist in San Francisco who smells like fried bologna.
John: You think I like it? Your Ex and my Ex living in a room behind my shop.
Ada: (Pouring coffee) Darling....I own the building. The smell permeates. And I hate the way it curls up...
John: (Tossing yesterday's wilted flowers aside)... Everything curls up...
Ada: ...Bologna when it fries, curls up. I hate it.
John: My customers buy with their noses.
Ada: Business is off? It's Christmas!

John: They buy roses. They buy bayberry soap. They smell bologna.

Ada: I know what Curtis is telling Kweenie.

John: Flowers are one thing. Meat is another.

Ada: Those two have to move.

John: Said Mohammed to the mountain.

Ada: They've crashed here long enough.

John: Once you loved Curtis.

Ada: Once you loved Kweenie.

John: A good case of changing partners.

Ada: Two bad cases of unrequited love. They've got to move.

John: A crime of passion might make us colorful in the neighborhood.

Ada: The unveiling of the mysteries inside all these marvelously restored old Victorians!

John: Curtis and Kweenie cling to each other...

Ada: ...because I love you and Kweenie loves you and you love me and Curtis loves me.

John: May I have the envelope please?

Ada: I never told you why I divorced Curtis.

John: Because Curtis likes...

Ada: ...what Curtis likes. No. Particularly why I divorced Curtis.

John: You promised to spare me the gory details.

Ada: You pumped Curtis about me.

John: You pumped Kweenasheba about me.

Ada: So what?

John: Fair is fair.

Ada: A dump is a dump.

John: What are you teaching this morning?

Ada: Children's literature.

John: Nice...

Ada: Kiddy litter.

John: Don't be cute.

Ada: To a bunch of reluctant adolescents who think they want to teach when they grow up. Hell. I don't even know what I want to be when I grow up.

John: You are a real junior-college thrill.

Ada: Listen. Curtis and I were on our first vacation. Driving down

Route 1. Eating Four-Bean Salad from a Safeway can. I was feeding Curtis...

John: Now *that's* cute!

Ada: ...because he was driving. I'd eat a bite, then lean over and feed him a bite. He'd open his mouth and I'd fork in the beans.

John: That's why you were never invited to the French Embassy!

Ada: A whole year we'd been married and it hit me. Who is this person? How'd we get to be driving in the same car? Me feeding him.

John: Things happen.

Ada: How do things happen? I hardly remember meeting Curtis. I sort of always knew him. One day he said it seemed like a good idea to get married.

John: So you tied the bean cans to the car and took off to the No-Tell Motel.

Ada: Curtis made me promise to tell him all my fantasies.

John: Did you?

Ada: At night. In bed.

John: Sort of a game?

Ada: Sort of therapy. It got to be fun.

John: You were made for each other.

Ada: He seemed to love me better if we played games.

John: He performed better?

Ada: He seemed to love me more.

John: What kind of games?

Ada: Children's games, really. He called me "The Doll Lady" and once every week or so he became one of my baby dolls.

John: Freud lives...and he's dating Tennessee Williams.

Ada: Don't try and stop me now.

John: Not for the world.

Ada: He had two favorite dolls he liked to be. One was Baby Bunting.

John: You'd be his mother.

Ada: I'd bathe him and talcum him with baby powder. It was as exciting as...

John: ...*Oedipus Rex.*

Ada: I'd diaper him and we'd cuddle on the bed while I sang to him and he kissed me here. (ADA touches her breast) He made me feel like a Madonna. Then we'd make love.

John: Baby Bunting stuck it to Mommy?

Ada: No! When the loving started the gaming stopped.

John: It was always foreplay?

Ada: For me. But Curtis let the fantasy part stretch on longer and longer. He invented a new doll called Gladys Mae. I had to dress him up in little girl clothes from Macy's.

John: Curtis as Shirley Temple?

Ada: He kept the motions of loving me.

John: Sweet Jesus and Dear Abby!

Ada: He needed mothering.

John: He should marry Kweenie.

Ada: No more than I should marry you.

John: You played along?

Ada: Till I went mad.

John: Sure.

Ada: One of my liberated lady students wrote in her term paper, "With a man, a woman enters as Juliet and exits as Ophelia."

John: Virgin to virago.

Ada: I complained to him.

John: What did he say?

Ada: That I wanted to tie him down. That I was tying him down.

John: What did you say?

Ada: I was furious. I'd been a good sport all along.

John: I'd say so.

Ada: He made me so mad standing there looking so goddam cute, so ridiculous in the cotton pinafore and white kneesocks. He stuck his tongue out at me. So I hit him.

John: Punched him?

Ada: Slapped him. Knocked him stunned into my vanity chair. He just sat there.

John: Really turned you off?

Ada: Then I tied him into the chair.

John: Tied him?

Ada: With cord from the electric blanket. Kind of poetic revenge. "Tied down?" I said. "I'll show you tied down."

John: He whimpered?

Ada: He cried.

John: You liked it.

Ada: I loved it. I faced him into the mirror and brushed lipstick and rouge all over his face. The powder caked in the tears on his cheeks.

John: You hurt him.

Ada: He was happy. I let him alone. I made him stare at himself in the mirror. I went into the kitchen and scoured the sink till the pad disintegrated.

John: How long?

Ada: I don't know. Twenty minutes. Then I started to worry about the circulation in his hands.

John: So you went back to the bedroom.

Ada: He was grinning.

John: From earring to earring.

Ada: I said: "What are you smiling at?" He wouldn't answer me. So I hit him again. You know what he said?

John: What?

Ada: This grown-man's voice. It came out of his powdered, dimpled dollface and all he said, so matter-of-factly, was: "Curtis just came in Gladys Mae's panties.

John: That's the Big Secret? Pantyhose.

Ada: I never let him touch me again.

John: Because of the games?

Ada: Because at that point I was included out.

John: Joe Namath wears pantyhose.

Ada: Curtis' only love object was Curtis.

John: You gave up too easy.

Ada: Easy!?

John: You could have dressed up like Gladys Mae yourself.

Curtis: (Enters through floraled drapery door) And to think students think their teachers hang in suspended animation between classes.

Ada: Curtis, I want you to move.

Curtis: Who kisses and tells? Walls have ears, doll. Good morning, John.

John: Hello, Curtis.

Ada: You and Kweenie both. Out!

Curtis: If they fired the weirdos, they'd have to close down every school in California.

Ada: Don't threaten me.

Curtis: Do you feel threatened?

Ada: I feel crowded.

Curtis: Crowded? By a cast of thousands.

John: It's San Francisco kharma. If you've got an extra bed in your apartment, somebody from the Midwest will crash in it.

Curtis: The Midwest is the pits. Whatever happened to the Midwest?

John: I'm still figuring what happened to you.

Curtis: Someday I'll tell you the whole truth. If awful "Ophelia" doesn't tell you first.

Ada: Someday I'm going to cut you up in itsy bitchy pieces. Very little pieces.

Curtis: Your favorite size.

Ada: As John Wayne said in *Red River*....

Curtis: I live and breathe movies.

John: Movies are such garbage.

Ada: As John Wayne said, Curtis, in *Red River* to all the fat cows: "Move out"

Curtis: Ada Tomata!

Ada: Curtis Schmurtis!

John: Kiddies!

Ada: How can an adult respond to THAT?

Curtis: You're just jealous because my parents live on the planet Krypton.

Ada: As I recall your parents....

Curtis: My mother said you'd do for a first wife.

Ada: She did?

Curtis: You didn't.

John: Before dawn I was at the Flower Mart on Harrison Street. I watched the sunrise over the East Bay.

Curtis: You're so pure.

John: I saw wet dew in Dolores Park.

Curtis: You felt "peace."

John: I hosed down the sidewalk out front.

Curtis: May the Castro Street merchants pin a rose on you.

John: But my head cannot get behind the trip you two lay on each
      other.
Curtis: Still crazy after all these years.
Ada: I'm sorry.
John: This is a big house and we're adults.
Ada: Adults!
Curtis: Keep saying it, Ada. Adults! Clap your hands and believe
      with all your heart and Tinker Bell will menstruate.
Ada: (Pulls on her sweater with a vengeance. She moves in on
      CURTIS, thumb-tip to thumb-tip, forefingers up at right
      angles to her thumbs framing CURTIS' face for a mocking
      movie close-up) How's that, Mr. DeMille? Is it a take? Or is it
      a fake?
Curtis: (Blows the sounds of "raspberries" all over ADA's palms)
Ada: (Retreating) Some adult!
Curtis: My diary entry about you today won't be nice.
Ada: It never is.
Curtis: You've read it.
Ada: You leave it lay out on purpose. (She tosses the diary to him)
Curtis: It was a test.
Ada: Then I failed.
Curtis: God will get you.
Ada: Curtis?
Curtis: Yes, darling?
Ada: Move out. You and Kweenie. Together. Separately. Bag,
      baggage: out! I want you and Kweenie gone. I want to smell
      John's roses. I loathe your fried bologna. I want my privacy
      back. (ADA picks up books and satchel, slams door, and exits)
Curtis: She once was so sweet.
John: What happened?
Curtis: She became a teacher. Why Ada teaches is beyond me.
      Sensitive people used to go into teaching. Kindly gentlemen
      like Robert Donat in *Good-bye, Mr. Chips* and nice ladies like
      Jennifer Jones in *Good Morning, Miss Dove.*
John: Sensitive people still teach.
Curtis: For sure. If they can balance a textbook with a whip, a
      chair, and a pistol. I personally am thinking of turning to a
      life of crime.

John: You could use a career.

Curtis: A career I got. A job I need. All these film schools turning out hundreds of little Francis Ford Corpulents.

John: Class tells.

Curtis: What's that mean?

John: Get a job. Get an apartment.

Curtis: There's not much call for film editors right now.

John: Use your connections.

Curtis: What connections?

John: Your famous gay underground.

Curtis: *My* famous? *My* gay? My *underwear!*

John: Come on, Gladys Mae; admit it. *Newsweek* says the gay mafia controls the media.

Curtis: I'm not gay.

John: Neither is your closet full of underwear. Pour me some more coffee.

Curtis: You ought to have your consciousness raised.

John: Women raise my...consciousness.

Curtis: (Pouring coffee) We also shovel who only stand and pour....Your consciousness about men.

John: I never think about men.

Curtis: About alternative ways of being a man.

John: I'm sick of your gay *schmerz*.

Curtis: I'm sick of your macho paranoia.

John: Okay, Curtis. The Bottom Line: as a person, I like you. As a fag, you're a drag.

Curtis: ...said the Flower Queen. (JOHN threatens) Excuse me. King. Flower King.

John: Men used to box.

Curtis: I didn't mean because you were interested in flowers that you were a "flower." I swear by St. Genet, NO!

John: You implied.

Curtis: You inferred what I did not imply.

John: I love women. Like I love Ada.

Curtis: I can love anyone.

John: How catholic.

Curtis: You really get your rocks off dumping on me.

John: You make good coffee.

Curtis: Someday you'll have the empathy to understand.
John: Coffee-making?
Curtis: When a man and a woman make love....
John: "Strangers in the night, beedoobeedoobee."
Curtis: ...among other things they do is celebrate their co-sexuality.
When two women make love...
John: Interesting!
Curtis: ...they celebrate, yes, celebrate their femininity.
John: Why don't you wake up Kweenasheba?
Curtis: She's tired. We were...celebrating.
John: Kweenie's tired all right.
Curtis: Kweenie's a hot woman.
John: And I thought it was burning bologna!
Curtis: What you won't let me say, John, is that I'm freer than you.
John: Freer and queerer.
Curtis: Hold on to this wire.
John: Why?
Curtis: So your death will look accidental.
John: Go arouse Lady Astor.
Curtis: When I want to celebrate manhood, I bed down with a
man.
John: I admit: you're honest.
Curtis: I'm natural.
John: You're not normal.
Curtis: I'd rather be natural than normal.
John: I think you're unemployed.
Curtis: Film companies are hiring only women editors.
John: Go roll out Kweenasheba.
Curtis: Women are chic. From the silent movies on, they've always
been the best editors. Dede Allen cuts all of Arthur Penn's
films: *Bonnie and Clyde*.
John: I need her to dust up the shop.
Curtis: Kweenasheba?
John: The one, the only, the original.
Curtis: Get off Kweenie's case.
John: "A case of do or die..."
Curtis: Shut-up.
John: I run this shop.

Curtis: Ada owns this house.

John: So I should shut-up?

Curtis: I'm going to marry Kweenie.

John: You and the Marines.

Curtis: I'm going to marry her and move her out of this house.

John: In a world of terrorists and pay toilets, you want to marry Kweenasheba?

Curtis: We'd be a team. A couple. Judy and Mickey. Tracy and Hepburn. Sonny and Cher.

John: A fag and his hag.

Curtis: Those words today are not acceptable.

John: May you have twins. You can name them Butch and Nellie.

Curtis: (Amused) Why do I like you?

John: You think marrying Kweenasheba will make you straight?

Curtis: But I *do* like you.

John: Your brain's in neutral. Your mouth idles on.

Curtis: You are a Straight Chauvinist. (Expansively dramatic) "The Adventures of Macho Man"!

John: Sue me. I'm a white Anglo-Saxon male.

Curtis: Macho do about nothing!

John: We males are an endangered species.

Curtis: I can see why.

John: Just man-to-man trying to protect you, boy. Kweenie's been around and she's winded.

Curtis: You whirled her around in the Haight-Ashbury when she was still Mary Margaret Chase.

John: And I fed her valiums for a month after a freaked-out methadone Marxist baptized her in acid. He told her she was the reincarnation of the one, the only, the original Queen of Sheba.

Curtis: And she's loved you ever since.

John: You drill that old rig, Curtis, you better dynamite through a million layers of old deposits.

Curtis: *Oklahoma Crude*!

John: You'll really get off thinking of all the dudes who beat you to first base. Hell. To Home Plate.

Curtis: All four of us have been around.

John: One rock musician after another.

Curtis: Is that all? Kweenie's dated the United Nations. With your bad-boy vocabulary, I expect you can peel off some really cute names for Blacks, Latins, and Asians.

John: Besides a Turk or twelve. And now a reformed faggot. That figures.

Curtis: So she has a talent for loving a lot of men.

John: Armies have marched over that chick.

Curtis: You stood in line.

John: Poor old cow.

Curtis: Stop, pig!

John: I guess I loved her once.

Curtis: I guess you maybe still do.

John: In a way....You freak me out, Curtis.

Curtis: Why?

John: I guess I'm a little jealous. Kweenie will marry you. Ada won't marry me.

Curtis: Sure.

John: I guess I'm a little shocked.

Curtis: I'm a little shocked myself.

John: Ada will freak out when I tell her.

Curtis: I know. So will Kweenie.

John: You haven't asked her?

Curtis: Marriage just seems like a good idea at this time.

John: You better go wake her up.

Curtis: Sleeping Beauty.

John: What will she say?

Curtis: She'll say, "Wow!" She'll say, "Far out!" She'll say, "YES!"

Kweenie: (Appearing grandly through the floral draperies and holding a big bologna sandwich) I'll say, "NO!"

Lights hold three solid beats
freezing the action to
END SCENE ONE

Lights fade down for five beats
and then come up on
SCENE TWO

Evening of the same day. The shop is closed. Incense is burning.

Christmas lights are a glow. Alone, KWEENIE whistles boisterously a couple lines of "Silent Night." She has obviously been photographing, without much satisfaction, a still-life of soap and flowers. She seems ponderous and pondering. She addresses her soliloquy to the absent ADA and JOHN and CURTIS.

Kweenie: May I speak? May I speak without being spoken to? May I make a personal remark?...A personal remark? Oh my....Oh yes. A personal remark? Please do. (Then flatly) I think I'll go kill a rock star....Nothin', huh? How do you get somebody's attention? "You can tell us anything." (She snaps a flash picture) My parents always said that. I'll bet every parent on the block, every parent in the nation, in the western hemisphere, in the world, in the mind of God has said, "You can tell us anything. We'll understand." Call *The National Enquirer*! EXTRA! EXTRA! Read All About It! BLIND PARENTS RAISE INVISIBLE CHILD!" I'll bet even killer sharks pump their kids for information. (She lines up another picture and snaps it) Personally, I prefer still-life. (She whistles one more line of "Silent Night") I must not whistle. What was it the nuns at good old Misericordia taught us? "When a girl whistles, the Blessed Virgin cries." (She whistles a fast "wolf" whistle) Who runs the Kleenex concession in heaven? "Bless me, Father, for I have whistled." I am the by-product of a long procession of parents and priests and nuns. They told me to be good. I'm good okay. Very good. But, mommy, what's "good"? Be good. You and daddy never finished that sentence. Be a good what? A good lawyer. A good doctor. Anything but a good virgin-martyr-saint. Right now I'm good...and pregnant. (Sings) "Round yon Virgin, Mother and Child." Tch! They'd never believe that!
Ada: (Entering) Is this the mad scene from *Hamlet*?
Kweenie: Just helping an old lady across the street...of her life.
Ada: Found an apartment?
Kweenie: You missed supper.
Ada: A-part-ment. As in a-part.
Kweenie: Maybe I should marry Curtis and be a housewife in Daly City.

Ada: Somehow that must be against zoning laws.

Kweenie: My nose hurts.

Ada: That's more barbaric than pierced ears.

Kweenie: It's PRIMAL!

Ada: Primal? It's positively Neanderthal.

Kweenie: It's only my left nostril.

Ada: ...and what a lovely saffron robe.

Kweenie: I may join that Dervish group.

Ada: And shake your tambourine for the tourists down at Powell and Market.

Kweenie: The same old Ada. (KWEENIE pulls out a joint)

Ada: The same old Kweenie. (ADA tosses KWEENIE a box of footlong fireplace matches) Where's John?

Kweenie: Out. (KWEENIE has struck the match and lets it burn close to her face)

Ada: Just us girls then.

Kweenie: Am I just another candlelight beauty? (KWEENIE waves the match before her face. She is baiting ADA as the "older" woman) What does youth do to a face?

Ada: Usually it leaves.

Kweenie: (Blows out match) Say, does Johnny still leave the toilet seat up?

Ada: We're off and running.

Kweenie: Johnny always used to leave the toilet seat up. More than once with that man I crawled out of bed in the dark of night and plopped my fanny down into the cold water.

Ada: How refreshing. Did you have to change your jammies?

Kweenie: Peroxide. I need peroxide. For my nose.

Ada: John stores a first-aid kit under the counter. (ADA busily waters plants)

Kweenie: Let me recite my latest poem.

Ada: You're so creative. Photography. Poetry. Hooking.

Kweenie:

> "Chameleons are not furious.
> They color themselves to fit their world.
> Suddenly, this long here...."
> What do you think so far?

Ada: Terrific. I hate it.
Kweenie:

"Suddenly, this long *here*,
I no longer speed on the urgency of *there*.
Chameleons are..."

Ada: Stop!
Kweenie: You'll make me forget.
Ada: You and Coleridge.
Kweenie: He was into opium.
Ada: He was also a poet. Let me squeeze this cotton over your
    nose. Someone interrupted his composition of a poem. Hold
    still. He never could finish it.
Kweenie: But I finished mine.
Ada: Like I said: he was a poet.
Kweenie: "Chameleons are adaptable."
Ada: Move aside.
Kweenie:

"Chameleons will be here long after
the rest of life,
extinct,
has died of a bleeding ulcer."

Ada: That's it?
Kweenie: Far out, isn't it?
Ada: Care for some tea?
Kweenie: I have some ginseng in my tote.
Ada: Thanks, dear, I'd as soon not swallow anything in your bag.
Kweenie: Don't act superior. Just because your toilet seat is down.
Ada: (Very angry) You were forbidden ever to go upstairs!
Kweenie: You've broken Johnny, paper-trained him like a little
    dog.
Ada: Ridiculous.
Kweenie: Signs and omens are everywhere.
Ada: When I was eleven, I connected a wire between two soup
    cans. I could barely hear my best girl friend.
Kweenie: In the universe. In the cosmos. It's all allegorical.... My

horoscope says I should leave San Francisco.

Ada: Good-bye. Good luck.

Kweenie: Good riddance, you mean. You've never liked me.

Ada: I could cheerfully murder you. Hand me your cup.

Kweenie: I tried to leave once before.

Ada: Try again. Try moving tomorrow.

Kweenie: I tried to leave when I thought that Johnny had married you.

Ada: Hurry. I have a short attention span.

Kweenie: I called you from the bus station in L. A.

Ada: Collect.

Kweenie: You've never liked me.

Ada: I accepted the collect call John had refused....Why should I like you? John's old....

JOHN AND CURTIS ENTER TOGETHER

John: (Pushing CURTIS aside) May I cut in?

Ada: Kweenie-says-she's-leaving-San-Francisco-She-promises-never-to-call-again-Not-even-collect-and-she-said-she-is-a-chameleon.

Kweenie: Ada, you're a stitch.

Ada: In time, I'll save nine. What's wrong with Curtis?

Kweenie: Curtis wants me to marry him.

Ada: Wonderful. You can move out bride and baggage.

Kweenie: I won't marry him.

Ada: That's wonderful too. You can move out separately.

Kweenie: Never will I marry him.

Ada: You're nobody's fool.

Curtis: (To ADA) You married me.

Ada: Curtis, you and I weren't married long enough to fight for custody of the cake.

Curtis: Kick me when I'm down.

John: (To CURTIS) Were you beaten as a child?

Ada: For the extra point, I could dropkick you into the street.

Curtis: I'd feel right marrying Kweenasheba.

Ada: Sometimes "no" is a positive answer.

Curtis: (Pulls KWEENASHEBA into a clinch almost like tight

dancing) Marry me, Kweenasheba.
Kweenie: Let go of me, you big ape.
Curtis: Marry me.
Kweenie: You're suffocating me.
Curtis: Marry me.
Kweenie: I'm getting claustrophobic.
Curtis: I can't let go of you.
Kweenie: Let go of me.
John: (To ADA) Let's go watch Channel 12's Big Time Wrestling.
Curtis: I need you.
Kweenie: I don't need you. Let loose!
Curtis: You can change your mind.
Ada: Five'll get me ten, she won't.
Kweenie: Wicker bedpans in hell!
Curtis: We're never too far into anything that we can't turn back.
Kweenie: I got along without you before I met you.
Curtis: I can't get along without you now.
Kweenie: Let loose.
Curtis: I can't let go of you.
John: May I have this dance? (JOHN softly hums "Silent Night")

JOHN AND ADA DANCE SLOW, CLOSE

Kweenie: Can't you tell where you're not wanted?
Ada: Neither one of them can tell where they're not wanted.
Kweenie: You have to let go of me.
Curtis: No!
Kweenie: I'm leaving you.
Curtis: No!
Kweenie: I'm leaving San Francisco.
Curtis: I can't deal with this.
John: (Sings *sotto voce*) "Sleep in heavenly peace."
Kweenie: Let go of me.
Curtis: I'll go with you.
Ada: Go get their suitcases.
Kweenie: No.
Curtis: Why can't I go with you?
Kweenie: I won't let you. You *must* let go of me.

Curtis: I'll never let you go.

    John and Ada, dancing, are just going into a dip. The next line freezes them at the bottom of the dip where they do a "take" until John's line.

Kweenie: Speaking of 'round yon Virgin and Child…I'm going to
    have a baby. (Curtis releases Kweenie)
John: That's good. We were about to go to sleep.
Curtis: I don't believe it.
John: Cute. A baby brother for Gladys Mae.
Ada: Look at her face, Curtis. You can tell a pregnancy in a
    woman's face.
Curtis: You have a ring through your nose.
Kweenie: I had it pierced this morning coming from the clinic.
Curtis: I don't believe it.
Kweenie: Curtis! The rabbit died!
Curtis: Honey-babe, we're never into anything so far we can't
    change our minds.
Kweenie: My mind's made up.
Ada: Like a hide-a-bed.
Curtis: Now you have to marry me.
Kweenie: No.
Curtis: Then you have to chuck the brat.
Kweenie: Says who?
Ada: That-a-girl.
Curtis: I say.
Ada: "The little Bummer Boy."
Kweenie: You constantly antagonize me.
Ada: Curtis calls it foreplay.
John: I think, Ada, we'll take a walk.
Ada: Says who?
Kweenie: You don't want to see a man nag a pregnant woman?
Curtis: I once let go of a balloon in St. Louis in 1957. Where did
    it go?
John: The same place electricity goes when the lights go out.
Kweenie: Don't try to worm out with your philosophy, Curtis.
Ada: We're all on to your rhetorical tricks, Curtis.

Curtis: I ought to belt you.

John: If you want to box....

Curtis: I mean her.

Ada: Curtis wants to hit Kweenie. That's one of the ways Curtis turns on. It makes a big man of him.

John: I don't want to hear this.

Ada: You wanted to know why I divorced Curtis.

John: Because of Gladys Mae's pantyhose.

Curtis: You have to repeat everything!

Kweenie: Shut up, Curtis.

Ada: Shut up, Curtis.

Curtis: What is this, the OK Corral?

John: Shut up, Curtis.

Ada: Do what you want, Kweenie.

Kweenie: I'm beginning to.

Ada: But don't listen to him.

Kweenie: I can't even hear him.

Ada: He beat me up and then he knocked me up.

John: You were pregnant?

Ada: Give me a cigarette. (JOHN starts to light it for her) For godsake, I can light it for myself.

John: You were pregnant?

Ada: Yes.

John: Curtis made you pregnant?

Ada: In a motel on Highway 1. Right after the Four-Bean Salad.

John: But I thought Curtis was...

Curtis: You are what you plug.

John: I ought to belt you.

Curtis: For making my own wife pregnant?

John: Really belt you.

Curtis: For making both these ladies pregnant?

John: Really hit you.

Curtis: I could punch you out with one hand.

John: Says you.

Kweenie: (Disgusted) Omigod!

Ada: You're worse than little BOYS!

John: So where's "Little Curtis"?

Ada: Curetted down some drain. God. I hate smoking. (ADA begins to cry) What do you mean "Little Curtis"? It might have been "Little Ada."

Kweenie: This night is going to run up a lot of karmic debts.

 Ada: You're the same as Curtis.

John: Don't get down on me.

Curtis: There isn't enough soap in this shop.

Ada: I'm not any man's incubator.

Kweenie: Who says I am?

Ada: I know, John, what you borrowed from Curtis. Those magazines of Asian women bound in tied-up situations.

Kweenie: Curtis keeps that disgusting junk under the bed.

Curtis: A man needs fantasies.

Ada: Signs and omens are everywhere.

Kweenie: For sure.

Ada: Move out! This is my house. You, Kweenie, out. You, Curtis, double out ...and now that I think about it, you, John, you... out too!

John: Why me?

Ada: Why not you?

John: I'm supposed to be your lover.

Ada: You're a tenant with a lease on a shop.

Curtis: Primitive people always eat the god they worship.

Ada: I'm going to my room.

John: It's *our* room.

Ada: Tonight it's my room again. I'm going up there and have a good cry for Little Ada.

John: This is all a guilt syndrome.

Ada: Out! All of you!

John: No woman should feel guilty about an abortion.

Ada: You utter idiot! I'm not whining for that little Ada. I'm letting it out tonight for *this* Little Ada. The one who counts. Me. The one who lives and breathes and teaches and tries to give up smoking while her lover wants to box, for godsake, with her ex-husband.

John: Don't dare go up those stairs alone.

Ada: Try and stop me. You or the Queen of Sheep Dip.

Curtis: I rather enjoy this.

John: We promised never to end an argument with separate beds.

Ada: This isn't an argument. This is a decision.

Curtis: Ada means not tonight, John. She has a headache.

Ada: Ada means sometimes people just need "alone-time."

ADA EXITS

Curtis: Good-night, Greta Garbo.

Kweenie: So here I stand with the two men in my life. One the
soul of the middle class. The other, the heel.

Curtis: What's next?

John: (Pointing upstairs to ADA) First: getting out of Ada's life.
(Pointing to Kweenie) Second: getting out of Flower Girl's
life.

Kweenie: Not on my account, Johnny.

John: I'm taking my motorcycle out. I'm going across the Golden
Gate. I want to feel fog in my face.

Kweenie: Why don't you just go upstairs to Ada.

Curtis: That wouldn't be fog in his face.

John: I'm not in the mood to rape.

Curtis: What about these wilting roses? What about this awful
herbal soap?

John: (Tosses Kweenie some keys) Kweenie, open up tomorrow?

Kweenie: Sure, Johnny.

Curtis: I mean what about the shop?

John: My lease has three more months. Curtis, why don't you buy
me out? Lock, stock, and barrel.

Kweenie: Maybe Ada will change her mind.

Curtis: Ada Vicary started life as a parson's daughter. Once she
starts moralizing on that....

Kweenie: Ada is an Aries with Scorpio rising. She'll change.

John: Ada can sit upstairs in her restored Victorian rocker till she's
90...

Kweenie: Ada will always be full of surprises.

John: ...till she's 95 and drooling in her needlepoint.

Curtis: Remember when making love was fun?

Kweenie: Fun gets complicated.

Curtis: In every grade-B mummy movie, the diamond in the tomb
always has curse on it.

John: ...or a Curtis.

Kweenie: Where will you go? It's late.

John: It's early. To the Russian River. A friend has a cabin. The key's under a rock by the porch.

Kweenie: You'll come back?

John: Probably. For awhile. Then I may cycle up the coast to Vancouver.

Curtis: Ada likes plays the way I live movies.

Kweenie: She thinks everything is *Romeo and Juliet*.

Curtis: A good thing those two kids aren't alive today.

John: You guys better pack up your bologna and move.

Curtis: "Years from now when you speak of this, and you will speak of this, be kind."

John: Curtis, if you couldn't quote movies, you'd be silent.

Curtis: What silent movie would I be?

John: Whatever, you wouldn't be original. (To Kweenie) So long, kid. Do it. (John pecks her on the cheek)

Kweenie: I can live on *that* for a month. (John smiles, shrugs)

JOHN EXITS

Curtis: (Musing) What silent movie would I be?

Kweenie: *Intolerance*.

Curtis: And you're beginning to look like *Birth of a Nation*.

Kweenie: Why have you always wanted to change me?

Curtis: To perfect you. Why, Eliza, don't you recognize Henry Higgins?

Kweenie: You're hateful.

Curtis: I'm Pygmalion.

Kweenie: You're a pig.

Curtis: You're never happy unless you're miserable.

Kweenie: You're never happy unless you make me miserable.

Curtis: Made for each other. What's the matter?

Kweenie: My film seems stuck in your camera.

Curtis: Have you rewound it?

Kweenie: Of course.

Curtis: You probably pulled the last picture too far and yanked it from the cannister.

Kweenie: I wound it right.

Curtis: Let me see. Was the little light on? Could you hear it click when you rewound it? I hope you didn't wreck the strobe. (The flash camera goes off.) You have to pay attention.

Kweenie: I'm blinded!

Curtis: You're also irreversibly deaf and dumb.

Kweenie: Everytime I get near something electronic, you condescend.

Curtis: Dearly beloved, we are gathered here tonight because Kweenasheba's film is caught in my camera.

Kweenie: I surrender, Curtis.

Curtis: Surrender?

Kweenie: I never thought I'd come to this.

Curtis: You can't surrender.

Kweenie: I can. I do. I'm beat.

Curtis: You're backing away.

Kweenie: I accept you, have accepted you...the way you are.

Curtis: Time with you is better than time without you.

Kweenie: I'm tired....

Curtis: ...You're chicken...

Kweenie: ...of trying to change you.

Curtis: SQUAWK!

Kweenie: You'll always be lower class.

Curtis: We have that in common.

Kweenie: The only thing we have in common is neither of us has ever been married to Elizabeth Taylor.

Curtis: Touch your tummy and say that.

Kweenie: The little bugger's mine.

Curtis: How about marrying me?

Kweenie: I think I'll strangle you.

Curtis: I knew you couldn't surrender.

Kweenie: Go to bed.

Curtis: Tuck me in, mommy?

Kweenie: Go to bed.

Curtis: You used to say, "Come to bed." ...I love you, Kweenasheba.

Kweenie: You mean you want me to love you.

Curtis: I do no kidding love you.

Kweenie: Am I supposed to bat that ball back over the net for a
   love, game, set?
Curtis: When a person says "I love you," it's civilized to say you
   love that person back.
Kweenie: I don't.
Curtis: Kick me some more.
Kweenie: I won't.
Curtis: Kick me.
Kweenie: I can't.
Curtis: Why not?
Kweenie: I surrendered.
Curtis: Then for sure kick me.
Kweenie: Why should I?
Curtis: To the victor go the spoils.
Kweenie: I didn't win, Curtis. I surrendered.
Curtis: If you won't make love to me anymore, then you have to
   kick me.
Kweenie: No!
Curtis: Hit me!
Kweenie: I said no!
Curtis: For godsake, Kweenie, hurt me.
Kweenie: When something's over, whatever happened to shaking
   hands and saying good-bye?
Curtis: Please.
Kweenie: (Amazed) I'm finishing an affair with a punching bag!
Curtis: Time, space, flesh have passed between us.
Kweenie: What's that mean?
Curtis: I can't deal with you leaving San Francisco.
Kweenie: Well good-bye, dear, and amen.
Curtis: Come to bed.
Kweenie: I haven't given up my free-will.
Curtis: I'll be under the covers when you're ready.
Kweenie: You're not hard to get.
Curtis: (Exiting) It's dark back here.
Kweenie: Get a nightlight.
Curtis: Where will you sleep?
Kweenie: Here on the couch.
Curtis: *Voulez vous couchez....*

Kweenie: Pack your pickup truck tomorrow morning.
Curtis: Orders straight from Wonder Woman.
Kweenie: You heard Ada.
Curtis: I hear you, Kweenie.
Kweenie: Sleep tight.
Curtis: I'm glad we don't have to bother to get a divorce.

CURTIS EXITS

Kweenie: (Making up the couch, sings) "...God rest ye merry
    gentlemen. Let nothing you dismay..." Everyone has gone off
    to sleep. Alone. (She toys with the blankets, then stands stock
    still as the realization fills her. She folds her hands across her
    stomach) I will see...I promise I will see my invisible child....I
    love you...I love you...I love you, baby. I am. I am the one. I
    am the only. I am the original Queen of Sheba.

LIGHTS SLOW FADE

CURTAIN

**One San Francisco Play's Gender Journey
From the "Neli-Deli" Sandwich Shop
at Dave's Baths to the Queer Stage...**

Lost Photographs, Found Genders

Pioneering Gay Theater in San Francisco in the 1970s

**Coming Attractions: Kweenasheba (1975)
was adapted by the author from his story
"Sweet Embraceable You" (1972).**

The beloved San Francisco character actor Michael Lewis introduced me to producer and actor Joe Campanella of the all-male Yonkers Production Company that produced my play *Coming Attractions* (aka *Kweenasheba*) in 1976, the year after Campanella himself co-starred in *My Fair Laddie* with head-liner Empress-ario Jose Sarria at the Royal Palace, 335 Jones Street. That Tenderloin venue was not far from the South of Market "Society for Individual Rights' SIR Center Theater," 83 Sixth Street, known, because of its spill of derelict winos propping up the sidewalk, by its camp name, "Wine Country," because that block of Sixth was then a filthy Skid Row providing perfect sanctuary for gay theater coming out of the closet.

The SIR organization produced theatrical events from 1964-1976, and published *Vector* magazine from 1965-1977. In a line of theatrical descent, the year after the free-styling SIR organization closed camp with its double-bill of Lanford Wilson's *The Madness of Lady Bright* and my play, the newly founded Theater Rhinoceros opened its doors with its own remounting of Wilson's riff on Tennessee Williams' Blanche DuBois in *Lady Bright.*

The five-foot-six elfin Michael Lewis was a great performer of any gender. He was legendary as the Lion in the San Francisco camp staging of *The Wizard of Oz.* We met one rainy December afternoon in 1975 at Dave's Baths across from the foot of the new TransAmerica Pyramid in the 500 block of Washington Street, a couple doors west of Sansome Street. Michael ran a little shop inside Dave's Baths where he whipped up desserts and coffee. He called it with a wink: the Neli-Deli. I ordered a sandwich, soup, and decaf. It was a slow day at the tubs, and, between gentlemen callers, I had been editing my script in my tiny dark cubicle which was no beach *cabine*, and brought it with me to sit on a well-lighted barstool at the deli service-counter window. I was barefoot with a white towel wrapped round my waist. We struck up a conversation.

As in all good show business stories, within an hour, we had met cute and were bonded and discussing pairing my one-act with a second one-act, *Lady Bright*, in which Michael was already cast to play the title role.

Pirandello would have approved: Michael was one character in search of an author.

He needed a companion play that would not charge royalties. Seeing that he was the force rather much in charge of creating a double bill for a proper evening's entertainment for Yonkers, I suggested he do a kind of dual-role double feature, and play the lead part of the flamboyant Curtis in my play because he was perfect, to the point of type-casting, for the part.

He and Campanella and I discussed, with Jose Sarria (SIR founder, 1963), the fact that my play featured two evolving men, and two straight women, living together behind a flower shop on Castro Street in 1972. I based that shop on my pal Tommy Zalewski's pioneering urban nursery and gardening shop "Tommy's Plants" at 566 Castro Street where the hale, hearty, and handsome big blond Tommy—come to Castro from Wisconsin—entertained hot locals and tourist tricks with fat joints and quickie fun in his upstairs office.

Yonkers wanted to cast four men from their talent pool which would have essentially changed the psycho-sexual narrative of my play while adding little but camp to it—which all these diverse years later might be great fun to try. In those olden days, I had been warned against such stunt casting by the example of Edward Albee who, while he approved interracial casting, insisted on cisgender casting for *Who's Afraid of Virginia Woolf.* I had composed for two male actors, and two female actors, because I envisioned a "coming out" comedy whose crusading political point was to *include* and *dramatize* the women—Ada, straight middle-class, and Kweenie, fluid counter-cultural—who in the emerging antics of gay culture in the 1970s were too often forgotten as collateral damage when men, like Robert Mapplethorpe, went gay leaving them, like Patti Smith, all too often behind. Hence, the cautionary title: *Coming Attractions.*

I wanted to examine that particular situation comedy of errors. So when Yonkers understood why I requested gender similitude dramatically and politically, these liberationist theater folk who were anxious to evolve on the subject of gender, made note that although they identified as an all-male company, they were happy to assist such diversified casting. Producer Joe Campanella wrote in the program: "You may ask why Yonkers is involved in serious theatre at this time. The answer is that we, as a production company, feel it is time to express ourselves in a different light. Why should we limit our goals to all-male drag and camp when there are other areas of entertainment to explore. We have a responsibility and commitment to the audience to provide worthwhile theatre, and we feel that tonight's presentation is worthy of your time. As Chairman of Yonkers, one of my first accomplishments was to revise our by-laws so that any person, male or female, would be able to audition and take part in any future production. My basic theory is that the best person for the role—male or female, if that person is the best, then he or she deserves the part. We need to branch out in our casting."

Even so, I was pretty much on my own to find such women.

I had to get creative. I asked my hip and hippie sister and house mate, Mary Claire Fritscher, who at age eighteen was eighteen years younger than I, and a star newly graduated from her high-school and community theater experience of performing the femme fatale "Appassionata von Climax" in *Li'l Abner* and choreographing *Oklahoma!* to stop by the open casting call, and walk right in and audition anonymously on her own merit, identifying herself simply as "Mary Claire," for the role of Kweenie, which was rather much based on her alternative feminist personality in the first place. Her example helped me create two strong roles for women. Without any input from me, Michael Lewis, Joe Campanella, and director Jack Green made all casting decisions. Two weeks into rehearsals after Mary Claire had proven her acting chops and her geniality to all concerned, we siblings announced our backstage ploy to much approving laughter and applause.

Secondly, when Jack Green's choice for Ada, Jeanne Nathans, suddenly got a part in a film, I asked my pal, the elegant Catherine White, to audition for Ada because of her own personal sophistication and because we had the time of our young lives playing the pregnant hippie bride and beaded hippie husband leads in Broadway playwright and screenwriter William Goodhart's 1965 "Generation Gap" comedy, *Generation*, at the Kalamazoo Civic Theater in May 1968. The production, directed by the British theatrical legend Bertram Tanswell, was well received and its run was extended. Catherine was also a dancer who had choreographed *A Funny Thing Happened on the Way to the Forum* for the Civic Theater. She and her husband, with their new baby, had just moved to San Francisco, and she agreed to "come out of retirement" as a favor since we had gotten along so well on and off stage during *Generation*.

Then there was the role of the straight John Vicary. For a year, I had been friends with the actor Bob Paulson who leased an old-fashioned open-air sidewalk florist kiosk across the street from the Castro Theater. We first met, also cute, standing under his colorful canvas awning in a soft winter rain while I bought one of his delicate rose bouquets. He and I also bonded taking an exam together when the San Francisco Sheriff was recruiting gay men. We both scored. I came in as Deputy Candidate number eleven, but I turned down the job which he took. So he was an authentic new deputy sheriff who was a veteran actor in dozens of San Francisco plays including *Fiddler on the Roof, Pal Joey*, and *Little Mary Sunshine*. (His co-star Mary Claire had also starred the year before in another production of *Little Mary Sunshine*.) His manly presence, brooding matinee-idol looks, and gregarious personality were ideal for the role of John Vicary who also owned a flower shop.

When my longtime sporting buddy, Jack Green, a credentialed and experienced theater director, agreed to direct *Coming Attractions*, I was delighted because in our group of new immigrants reconstituting ourselves *en masse* in San Francisco, we were all inventing new lives, new roles, and new ways of befriending each other while transferring our talent, hearts, and humanity from homophobic towns and cities from which we had fled as sex refugees trying to carry on the natural narratives of our lives.

Late nights, after rehearsals and after performances, our cast and crew retired for food and drink at Pam Pam's coffee shop, open 24/7, one block west of Union Square, 398 Geary Street at Mason, mixing sometimes with professional actors from proper playhouses just across the street, like the American Conservatory Theater's Geary Theater, and the Curran Theater where film director Joseph Mankiewicz shot the "Broadway theater" exteriors and interiors for *All About Eve*.

Lucky for us happy friends rehearsing at SIR, Eve never showed.

In 2017, my dear friend, the photographer and author Jim Stewart was searching his files of negatives and found rehearsal photographs both of us had forgotten existed. We had met in 1973, and when he moved to San Francisco in 1975, he lived with me and my sister at our home for six months before moving to the artsy bohemian Clementina Street where he began shooting for *Drummer* magazine, which I had the good fortune of editing for three years (1977-1980).

Drummer often published plays like *Pogey Bait* and *Isomer* and *Corporal in Charge of Taking Care of Captain O'Malley*. *Pogey Bait* was written by 1960s Off-Off-Broadway playwright and Gay Games bodybuilder George Birimisa of Caffe Cino and Theater Rhinoceros who produced *Pogey Bait*. *Isomer* was by Richard A. Steel, a pioneer of New York's Circle Repertory Company, who was also an associate of Sam Shepard and a good friend of Lanford Wilson. My closet drama *Corporal in Charge* was the only play the revered publisher Winston Leyland included in his canonical anthology and Lammy Award Winner, *Gay Roots: Twenty Years of Gay Sunshine - An Anthology of Gay History, Sex, Politics, and Culture* (1991).

Stewart's lost negatives of *Coming Attractions*, shot on the SIR Center's stage, with available light, were dusty and damaged, and have been restored as much as possible for archival purposes by Mark Hemry. The perversatile Stewart, to whom I am so grateful, soon after, only a few blocks from the SIR Center, was the designer and carpenter who built the interior of Oscar Streaker Robert Opel's Fey-Way Studio, 1287 Howard Street, the first gay art gallery in San Francisco, where Opel was murdered in 1979. Author Stewart's 2011 hello-and-goodbye to all that was his best-selling memoir, *Folsom Street Blues.*

Back in that primitive first decade after Stonewall, *Coming Attractions* may have been the first play written on Castro Street (1975) about life on Castro Street. It played weekends to full houses for a month and was noticed on the cover of *The Bay Area Reporter* and in the arts "Pink Section" of the *San Francisco Chronicle*.*

The Bay Area Reporter, Volume 6 #5, March 4, 1976, and "Date Book Arts and Entertainment" Pink Section of the *San Francisco Chronicle*, Sunday, March 21, 1976

Notes for *Coming Attractions* from the
Yonkers Production Company Program
by Perry George

Coming Attractions [aka *Kweenasheba*] was first produced by the Yonkers Production Company, San Francisco, premiering March 13, 1976, at the Society for Individual Rights SIR Center Theatre, 83 Sixth Street, San Francisco. Joe Campanella, Producer. Directed by Jack Green. Photography by Eye-Onic. *Coming Attractions* was double-billed in a program of two one-act plays with *The Madness of Lady Bright* by Lanford Wilson, and was noticed as the cover of the weekly newspaper, the *B.A.R., The Bay Area Reporter*, Volume 6 #5, March 4, 1976, and in the "Date Book—Arts and Entertainment" Pink Section of the *San Francisco Chronicle*, Sunday, March 21, 1976. [*Coming Attractions* may be the first gay play written and produced in San Francisco reflecting the actuality of the gender mix in early 1970s emerging gay culture on Castro Street.

CAST

In order of appearance:
John Stack: Bob Paulson
Ada: Catherine White
Curtis: Mike Lewis
Kweenasheba: Mary Claire Fritscher

JACK FRITSCHER
Playwright

Jack is an Illinois Gemini who played in Peoria (and Chicago and New York) before arriving, five years ago, in the Gemini City of Oz. His first produced play, for which he wrote the book and lyrics with Lawrence Brandt, was the musical-comedy, *Continental Caper* (1959). He has acted in *Oliver!* and T. S. Eliot's *Murder in the Cathedral.* He played the lead in the hippie comedy, *Generation*, and the five male leads in the musical-comedy, *Canterbury Tales*, also appearing fleetingly in *The Streets of San Francisco.* He has published two books, *Television Today* and *Popular Witchcraft: Straight from the Witch's Mouth* (Citadel Press). Currently he is working on a collection of San Francisco short stories while writing a TV movie, *Duchess: Berlin 1928.* He lives it up to write it down. *Kweenasheba* is dedicated to his lover of seven years, the photographer, David Sparrow.

JACK GREEN
Director

Born the day before Thanksgiving to a theatrical family in Duluth—that's right, a theatrical family in Duluth, Minnesota, Jack fled from the frozen northland at an early age. At a more mature age, he received a B.A. in Theatre Arts at UCLA, after which he became Founder/Director of the "Fifth Corner" company in Los Angeles, an ensemble presenting Off-Off-Broadway plays. *Coming Attractions* makes both his Yonkers and San Francisco theatrical debut.

JOE CAMPANELLA
Producer and Chairman
Yonkers Production Co., Inc.

Yonkers is fortunate to have as its producer, the capable and talented, Joe Campanella, who has been active in all-male theatre in San Francisco for over ten years. Most recently, he played the male lead in *Blithe Spirit* for which he received a Cable Car Award nomination. His background in Gay Theatre includes two Yonkers productions, *That's Show Biz*, and *Michelle Plays the Palace*. Professionally, Joe works as a radio announcer at KEST Radio in San Francisco, and teaches a course in Radio and TV broadcasting. Since coming to San Francisco eleven years ago, Joe has appeared in productions with the Opera Ring, Interplayers, Playhouse, and at the Village in *Ready or Not It's Me* and *It's Me Again*. He also played opposite the famous Jose Sarria in many spoof operas.

Joe is current chairman of Yonkers, a titled member of the Royal Household of Grand Duchess Charlie, and the newly appointed Production Chairman of SIR Center. Joe writes: "You may ask why Yonkers is involved in serious theatre at this time. The answer is that we, as a production company, feel it is time to express ourselves in a different light. Why should we limit our goals to all-male drag and camp when there are other areas of entertainment to explore. We have a responsibility and commitment to the audience to provide worthwhile theatre, and we feel that tonight's presentation is worthy of your time. As Chairman of Yonkers, one of my first accomplishments was to revise our by-laws so that any person, male or female, would be able to audition and take part in any future production. My basic theory is 'the best person for the role—male or female'; if that person is the best, then he or she deserves the part. My hope with *The Madness of Lady Bright* by Lanford Wilson, and *Coming Attractions* by Jack Fritscher is to establish Yonkers as an open-minded theatrical company."

MICHAEL LEWIS
Curtis, *Coming Attractions*, and Leslie, *Lady Bright*
Producer, *Coming Attractions*

Mike has been a familiar face to San Francisco audiences since 1970, making his "Golden Award" winning performance in the Yonkers Production of *Hello Dolly*, only to be followed by a long line of memorable roles in *The Boyfriend, Dames at Sea, Feather and Leather Follies, CMC Carnival,* and *Little Me.* More recently, Mike claims a Cable Car Award for his unforgettable role of the Lion in *Wizard of Oz.* Active in charities, his characterization as the Lion has been delighting audiences from the Shriners' Hospital to the *Jerry Lewis Telethon.* Mike is re-creating the role of Leslie in *The Madness of Lady Bright* from a previous production staged last year at San Francisco State University. You can find him performing to SRO crowds at his own business, the Neli-Deli, at Dave's Baths.

MARY CLAIRE FRITSCHER
Kweenasheba

From Appassionata Von Climax in the Peoria (Illinois) High School production of *Li'l Abner* to the focal leading lady (and Yonker's first actual female leading lady) in Yonker's San Francisco production of *Coming Attractions*—that's how far the eighteen-year-old ingenue, Mary Claire has come. Her varied experience has touched on every aspect of theatre: dancing, singing, acting, even set construction and decoration, make-up, children's theatre, and directing. Now she adds gay theatre to her credits. Her credits specifically include the lead in *Little Mary Sunshine, Archie and Mehitabel,* as well as dance director for the choreography for a community production of *Oklahoma!* As a "backstage musical" note, for Yonkers, she auditioned anonymously, as "Mary Claire," winning the role of Kweenasheba, written specifically for her by the author, her brother. They revealed their relationship at a party during the third week of rehearsal. She is a psychology major at City College of San Francisco, studying advanced acting, directing, and philosophy.

CATHERINE WHITE
Ada Vicary

Catherine moved to San Francisco with her husband three months ago from Michigan where she was active in the Kalamazoo Community Theatre. Her credits there include an extended run in the hippie comedy, *Generation*, playing the female lead opposite Jack Fritscher who invited her to step into the role of Ada when actress Jeanne Nathans landed a part in an upcoming film. Six months ago, Catherine gave birth to her newest production, a son, who can sometimes be heard backstage, rehearsing.

BOB PAULSON
John Stack

Handsome Bob Paulson, is a newly sworn and openly gay San Francisco deputy sheriff, whose acting credits include fifteen musicals for Woodminster Summer Musicals in Oakland, notably, George Musgrove in *Little Me*, Hysterium in *A Funny Thing Happened on the Way to the Forum*, Mottel the Tailor in *Fiddler on the Roof*, and James Wilson in *1776*. He also appeared as Arthur Swan in *No Man's Land* and the Gardner in *The Vigil* for Producers Associates in Oakland. For SIR he has appeared as Ludlow Lowell in *Pal Joey*, Capt. Jim in *Little Mary Sunshine*, and Marcus Lycus in *Forum*. He also directed *Anything Goes* with Michelle, and has appeared in numerous SIR-lebri-te Capades and Revues for SIR. His set design credits include, for SIR, *Anything Goes, Madness '71*, and *Hello Dolly* for SIR and Yonkers. He also designed *Dames at Sea* for Kimo Productions. Co-incidentally "type-cast" as John, the owner of a flower shop, Bob, until he was recently picked for the first group of openly gay deputy sheriffs, was the manager of a flower shop on Castro Street.

"YONKERS DOES GAY THEATRE
WITH TWO DRAMATIC ONE-ACT PLAYS"
by Perry George
Reprinted from *Yonkers Free Press*

Yonkers is proud and happy to offer to our theatre-going public a whole new facet, for us, of theatrical endeavor in two one-act plays, *The Madness of Lady Bright* by Lanford Wilson, and *Coming Attractions* by Jack Fritscher. The pairing of these two plays, Yonkers Productions Company's Sixth major endeavor, is not an all-male musical comedy or revue. There is no expensive union orchestra, lavish sequined and feathered costumes, stunningly choreographed production numbers or singing, that have given us the spectacular reputation we have.

It is not Yonkers' intention to abandon this type of theatre, which we have pleased audiences with again and again from *Hello Dolly, The Boy Friend, Little Me, Michelle Plays the Palace*, to *That's Show Biz*, but to enhance this achievement with a branching out, a theatrical coming-of-age and an emergence to the dynamic times this theatre group, our City, state, and nation are arriving at in encouraging and recognizing the blossoming of relevant Gay Theatre where a positive and honest mirror image of ourselves and our friends, as members of the gay and general community, can have both entertainment and insight.

The first play, *Coming Attractions*, an original play by the local playwright, Jack Fritscher, will receive its world premiere and is a vignette of a life-style very likely to be familiar from the neighborhoods of San Francisco to anyone who sees this play. *Coming Attractions* deals with homosexuality in a matter-of-fact positive way, with the homosexual living "happily-ever-after"—no suicides, no murders, none of all the strangely unnecessary retribution that seems inevitable in most gay-themed drama we are exposed to in the "straight world" theatrical productions. It is our belief that the turn of this tide of negativity must start from the Gay Community as it does not seem likely it will from the Straight Community.

Also aware of the fact that all within gay life and the Gay Community is not like a "Gidget Goes Gay" kind of movie, and remembering our often traumatic and painful past, we offer Lanford Wilson's compelling drama, *The Madness of Lady Bright*, a study in the complete schizophrenic breakdown of an ageing fading failure of an effeminate homosexual on a very hot, hot night in New York

City. Everyone in the audience cannot avoid seeing a little, a lot, and perhaps too much of Leslie Bright in themselves or someone dear to them.

It is unwise to single out one performer from the many who work so hard to entertain the audiences who see our shows, but I cannot conclude without saying the compelling, powerful, and sensitive performances I have seen blossoming in Mike Lewis as Leslie (Lady) Bright, and as Curtis, "the real Kweeasheba," throughout rehearsals of these two shows will be worth the price of admission for all who see his double tour-de-force. *Lady Bright,* which also stars Shel Kovalski, is directed by Andrew Barron; assistant director, William Howard.

Tickets for this double-bill of one-act shows are available at Macy's Box Office, The Record House, and the Kokpit Bar. They are for unreserved seating and are $4 each, March 13, 14, 20, 21, 27, and 28. After the closing night performance, there will be a cast and audience party at the Kokpit Bar, 301 Turk Street.

CREDITS: *The Madness of Lady Bright,* written by Lanford Wilson, courtesy of Dramatists Play Service; directed by Andrew Barron. *Coming Attractions,* written by Jack Fritscher, courtesy of Spitting Image/Palm Drive; directed by Jack Green. Both plays produced for Yonkers Production Company by Joe Campanella; sets by Bob Paulsen; lighting and sound, Bill Hirsing; program notes and design, Perry George and Bob Cramer; stage manager, Rod Schaefer; crew, Randy Totten; photography, EYE-ONIC; special thanks to Jim Briggs, Mark Barrett, Record House, Kokpit, Dennis Coonan, Bert Arthur, Tadd Waggoner, SIR Board of Directors, and Exactly That Productions.

YONKERS PRODUCTIONS
presents
an evening of one acts

THE WORLD PREMIER OF JACK FRITSCHER'S "COMING ATTRACTIONS"

March 13,14; 20,21; 27,28

SIR Center Theatre · 83 6th St. S.F.

8:30 PM $4.00

TEL.RESERVATIONS 673-4258

AND LANFORD WILSON'S

The Madness of Lady Bright

Tickets Available at the Record House-Polk & Post,MACY'S Tickets or
FOR MAIL ORDER,ENCLOSE CHECK & SEND TO YONKERS PRODUCTION CO.,
c/o 785 McAllister St. "I", S.F. 94102.

Enclosed please find $________ for____($4 each) for the
evening/s of   MARCH 13 14 20 21 27 28 (circle)

PLEASE MAIL TICKETS TO:

NAME____

ADDRESS_______________________________ TELEPHONE__________

Phone reservations, please call 673-4258 or 474-6919

Top: (L) A pensive Bob Paulson (R) Michael Lewis and Bob Paulson
Bottom: Mary Claire Fritscher and Catherine White. Photos: Jim Stewart

Top: Catherine White and Mary Claire Fritscher rehearse on set
Bottom: Ada (Catherine White) challenges the ironic hipster Kween-asheba (Mary Claire Fritscher). Photos: Jim Stewart

Top: (L) Mary Claire Fritscher and Catherine White (R) Catherine White
Bottom: Director Jack Green and Mary Claire Fritscher. Photos: Jim Stewart

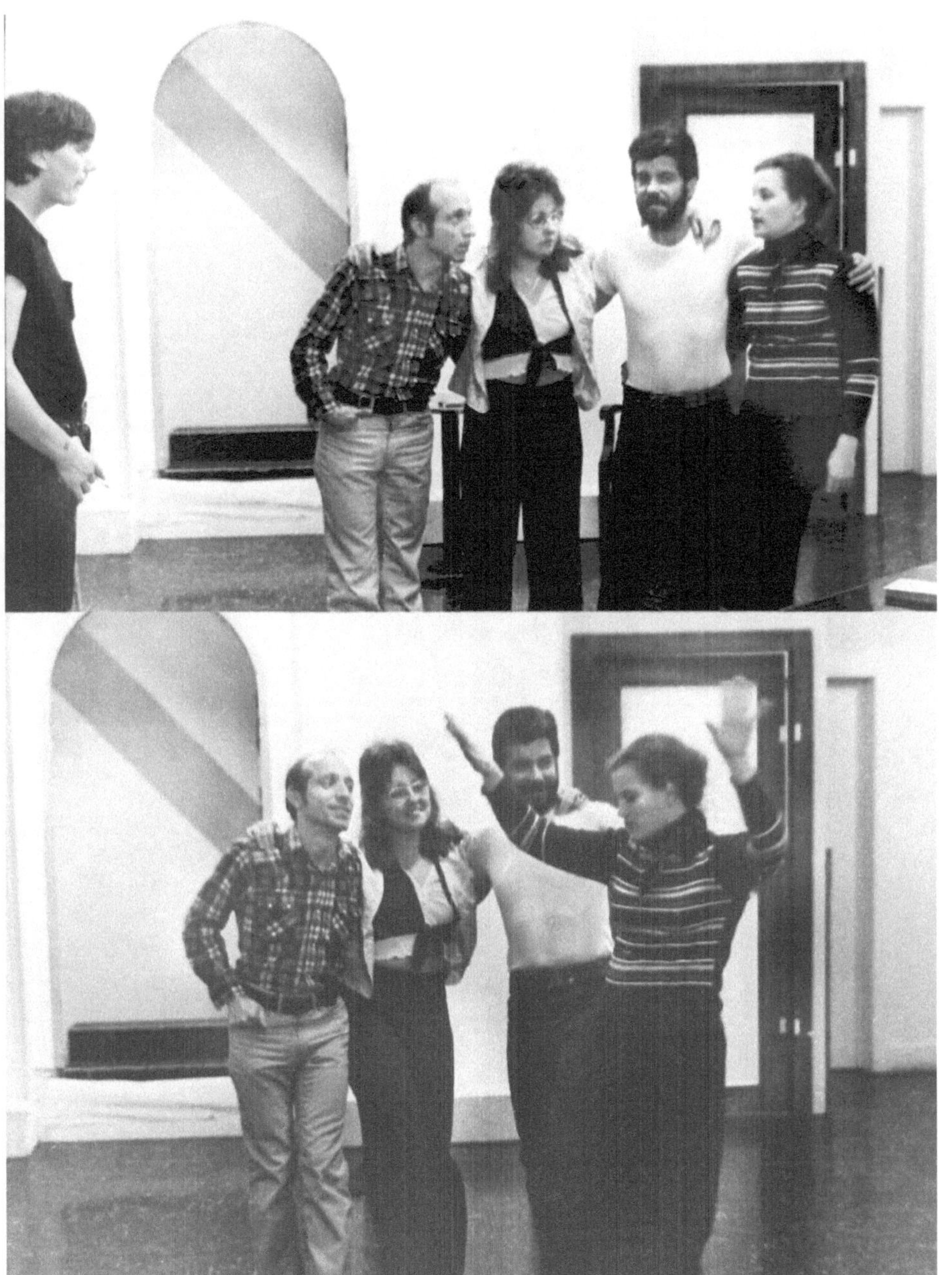

Top: Michael Lewis (Curtis), Mary Claire Fritscher (Kweenasheba), Bob Paulson (John Vicary), and Catherine White (Ada Vicary)
Bottom: Michael Lewis, Mary Claire Fritscher, Bob Paulson, listen atten-tively to Catherine White. Photos: Jim Stewart

Top: The always buoyant Michael Lewis with Mary Claire Fritscher, Bob Paulson, and Catherine White
Bottom: Rob Schaefer, Stage Manager; Bill Hirsing, Lighting and Sound; Randy Totten, Crew. Photos: Jim Stewart

With director Jack Green, tall and center, Michael Lewis, Mary Claire Fritscher, Bob Paulson, and Catherine White. Photo: Jim Stewart

Jack Fritscher, Catherine White, and Franklin Smith, *Generation*, May 1968, Kalamazoo Civic Theater

Top: Michael Lewis and Jack Fritscher, West Hollywood, 1989. Photo: Mark Hemry
Bottom: Jack Green, 1977. Photo: Jack Fritscher

B.A.R.
free
IN THE BAY AREA
.25 ELSEWHERE
VOLUME 6   NUMBER 5   March 4th   NEXT ISSUE OUT MARCH 18   NEXT DEADLINE: MARCH 12
THE LARGEST CIRCULATION AND READERSHIP IN THE BAY AREA
GAY HATE CAMPAIGN GROWS
... SEE PAGE 4
"Lanford Wilson writes with understanding and sensitivity"
THE NEW YORK TIMES
Yonkers Presents
"COMING ATTRACTIONS"
by Jack Fritscher
"THE MADNESS OF LADY BRIGHT"
by Lanford Wilson
March 13, 14 - 20, 21 - 27, 28 8:30pm   SIR Theatre
TICKETS: 673-4258

www.ingramcontent.com/pod-product-compliance
Lightning Source LLC
Chambersburg PA
CBHW030349200726
48286CB00013B/684